SHOHOLA FALLS

For Mikel —
in admiration and
friendship —

Shohola Falls

A NOVEL

Michael Pearson

Michael Pearson

 Syracuse University Press

Library of Congress Cataloging-in-Publication Data
Pearson, Michael, 1949–
Shohola Falls : a novel / Michael Pearson.— 1st ed.
p. cm.
ISBN 0-8156-0785-7 (alk. paper)
1. Twain, Mark, 1835–1910—Fiction. 2. Nineteen sixties—Fiction.
3. Race relations—Fiction. I. Title.
PR6066.E218 S46 2003
823'.914—dc21   2003012234

"As dreams are made on . . ."
EJPCS

Michael Pearson is the director of creative writing at Old Dominion University. He has written reviews and travel stories for a variety of magazines and newspapers. He is also the author of four earlier books. *Imagined Places: Journeys into Literary America* was listed by the *New York Times Book Review* as a Notable Book of 1992. His other books are *John McPhee,* a biographical-critical study; *A Place That's Known,* a collection of essays; and *Dreaming of Columbus: A Boyhood in the Bronx,* a memoir.

Contents

SHOHOLA FALLS

Prologue

*T*he first time I met Mark Twain he wasn't even Mark Twain. A long way
from it, as a matter of truth. He was just a skinny red-haired young pup with
freckles and a smile that hinted at the mischief about to come. He was in his
father's store, standing behind his mother, half peeking around her skirts to see
who she was talking to. My sister was asking for an extension of credit, and he was
craning his neck around to see just who was doing the begging.

I didn't see much of him that day because his mother waved her arm behind
her back without looking at him, like she was swatting at a fly, and said, "Scat
now, Sam." Then she shook her long red hair and turned toward her husband,
who stood behind the counter, stiff-necked as a preacher on Sunday, and said,
"Marshall, step over here to speak with this young woman, please." Mr. Clemens
wiped his hands on his apron and stepped around the edge of the counter. And
Sam was gone before I could see anything but the fire in his blue-gray eyes, aflame
like a cat's, as he turned tail and went out the door.

His home on Hill Street was uphill from the river and the front door to his
house opened directly onto a road that was only a stroll to the main street. My
family had moved across the way from him, along North Street, into a big old
barn of a house with as many pigs and dogs as children. We were as different as
moonlight and the illumination from a candle, Sam and me, but I could tell
from his glance the first time we saw one another that we had something in common and that our lives would be intertwined like those of brothers.

1

In a manner of speaking, I fell in love with Mark Twain that day, before he even truly existed, the way a boy can fall in love with another, admire him so much that he would follow him anywhere without losing a hair of confidence. He was nearly two years younger than me but he always seemed older and smarter than any of the boys I knew. From the very beginning, he struck me as a person who could imagine just about anything into life. I knew right away that he was the kind of boy who would make life interesting. If it hadn't been for the love and admiration I held for him from the start, it wouldn't have been as hard for me when he convinced himself that I had betrayed him.

NEW YORK CITY

1

My name is Tommy Blanks. Or at least that's close enough to the truth for now. I've found in the last few years that some lies are nearer to what's true than most of us ever expect to come, anyway. So I don't draw too many hard or fast lines between what's imagined and what's recollected. Sometimes what we dream up is real enough to live with and turns out to be the story of our lives. Our lies may turn out to be what was true all along.

Don't get me wrong, though. I'm no liar unless I'm forced to be. I'm just not sure what the truth is sometimes. And at other times there seem to be so many truths. Who can tell what's what? I can only guess, for instance, why my father disappeared or why I ran off across the country when I had every good reason to stay right where I was. But if I hadn't gone, I would never have gotten to California and met Welcome William Ward. That's where I met up with what I was running from, and deep down inside I know that I was fortunate that it caught up with me when it did—before I got lost entirely and fell so far I couldn't find my way back. I can't even tell you for sure why my great-great-grandfather's journal and his friendship with Sam Clemens were so important to me. Every once in a while you come across a story that's not about you but is anyway, and that's how my great-great-grandfather's journal felt to me. I've traveled a lot in the past few years to come to these conclusions. It seems as if you have to go a long ways to see what's right in front of you. Sometimes you have to step back far enough to shake the blurriness from your eyes.

Most of my life up until the last couple of years hadn't been action-packed. I'd lived inside my head more than I had in the physical world, I think. I'd gotten used to spending a good portion of each day reading or simply daydreaming, but then my mother died, my father disappeared, I got arrested, fell in love, and went on a cross-country journey in search of Mark Twain.

Well, not exactly, but that's near the truth—as near to the truth as one sentence can take it, I suppose—and as I said, it's hard to get anywhere but close to the truth anyway. Things are generally complicated and confusing no matter what way you explain them. It's not even easy deciding where to begin to tell a story. Stories rarely have straight lines. It's more likely that they're circles or mazes with all sorts of entrances and exits. So many beginning places are possible for this story— when my mother died or my father took off, when I was grabbed by the cops or the moment I glimpsed Nada, when I saw Shohola Falls for the first time or the last. Probably the real beginning place is when I found the journal and learned about my great-great-grandfather and Sam Clemens.

In order to make some sense of that, though, I need to tell about what led up to my discovering the journal. I need to tell it as it happened to me, if only to understand it myself. Before I found the journal, my life was mainly made up of other people's stories. After I found it, I started to understand that my dreams were a way of making sense of the world and that each person narrates his own life by deciding what that dream is and how it connects to the stories of others. Often we can't control what happens in our lives, of course, maybe only rarely can we do that, but we can decide what it all means. Life isn't all that different from our dreams. Who knows what's coming in either? Who's brave enough to know? Most days it takes courage just to face the past and make sense of it, let alone the present or the future.

What I'm really trying to explain, to myself mostly, is how I came to be here, where I am now, in Yulan, New York. This all happened only a few years ago, but it seems as if it were another life, someone else's life. Yulan is a village nestled in the Catskill Mountains just a few miles from a bend in the Delaware River that separates New York from Pennsylvania. The town is surrounded by beautiful country, not far from the hill on which Zane Grey built a house overlooking the silky green waters of the Delaware, and not many miles from the Methodist church in which Stephen Crane listened wide-eyed to his father's fiery sermons. The tourist brochures describe it as the "laurel hamlet" and mention all the boarding houses and lakes in the area. I've seen people roll their eyes and call it the Irish Alps with the same inflection that they use to describe Rockaway Beach as the Irish Riviera. It's supposed to mean that the place is butt-ugly and fit only for people who can't afford anything better. There's no question that this part of the Catskills has its share of McNamaras and Donahues from the Bronx, tile setters and tin knockers galore, and that it's a middle-class resort, but it's beautiful, too, I think. The houses aren't always grand or recently painted, but the mountains and rivers are straight out of a storybook.

I guess you'd have to say that when I first came to see Sullivan County I was in jail, which, surprisingly, didn't seem to change the loveliness of the place at all for me. I was in jail and I guess I deserved to be.

The first week I was there, in the early summer of 1966, I got tangled in some poison ivy vines as I drifted through the woods with thoughts of escaping to New Orleans or Key West dancing around in my head. I looked like a movie criminal or a cartoon character or maybe both at the same time. My nose was swollen, red, and blistered like an old drunk's. My right eye was shut into a slit. A rash cut into my neck a few inches below the folds of my swelled chin. My earlobes were as big as orchid petals. Everything itched, but I refused to scratch, so I had a look, I suppose, of grim determination on my face. Newcomers to the camp seemed to read it as a readiness to do some sort of brutality. I could see why they made that mistake (the boys who had been there when I had arrived had better reason to suspect that I was violent, but I'll get to that later). I did sit on the edge of my bunk or the edge of a tree stump or, for that matter, the edge of whatever I was on— but it was not out of some kind of belligerence, really, or even a readiness to act, but because I couldn't stand feeling the fiery itchiness that inflamed every single inch of my body. I didn't have the nerve or the flexibility to examine all the folds and soft tissue too closely, and for that reason it was hard to tell what itched and what didn't. I had to lie in my bed at night, splayed out like some half-wit martyr staked to the ground just to get some relief from the heat that was radiating from parts of my body that I'd need one of those dental mirrors to see.

That poison ivy gave me a new way of presenting myself to the world, though: damaged and more than willing to fight. Of course, this was a lie. I wouldn't call myself a man of action. I had read a lot more about life than I had actually been willing to live it. And even though I wasn't a coward, exactly, I was much better at avoiding confrontations than I was at engaging in them. Even weeks after the blisters disappeared, the scars hung like shadows on my arms and face, and I leaned in a way that probably looked as if I were getting ready to launch an attack or shed my skin. In reality, I wanted to hide deep inside my skin and stay as motionless as possible.

So at sixteen years old I got to feel what prison was like. My whole body was a prison. I was walled in even inside my own flesh. Remaining still was the best way not to feel any discomfort. It also gave me plenty of time to think about what I was doing in Yulan, a town with a Chinese name but an Irish—and German-American population of about three hundred. Nobody seemed to know for certain where the name came from, but *yulan* meant magnolia or mountain laurel in Chinese, I was told. Probably some Chinese laborer on the railroad that was built through Port Jervis in the nineteenth century saw the pink and white blossoms on the lacquered leaves and was reminded of the mountains and flowers of his homeland. In a wave of nostalgia he may have moaned *yulan, yulan*.

There's no way of saying why the people who settled there decided on that name. There never would be a Chinese family who lived there. Not even a place that served Chinese food, as far as I knew. Maybe some Irish settlers heard the coolies repeating the word *yulan* as if it were an incantation, and they latched onto it for good luck in the hardscrabble world they faced. I don't blame them for reaching out for any kind of luck that might have seemed near at hand—even if it was an illusion. The name made me feel that I had been transported out of the Bronx to some nether world, a dark fairy-tale landscape breathlessly real and unreal at the same time. It was like living in a storybook, a dream drifting into a nightmare and back to a dream. For me, the word *yulan* had a magical incomprehensibility to it, like *shazam*.

In those first weeks in Yulan I had a lot of time to think about how I came to leave the Bronx. There's no question that leaving that part of the world is a pretty common tale. The Bronx is all exits and no entrances. If there's a place that has "departure" written all over it, it's the Bronx. Not many people stay there unless they have to, unless they're too poor or too old to make their escape. If you were over twenty-five years old and still living in my neighborhood, you were either a junkie or too stupid to know better.

I'd just turned sixteen when I left, and even though I had dreamed of getting out of there for years, my leaving came abruptly and as a complete surprise to me. By a strange coincidence that I'll explain a little later, it was Mark Twain who led to my leaving.

2

I left the Bronx on June 21, a day before my birthday, on a morning so hot that the pigeons tiptoed across the sticky tar on the roofs of the apartment buildings. By noon the temperature was in the high nineties, without even a breath stirring the marsh reeds on Clason's Point. On a day like that in the Bronx, the sky looks white-hot, and anything with a brain lurks in the shade. The month before, President Johnson had come on the television, a sad-faced cowboy, appealing to all Americans to stand together in supporting the draft and the fight in Vietnam. At a certain point in his speech, I thought he was going to howl in sorrow, like a hound dog caught in a steel trap. I felt bad for him. He reminded me of the old men I saw slouched in the back of Ahearn's Bar, liquid-eyed and loose-fleshed. He made me remember that I didn't want to feel that kind of sorrow, that I didn't want to feel caught in that way. He also made me remember that the war may have been thirteen thousand miles away, but it was getting closer to me every day as I moved toward my eighteenth birthday. It was a storm heading in my direction. And I couldn't do much more than watch its progress. It was just one more thing I couldn't figure out. One more thing I couldn't do anything about.

I spent a lot of time in my last few months in the Bronx on the roof of my apartment building, reading comic books and newspapers that I stole from the candy store around the corner and books that I lifted from the library. I might not have been ethical (as a matter of fact, I was pretty much in a constant state of Catholic guilt during those days, so much so that feeling guilty about things in general seemed as natural to me as being hungry at dinnertime if I hadn't eaten lunch that afternoon), but I did have an aesthetic conscience that I was scrupulous about: if I didn't like what I had stolen, I'd return it. Sometimes it was harder getting it back in without being caught than it was taking it out. I just didn't want to hold onto books that I didn't value. Even if I didn't like a magazine or book, though, I always read it before I brought it back. I'm not sure if I didn't want to judge things rashly or if I worried that I might miss something, maybe even one good sentence in a book that was otherwise a piece of shit. So I read everything just in case.

I had plenty of time to read because I rarely did my homework. I loved books, still do, everything about them, from the faint smell of wood pulp and desire in the new ones to the musty odor of a damp attic and memories in the old. Opening a book is like starting a new life. The pleasure of reading any book for the first time is deep and somehow filled with both happiness and regret. If it were a physical feeling (and sometimes it is), I think it might be like the faraway pain that you get in your chest after you've been swimming too long and take a deep breath. It hurts, but it lets you know that you're alive. I still hesitate sometimes with a closed book in my hands, as I often did then, trying to prolong the moment, anticipating the rush of excitement that the first sentence, if it's the true one, can produce. Then, once I read the book for a while, if I like it, I'll slow down, close the covers, hold the book against my chest and let the story drift under me and through me. At those moments I feel like I've fallen off a cliff but the words hold me up, keep me afloat for as long as I can stay in touch with the voice telling the story. It's sort of my voice I hear, or at least the voice of someone familiar enough to be my twin brother.

Early on I realized that I couldn't change what was about to happen in a story, but I could make it wait to happen. I could tease it and myself at the same time. It was like experiencing life without any of the real jeopardy. It seemed to be a practice for living, a way of getting ready for what life could hold, even though I came to realize there was no way to get fully prepared. Still, it was a way of practicing on other people's happiness and sorrow. A way of making something inside you lighter and stronger. At times it felt like experience itself, more real than any stickball game or subway ride, as true as any love or fear. And, besides, once I'd read the story, I could make it happen over and over again just opening the book one more time. I liked the way the world felt when I could tell exactly what was going to happen, even if I didn't understand why it happened. In some way, the kind of knowing that comes from reading a story seemed to make things clearer. Or at least it kept the confusion at a distance for a while.

And most of the time things just didn't seem clear enough to me. My mother died a year and a half before I was sent away, and everything fell apart around then. She was sick for a long time, for nearly three years, turning shades of white and yellow, her stare becoming flat and fish-eyed, and the bones pressing against her skin as if they were alive and wanted to crack through the flesh. It was hard for me to take my eyes off her. And, of course, that was one more thing to feel guilty about—not being able to stop watching my mother die.

If you've ever watched someone die of emphysema, you'd never smoke. You wouldn't want to see anyone light up a cigarette. You might even wish you'd never been born, then you wouldn't ever have the chance of suffering like that or seeing someone you care about have to suffer in that way. Dying should be easier. It would still be scary as hell. All the questions about what comes next and whether our bodies come with us and if our loved ones all meet would still be unanswered, but we could just float away like in a cartoon, the spirit image lifting from the body. I probably should have spent less time in front of the television on Saturday mornings as a kid, but if we paid attention cartoons might provide us with solutions to a lot of our problems.

Dying doesn't have much to do with cartoons, though. A person with emphysema drowns in his own phlegm. For months, maybe years, you can hear the crackle and gurgle in the lungs. The cough turns into a bark, strangled by mucus and fear. The person gets dreamy-eyed and desperate. You find yourself looking everywhere but into the person's eyes.

Anyone who says dying is fast and simple is either crazy or working in Hollywood. I suppose it can come now and again like a thunderbolt, a stroke or a bullet to the brain, but I'd bet that most of the time it happens the way it did with my mother, slow and terrifying. My mother fought it the whole way, every day for those years. She fought to catch her breath, to give up cigarettes, to uncramp her hands after dialysis. Each day was a battle with pain and fear. Each day she fought to regain the life that had been stolen from her by disease. Her disease became as real to me as any of our neighbors in the apartment building in which we lived—even more so. The disease had a personality of its own—smirking and arrogant. And cruelly deceptive, allowing itself to be defeated just enough to give my mother shreds of hope as she deteriorated. I found myself hating her disease the way you'd hate another person, imagining its face as I slit its throat or plucked out its eyes. You get to hate the disease the way you'd hate an anonymous caller that dials your number at all times of the night relentlessly for months, someone who doesn't have the courage to leave his name or meet you face to face.

The body doesn't give up easily. It struggles even when it seems embarrassing to do so any longer. That's the way my mother's body struggled, and after a while I started to think of her body, like the disease, as something separate from her, an alien, a monster in league with her illness who had laid siege to her and kept her walled inside. The idea of building a wall began to feel to me like the only smart way to stay alive. So when I came across magazines with pictures of Vermont scenes, my eyes lingered on the images of stone walls, the higher, I thought, the more beautiful.

My father began to drink around the same time my mother first got sick. I couldn't recall him having much more than an occasional beer before that. Once she took to bed pretty much permanently, he had a drink in his hand whenever I saw him. It became hard to remember ever seeing him without one. A can of beer was as much a part of his hand as the gold wedding band was a part of my mother's. With beer he was okay, though, even when it was two six-packs a day. It was when he drank hard liquor that he became someone I didn't recognize at all.

He found some way of keeping his job as a carpenter, or at least he kept finding new ones when he was laid off for not getting to the work site on time or at all. He was good with tools and loved working with wood. And by what he was able to do with it, it seemed that the wood shaped itself to his touch, as if it loved the feel of his hands. His foremen treated him like a child who knew an important secret. They spoiled him until he finished his job or until they couldn't accept his behavior any more and keep face among the other workers. Then they dismissed him with the sort of regret men usually reserve for their own wasted talents. Nobody ever seemed to dislike him. They always began the "you're fired" speech by saying, "James, I wish I didn't have to do this. I've never seen a better finish carpenter than you in my life. But . . ."

In the last two months of her sickness, I can't remember my mother leaving her bed, except when she had to be taken to the clinic three times a week to be hooked up to a dialysis machine. My father said that it had something to do with the medicine they gave her in the hospital once, causing her kidneys to fail. The skin on her arms and legs was sheer as sunlight except for the dark purple bruises that seemed to be there to remind the world of the constant pain she was in. The last time she went into the hospital she knew that she was going to die, but she got my father to sign her out because she wanted to do it at home.

Her bedroom window opened to a view of the back alley of our apartment building, and it was late spring, when everything should have been in bloom. Of course, there wasn't much to blossom in our neighborhood, a few chestnut trees on Garrison Avenue but not much else. It was all buildings and concrete until you got down to the river. But she liked looking out the alley window. She said it was peaceful and every now and then this guy would come along and play the saxophone. He played it so sweetly that it was easy enough to imagine birds chirping and the wind whistling through a bank of trees. Maybe that's what she did imagine because when the old guy came around, unshaven and squint-eyed, she always smiled. It might not have been a smile exactly but something closer to a relaxing of the muscles in her face. She'd have me prop her up with a couple of pillows, and when he was done playing, she'd tell me to toss a quarter out the window. As it left my hand, his eyes tilted up and he always tipped his sax in our direction. He probably played a lot of songs over the months he came to the alleyway, but I remember only "Let the Rest of the World Go By." It was my father's favorite song. He used to sing it all the time when I was a little kid, but I hadn't heard him sing in years.

My mother had been a beautiful woman when she was young. The photographs I had seen of her reminded me of Gene Tierney. Her name was Mildred, a name that I always thought too dull for her mysterious kind of beauty. Dark hair and foreign eyes. A doe's eyes caught by some photographer for *National Geographic*. Watchful. By the time she was dying, her eyes looked out from some place distant and unreachable. She got very sad at times and scared too. You could see it in her eyes. Her life seemed to be concentrated in her eyes. They filmed over and narrowed in terror at night. But she never completely lost her sense of humor or her sense of wonder. She was curious about everything, about books and politics and what the neighbors were doing. You could almost believe that sort of curiosity could keep you from harm. But I learned better, of course. I found out during her illness that wonder was like innocence. It didn't protect you at all.

Every time she heard a strange noise in the alley or a shout in the hallway, she'd say, "Tommy, go ahead and look. I know you're dying to see what that is." We both knew that she was the one who really wanted to see what was happening. And whatever it was—Mrs. Borneman sweeping up a broken vase or Jimmy Hanley arguing with his sister—she had to have the details. She needed to know who was on the front stoop and what Mrs. Civetelli was wearing to church. Before she got too sick to go, I'd push her to Mass in a wheelchair. "I should have worn my polka dot dress," she'd whisper. "It would match my arms." Then she'd smile and say, "Move faster, mister, or we won't beat Mrs. D'Angelo to a seat in the last pew."

It was difficult for me to imagine—and perhaps for her as well—how she could actually be dying when everyday life was continuing as if nothing out of the ordinary were going on. It made me consider the possibility that my fears for her were unfounded, that this was just another childhood nightmare that would disappear in its own course. I was afraid that she would die and I was afraid that she wouldn't, that her sickness would turn her into a stranger who couldn't even recognize herself. Each morning I woke up and held myself perfectly still, not sure for a moment if I had dreamed her illness into existence and if I couldn't, by not moving a muscle, unmake it.

Every now and then I'd catch her looking at herself in her compact mirror, a look of surprise washing over her, as if she couldn't figure out who this was in the few square inches of glass or what had happened or when exactly the change had begun. Her thick brown hair had turned brittle, her ivory skin all chipped and discolored, her lips dry and thin. If she caught me glancing at her, she'd purse her lips and then say, "What do you think? A new hairstyle? Or maybe I should dye it red and then I could be a stand-in for Lucille Ball. Eh, Ricky?" One time when she was in the hospital and I was sitting there while a nurse took her blood pressure, she looked up into the bored face of the woman holding her arm and said with the kind of matter-of-fact tone most people save for simple questions, "You know, I used to be beautiful once." Then she said it again, this time as if it were a punch line to a joke, her inflection rising to a vaudeville rhythm, but to me it sounded wistful. The whole sentence seemed to be a sigh.

Toward the end, she didn't ever want to sleep, even though she was in her bed most of the time. Her lips had turned a shade of blue, and her hair was as dry as pictures I'd seen of late summer wheat. She wanted to listen to me talk or to play cards, even if she wasn't able to concentrate on either. Or she would say, "I'd bet you'd like a nice cup of tea, Tommy, wouldn't you?" I didn't like tea, but I knew that she wanted to hear me rattling pots and filling cups of water in the kitchen. She wanted to fill her moments with our life together. She never took more than one sip of the tea or a bite out of the toast that she had asked for.

When my father came home from work, he was silent. He seemed angry at her for being sick and at me for being healthy. He never yelled, though. It was as if the beer went down his throat in a stream, a current, that wouldn't permit anything to come back the other way. He just floated away from us until he was not much more than a pinpoint on another shore. I'm not sure exactly when he started to disappear, but it was right around the time of her first hospital stay. I've thought a lot about why he began to disappear, like a man intentionally going deeper and deeper into a fog, but I still don't have any absolute answers—just guesses. Of course, partly, it must have been the fear of losing my mother that made him turn away but it may have had something to do with his jobs as well. He loved making things out of wood, but I suspect that he found no light in the big office buildings he worked on for one construction company after another. I could tell that he hated our neighborhood, too. The Irish and Italians were leaving and being replaced by Puerto Ricans and blacks. He never said much, but I could see it in his eyes as he sat at the Formica table in the kitchen and gazed out of the window into the dusk. By the time my mother fell gravely ill he was already gone—he had just left his body behind. I think he felt guilty that he had deserted her, but as she got sicker he was like a lost hiker on a cold mountain who had given up on finding his way back. Maybe he didn't want to find his way back. It was easier and less painful to be lost, to let himself drift sweetly into the cold night.

As he retreated from our lives, my mother came into sharper focus. She filled the silence he left behind. Where he seemed lost, she always appeared to be on the edge of discovering something. One of the last things she said to me was, "I wish I could know everything, Tommy. I'd like to see everything in the world over and over again. Everything seems new to me now. Even you."

She fought for two weeks after she got home from the hospital for the last time. It was hard to understand where she got the strength. She still smiled at me every once in a while, but most of the time she just clutched her blue prayer book and stared in the direction of the alley window. The chaplain from the hospital came every day, carrying a small circular gold box, which was large enough for earrings but that held the Eucharist. He looked like the kind of man who had done well in spelling bees throughout elementary school and then found it puzzling trying to figure out what to do with the rest of his life. But he didn't seem depressed about it, just a little bemused, as if everything were slightly silly but not really sad. I liked him a lot, and I know that my mother did too. Her eyes brightened when he entered the room, and she became girlish in an awkward way, as if she were trying to remember how to flirt.

The doctor who came every other day was about the same age as the chaplain, middle-aged only younger than my mother, and where the chaplain seemed vague and wonderfully shapeless, the doctor was all sharp angles and clear edges. But I liked him too because he appeared ready to defeat any disease by simply facing it down with common sense and science. He wasn't going to let anything scare him away. When my mother couldn't catch her breath and her eyes widened with knowledge, he acted as calmly as a TV repairman, plugging and unplugging tubes, placing a mask over her face, and turning on a boxlike machine that he had left days before in the corner of her room.

He looked down at her, smiled, and talking so loud that it seemed as if she were not dying but deaf, said, "You'd probably like to put this mask on me, wouldn't you?"

He paused, looked out the window, and then lowered his voice to a whisper, "Doctors create more ways to torture people keeping them alive . . ."

I shifted in my chair and when he looked at me he appeared surprised that anybody else was in the room. It was as if he thought the room was crowded enough with my mother, himself, and her disease all sharing such a small space.

She died on Ash Wednesday, in the afternoon. The ashes were a check mark on my forehead. It looked like one of those stickers people get for voting. I was checked off. I had done my duty. Of course, the ashes were supposed to remind me of my mortality, that from ashes I came and to ashes I would return. But like a lot of lessons that I learned in school or church, it made me wonder what the catechism had left out. Communion made me part of something, but it also implied that only some were saved. Confirmation made me a soldier of Christ, slapped into battle, prepared for one more form of obedience. But school and church didn't offer answers to complex questions as much as they demanded silence. God's silence was my father's silence during my mother's illness. It was a Catholic silence. It seemed to me then to have less to do with faith than it had to do with submission. After about a year of watching my mother suffer, not believing came to be a sort of faith for me, a way of knowing that suggested the world couldn't do much more harm to me than it was already doing. But I got my ashes anyway so that my mother would see them and know I had gone to church. I didn't need the ashes to help me understand some lesson about mortality, and this is what bothered me about the church. It seemed to provide a lot of information about things I already knew, but it didn't help much with those I didn't. I knew my mother was going to die. I just didn't understand why or how I was supposed to live afterward. In all honesty, I'm not even sure if she cared if I got the ashes or not. In the last week, she seemed to have gotten tired of living, plain and simple, and not much interested her. For me, this was the saddest part of her dying—her imagination during the last few days turned on itself and disappeared. She just wanted to be gone. It was as if she had already left and forgotten to take her body with her.

I was never too scared during the afternoons with her because it didn't seem possible to me that anyone could die in the sunlit middle of the day. Death seemed possible only in the night. Decency demanded that death wait for darkness to fall. I had just gotten home from the playground of St. Anne's Elementary School, and the chaplain and the doctor were both in her room. Everyone looked around as if they were embarrassed when I walked in. I was embarrassed myself to have been out playing punchball with my friends. It didn't seem fair that anyone should be playing while my mother struggled to breathe. But for a second it seemed as if she weren't really sick at all but instead was a character in a Victorian novel caught entertaining two gentlemen callers who should not have been there.

As if to shatter the awkwardness, she whispered, "Play cards with me, Tommy."

I sat down next to her bed as the men backed away toward the oxygen machine like two stockbrokers moving together to discuss the latest price quote, acting as if they had ordinary, practical business to attend to before the lunch hour. Death seemed out of the question in this no-nonsense afternoon world where little things needed to be done, where my mother and I would be concentrating on how many hearts were in our hands and how we could avoid being left with the Queen of Spades.

For about ten minutes the universe collapsed into our game. If we could keep on playing, my mother would never die. Who could die in the midst of a game of hearts? The game would save her. It would save us. As long as we continued to perform our ordinary tasks, how could anything extraordinary happen? It would have no place in such a world.

But we didn't finish the game. I saw her make one last effort to hold her concentration on the cards, and then she closed her eyes and lay her head back on the pillow.

"I don't think I can finish the game," she said and opened her eyes to look at me.

The chaplain and the doctor were back at her bedside before the word "sure" was out of my mouth. They bent over her, one on each side of me. Outside, the old sax player had returned, filling the alleyway with a faraway sound.

The light in the room had already begun to break apart. It seemed to be cast into little pieces like the noisy illumination spit from a movie projector. It was more dreamtime than daytime, with words and movements floating on the brittle ridges of light. My mother looked past the chaplain and the doctor through the shards of light at me. Her eyes were clear and calm.

"Get me that, Tommy," she said, and I knew she meant her little blue prayer book even though she never made a gesture and didn't try to raise her hand to point toward the table next to her bed.

I gave it to her, and for a minute she clutched my hand and the book. When she let go, her eyes closed again. With her eyes closed, she seemed about to speak. A sound, a cough in preparation to say one last thing, came from deep inside of her.

The words broke like glass against her chest—"I . . . no" or "I . . . know"—and I leaned in to rest my ear near her lips.

But there was nothing but the echo of the words in my head. I placed my fingers against her cheekbones and let them slide to her mouth. Her breath pulsed and wheezed against my fingertips, and I was a blind man reading a message in Braille about the end of the world.

She slept for about a quarter of an hour. When she woke up, her breathing had gotten much worse. Her eyes had a film over them and were both distant and brutally clear at the same time. She looked at me and through me.

"Let me breathe," she whispered. Then urgently, "Tommy, make me breathe. Let me breathe."

For half an hour, she wheezed and pushed away the oxygen mask that the doctor and I tried to hold onto her face. I kept saying, "Take the mask, Mom. I'm trying to help you. Let me help you."

But she pushed it away, saying, "Make me breathe. Make . . . me . . . breathe." Until the words seemed to take all the air out of the room. I wanted her to live, and I wanted her to die. I wanted to forget for a minute how much I loved her. Or maybe I didn't love her enough to see her live.

And then, as if she read my thoughts, she squeezed my hand and said, "Let me go." She closed her eyes, her lips parted by the last syllable like a singer holding a note, soundless, in the air forever.

When I touched her, I knew right away that she was gone. There was something about her skin. It didn't feel real anymore. It was a doll's, a cool plastic. In one second, a pulse of breath, everything had changed. She had been with me and now she never would be again. The doctor and priest began to move busily around the bed, the doctor holding his fingers against her wrist and listening to her heart with a stethoscope and the priest drawing a cross in oil on her forehead and muttering prayers. I just sat on the bed, not listening to either of them. I felt the priest put his meaty hand on my shoulder. Then, outside, the music stopped, and I went to the door, opened it, and walked down to the river.

3

When my mother died, my father left completely. I mean he stayed at home and drank or went to work when he had a job, but he was more of a stranger than he had ever been before. I wondered at times if we were really related at all. We had the same wheat-colored hair and light blue eyes, but at nearly fifteen years old I was only a shade over five feet tall and barely weighed one hundred pounds, and he was six foot two and barrel-chested and had forearms cabled with muscles. He looked to me like the drawings in the advertisements for Charles Atlas strength products in the weightlifting magazines I sometimes bought. At other times, I wondered if I weren't just a copy of him in miniature. It was only a matter of time, perhaps, before I became him, and although I wasn't certain exactly what that meant, it scared me.

My father and I lived in a perfect silence that was almost as soothing as floating on water. He was just a body next to mine on a great salt lake. We were both doing the dead man's float, holding our breath. Every once in a while we spoke a few words, but it seemed if we dared to turn and face one another or if we said too much, we might cough and sputter and sink forever. Most of the time we kept our mouths closed.

Much later, when I read my great-great-grandfather's journal, I began to sense the meanings and consequences of silence, how silence is a language of its own and speaks with as much subtlety and force as words. But then silence seemed a way of escaping the responsibilities of meaning. When my father did speak to me, most of the time it was in the form of directions or questions he had already answered. "Tommy, go get me a pack of Chesterfield Regulars around the corner, hey?"

And although it was only a five-minute walk, I'd go out for an hour, spending most of the time reading comic books in the back of the candy store. He'd never ask me why I had taken so long. He'd just nod, his face a silhouette reflected against the dark window, when I came in the door. I liked the feel of the cellophane as the package slid from my fingers onto the kitchen table. It felt like liquid, and the feeling stayed on my fingertips as I drifted back to the living room.

My father hadn't been good to my mother when she got sick. He hated her disease so much he began to hate her as if she had given her body over to another man. He hated her disease in the way he would have hated her lover and hated her for having one. And without his hatred he wouldn't have had anything to shield himself. So he despised her disease and then her and eventually everything. Hate became a form of love for him, I guess.

Of course, he never told me any of this, but I think that's the way it was. He wanted to speak about it, I could tell or imagined that I could, but there was something that wouldn't let him talk sweetly or encouragingly. In some strange way, he seemed to feel that losing his hatred would have been a betrayal of my mother. So hatred became his only way of showing how much he loved her, I think. I know that doesn't make too much sense. But that's the way the truth is most of the time.

I'd like to tell the truth, if the truth can be told, I mean. But writing these things about my father, I realize that he's become a character in my story, and I can't make him any more real or true than that. Once you start writing about someone, he becomes the person inside your head, just another part of your imagination and whatever truth is in that. There isn't a person who ever lived who isn't too complex for words, too mysterious for any sentence that can be devised. In ways, my father was a son-of-a-bitch—he made the air in our house hard to breathe at times.

But that's not the way things had always been in our house, and it wasn't the person he was—at least when I was a young kid. Or the way I've come to remember him. He'd been a good father and a loving husband. He'd always been quiet. No matter how many people were around, he'd seem to be sitting on the outside of the circle, an expression on his face that suggested he was only half paying attention to what was happening around him. He was dreamy-eyed, people said. But anyone who thought he wasn't there had a surprise coming, because he never missed a beat in a discussion, even if he didn't seem to be part of it.

He was funny, and he poked at a conversation like a kid on a river's edge with a sharpened stick looking for whatever was interesting in the grass. He could be silly, too, puns slipping and sliding all over his lips at the dinner table—"What, pickled beets again? Who am I, Jack Kerouac?" or "How about a steak tomorrow? Or do I need to become a vampire first?" My mother and I would groan, and he'd roll his eyes, "I vant blud."

At parties he'd bring out his four-string guitar and pick away so that each note was held outside any chord. Each note hung separate, like a carefully pronounced syllable. His singing voice was soft and sweet as a young girl's. He was like a man who has some lovely boyish quality to him and is more deeply masculine for it. At those moments his silences seemed like wisdom, a watchfulness that told a boy something about being a man.

He changed even though I'm sure he didn't want to. Sometimes I suppose that happens to people. No one plans to become what they don't want to be. You probably wake up one morning like Kafka's cockroach, trying to figure out how it all came about when you thought you had been aware of what was going on and where your life was headed. The whole thing—what your life has turned into—must seem like it has nothing to do with you or anything you can remember doing. But can that ever be true? I mean, can our character appear before us suddenly, a surprise, like some thundering fate, without our having a hand in it in some way?

When my mother died, he seemed to realize with catastrophic force how much he loved her, and that made him angry. He was furious with her for going away, for leaving him alone. He wanted to forget her completely, I think, because remembering made him realize that each of us lived with the consequences of our lives, and he saw too clearly into his own future. So for more than a year after she died, we lived in a humming silence. Until even the sounds I made closing doors or turning pages in books splintered the air and made him wince.

I understood how he felt. I wanted the same silence that he did, I'm sure. I didn't want to be hugged or have deep, emotional conversations. I was happy to be living with someone who was like a step uncle or third cousin, someone who could disappear without causing a ripple in my life. It felt fine not to have to get too close. I didn't want to love him any more than he wanted to love me.

When he did speak, most of the time it was talk about what was going wrong with the city or on his job. He loved to work with saw and lathe but hated the construction jobs he found himself in.

"The unions are falling to shit," he'd say. "The damn niggers don't want to work. But they have to have them. They don't work a half a day for a day's wages, but we have to have them on the job. If my foreman knew shit from shinola, he might know how to run a job the right way. He'd have to start by firing half the crew. And it's the same friggin' thing in this neighborhood. If we could get rid of half of them, it'd be a decent place to live. But it's going to hell and taking us along with it."

I didn't have any black friends. Black kids and whites kept apart as if it were a natural condition. It was as if we spoke different languages. We eyed each other carefully, enemy soldiers walking a border. We passed by each other in the kind of watchful silence that my father and I understood very well.

I loved my neighborhood, though, because it was so crowded that it was usually easy to be invisible. I lived on Longfellow Avenue in the Hunt's Point section of the Bronx, a thumb of land pointing into the East River. On clear days I'd go down past the Market toward the marshland and the river and watch planes angle over Riker's Island toward LaGuardia Airport. The river was the color of rusted metal and rotten vegetables, but every now and again it smelled like City Island and the Long Island Sound. I mean that it smelled like another kind of place, ripe and alive. City Island was only a few miles directly north of where I lived, but it might as well have been on another planet. It looked like the pictures I had seen in *National Geographic* of New England fishing villages with narrow cobblestone streets and beach houses with shutters and window boxes. Sailboats bobbed in the waters surrounding the town pier, the peremptory cries of gulls filled the air, and, I imagined, the salt air had the acrid smell of loneliness and possibilities.

Most of the time, the exhaust from the trucks grinding into and out of the big market filled the air near Hunt's Point, even down toward the river. There just wasn't any easy way of getting away from the foul breath of the city. When I played with my friends in the schoolyard of P.S. 48, the sounds of the car horns and tires screeching mixed with our shouts, the smoke in the air turned the spaldings a deeper shade of pink, and our bodies vibrated to the rhythm of the earth-rattling trucks and buses. There was always some kid yelling up to a fifth-floor window, calling, "Hey, Ma, throw down a quarter!"

Sometimes, on my way home, I'd go with my friend Michael Murphy up to his second-floor apartment in a building near the playground. His mother was out each afternoon, cleaning apartments on Park Avenue or Sutton Place in Manhattan. She would waddle in about 6:30, grease from the subway seats staining her coat, her stockings fallen around her swelled ankles, and smile at the two of us as if nothing in the world could make her happier than to get us dinner. I stayed a few times for hamburgers and french fries, but most often I left, saying that my father wanted me home for dinner.

The hours that I spent in Murph's apartment were difficult to measure by the clock because his stories, and his mother's when she returned from work, seemed to erase time. Past and present were all the same. O'Neill's Pub in

Youghal along the southern coast of Ireland and O'Malley's Tavern on Kingsbridge Road in the Bronx were extensions of one another. Ireland and America became one narrative, a geography held together by the voice telling the stories. The Murphys always had a tale of a cousin who had just come over from Galway or an uncle who should never have left Tralee. Tales of grown men finding themselves more lost than Odysseus, stumbling around in front of a three-family house near the convent for the nuns of Our Lady of Mercy School, the men singing drunk after a wedding at the VFW, shouting at each other until the nuns stuck their cropped heads out the windows at four o'clock in the morning, stunning the men into silence as they fell crashing, ass first, into separate garbage cans. Stuck fast and too drunk to care until the garbagemen showed up a few hours later to shake their heads, laugh, and eventually pry them loose.

Murph would start a story and his mother would shake her head in a well-rehearsed rhythm of disapproval, saying, "Och, och, a donkey's ass that Brian Byrne always was and his friend Connie O'Shea was no better. When we were children in Dublin, Connie fell into the Liffey one night on his way home from Temple Bar. But he sang like an angel, even with the filthy water gurgling in his mouth." And then she would begin to sing "Danny Boy," stopping only when Murph sang along with her, his mouth half full of Coke.

When I returned home on those nights, their stories crowded into my apartment with me. It didn't matter if their stories were true or not. They were as true for me as the ones I read in books, and in listening to them I began to suspect that it might be possible to tell a story that could become true, a story that could make the world instead of being made of it.

It might take hours for the tidal silence in my house to drag the sound of the stories under. Sometimes when I turned the lock in the door and walked into the living room, I'd say loud enough for anyone in the hallway to hear, "Hey, Dad, I'm home. How was your day?" Of course, when he was at home I never asked such questions and he didn't either, until one day in the late spring.

"How are you doing?" he said when I came home from the schoolyard. He looked out the window and cleared his throat.

"You're almost a man now." The words came out so fast that they seemed practiced. He had more than likely played variations of this conversation in his mind many times during the last months. I didn't know how to react, and he looked embarrassed that he had said anything. It was as if he were a relative who hadn't seen me for a long time and was surprised by my growth spurt and couldn't for a second place me as part of his family. I took off my jacket and draped it over the hissing radiator.

"I'm doing all right, I guess."

"Yeah, I can see that. You can take care of yourself." He looked over at the jacket, his eyes following the steam rising from it.

"Sure I can. Sure."

The sound of *sure* crept into the hiss of the steam and we sat there like two people trying to hear a conversation over the roar of the surf. He looked directly into my eyes and said, "Things, you know, aren't the way you want them to be all the time. You wish you could change them. But you can't. Right? You understand what I'm getting at? You can't do anything about certain things. You can't change what the world is."

"Sure. Yeah, I know."

But I wasn't sure that I did. I picked the jacket off the radiator and felt its warmth against my arms. It lay in my hands as if he had just handed it to me without telling me what to do with it. Like his words, the jacket seemed out of place. It made me nervous to hear him say that much, to speak so many words at one time. For a moment I had the peculiar thought that he was going to sing "Danny Boy" or some other song in an extraordinary imitation of Mrs. Murphy. But I think I was really afraid that if he started to let the words come out, he wouldn't be able to hold them back, and there would be a flood that neither of us could handle. But just as that first cold trickle of fear entered my chest and I placed the warm jacket beneath my folded arms, he went silent again.

Two hours later, before he went to bed that night, I heard him crush one last can of beer and let it clang against the others in the garbage bag in the kitchen. Then he walked into the living room and eased himself into his chair. He didn't look at me sitting on the couch. When he did speak, it sounded like a man in the middle of a conversation.

"You know, I never knew my father."

My mother had told me a little of the story, but I just kept my eyes steadily on him, waiting to hear what he had to say.

"I was born a month after he died in France during World War I."

"How did he die?"

"It was a few days after his twenty-first birthday. He died the way so many died in that war, fighting over a few yards of dirt between one trench and another. It was only a month before the Armistice, but I guess that doesn't make any difference, does it?"

"Why didn't you live with your grandfather?"

"Something happened between my mother and my grandfather. They blamed each other for my father's death, I think. I never got to know my grandfather any more than I knew my father, and my mother would never talk about the old man. My father she barely knew. They met when he was twenty, and he was dead a year later.

"A few times when I was growing up, my grandfather called when my mother wasn't at home and told me—when I was old enough to come on my own—to visit him in the mountains. But by the time I was old enough to understand things, my grandfather and I had our separate lives and it didn't make much sense to drag that forgotten life out into the open. I had my own war to fight in.

"I saw his house once in the mountains upstate after he died. He left a trust fund to take care of it until one of us—you or me, I guess—we're the only ones left—decides to live in it. That's how he has the will set up. He was a tricky old geezer, I suppose. The only way to inherit his house is to live in it full-time, at least for two years. That wasn't for me. All those skunks and bats. I'm not sure why the old man cared, but there it sits."

"Mom told me something about it—it's in the Catskills?"

"Yes, way back in the woods. So cut off from the world you'd think you were the only person on earth."

"Did he live there by himself all those years?"

"As far as I know he did. For some reason he wanted that place to stay up. He cared more about that place than he did his family, I think. Or maybe it was a monument to his dead son, I don't know. Or a way of getting one of us to return home.

"My mother didn't ever tell me much about my father, but I figured out from what she said that he didn't really have to go to war. He was married and had a child on the way. Who knows why he went.

"One story my mother told about him always stuck with me. He was a carpenter, like me, and he was working in an apartment on 63rd Street right off of the Park. He was rebuilding the window casement on the seventh floor, and he fell out and landed on the doorman below. He killed the doorman, a porridge-fed Irish kid named Billy McMann, who was bent over tying his shoelaces. Broke McMann's neck. Snapped it like a dry chicken bone. My father just stood up, though, looked at McMann long enough to see that he was dead, and walked away, not a scratch on him. People talked about it like it was a miracle, my mother said, and my father walking away without a word, well, they assumed he was in shock, I guess.

"But I think maybe he had accepted his own death on that seventy-foot drop. I've seen things happen to guys on construction sites where they become different people in the blink of an eye. I'm guessing that maybe my father had imagined the concrete of the sidewalk, and when it turned out to be a cushion of Irish fat, he didn't like the twist of fate—even though it meant he was alive. In a strange way I suppose he thought it broke faith with how things were meant to be. So he decided to find another way to die. There are plenty of ways to kill yourself. And a war will give you a lot of chances to die."

He stopped talking then, and for a minute I thought that was all he was going to say. He looked up at me as I sat on the couch, a book opened on my lap.

"What are you reading? Any good?"

"It's called *Henderson the Rain King*. Yeah, it's terrific. It's about this guy. . ." But I didn't finish because the expression on his face told me that he had something else to say, and, besides, he hadn't asked me what it was about.

"It sure looks thick. The paper's about all I can handle. I'm glad you like it. I'm glad you read the way you do. It puts you in a different place, I bet."

"Sometimes."

"Sometimes I think about that. Being in a different place, I mean. About the way some other people live. I try to imagine their lives in other cities. But all I can picture is my life. This place."

I looked hard at him, trying to see his features, for I sensed that I should try to memorize them for the future. But there wasn't much light on his side of the room and he was in the shadows. So I tried instead to remember what he had looked like when I was a little boy. Slim and blond-haired. A tanned face. Veins that stood out like blue streams branching along his forearms and biceps. Eyes so light they looked like sky mixed with clouds. I could see that image of him more clearly than I could see the person in front of me.

It seemed as if he smiled, it was so quick it was hard to tell for sure, and then he spoke one last time.

"I'm glad you can picture other lives. That's a good thing."

Then he went off to bed. That was the last I saw of him.

4

He didn't leave a note. He just took off. He did leave an envelope, though, with over a thousand dollars in it—enough to pay the rent and buy food for a good long time. He also left behind a deeper and more soothing silence, an emptiness that felt good to me. He left me with a feeling that there was nothing else for me to lose. And as long as I didn't break the wall of silence around me, I would be all right. At night sometimes, I'd think about my mother as I lay in bed. It often felt as if a dark wind were passing through me, a chill that swept into my bowels and up toward my chest. I prayed then that the feeling would stop, blow away into the night. I prayed not to feel anything. And after a while my prayers were answered. That dark wind stopped showing up at nighttime, and I stopped feeling anything when I thought of my mother's dying, and I didn't even think about where my father might be or what he might be doing.

I lasted about a year on my own. I let them cancel the telephone service, but I did pay the rent on time, bringing it in cash up to Mrs. Haffheimer, the landlady, on the second floor. Every once in a while a neighbor would stop me in the hall of the apartment building and ask, "How are you doing, Tommy? And how's your Dad? I haven't seen him around in ages." I'd say we were both fine, just pretty busy. These people were just making conversation and didn't want to know anyway, so no one disturbed my life. I did enough work in school to pass and not get any letters sent home. And, to my teachers, my behavior appeared to be good, if not exemplary, although it was really just a cloudy-eyed indifference. I was my father's son, all right.

My father's departure, then, hadn't caused even a ripple in my perfect solitude. I liked being alone. Loneliness was nothing new for me. It felt like home. I had gotten used to the ache that my mother's death left me with. When she died, I understood what *heartache* meant. It wasn't some figure of speech. It was a physical thing. Like a toothache. The pain swelled and contracted in its own rhythm, but it was always there. So even when I didn't feel it directly, I felt its absence. I guess you could say my heart felt sore, as if it had been hit by something, bruised as deep as it could without splitting open.

Then after a while it felt hollow and sometimes as if it were awash in icy water. The best feeling for me came to be that hollowness. It was like being on the edge of sleep, the feeling you get when you're lying on the couch watching television and you're just barely conscious of what's happening on the screen—it's all sound and flickering light—and you're there and not there at the same time. It's not like you're moving into another country. It's as if you're already gone.

I wanted someone to be angry with, but for some reason I couldn't get angry at my father. I felt sorry for him, but truly I didn't feel much of anything when I thought of him. There was just a blank space where feeling was supposed to be. I hated pretty deeply, though. I hated something distant and invisible and unnamable. Some idea of justice that seemed a shitty joke. I couldn't even believe much in the chance of good fortune, as I had when I was a kid. The only thing I had to hold onto was the cushion of silence that was part of everything I touched in my apartment. Silence became sweeter than sound. It was the sweetest sound in the world to me.

Or I had books. I wanted life to be like books—who wouldn't, I guess—something enclosed between a front and back cover, with a clear beginning and ending. In books even the confusion and pain had an order and meaning to them. Life was too cluttered and disorderly. And the pain was too real, too close. Sometimes I couldn't get a clear picture in my mind of what was happening in my own life, but in books everything seemed so clear—black marks arranged neatly on a white page. Always an order hidden in what might at first seem to be chaos. Any silence was filled by the voices that those marks on the page made in my head. It was like being in a cloister where the sounds filtered in from outside the walls, and I never saw who made the sounds. I had to imagine that part.

I didn't live like a monk, though. I was usually fairly busy in the world. I didn't even have much time to hang out with my friends in the schoolyard. I worked after school every afternoon in Drewsen's Deli. I rode one of those big bikes with the wide tires and the square basket welded to the front of it, delivering groceries mostly to older women in the neighborhood, flying up and down the hills, boxes of cookies and cans of beans splashing around in the bags. I'd hike up to a fifth-floor apartment, smile, and get a dime or a quarter tip. On Saturdays I worked from eight in the morning until six at night.

Weeknights and late Saturday I spent my time stealing things. I'd hop the turnstile and ride the subway into Manhattan and browse Brentano's or Scribner's. Within a month I had a complete set of Dickens. Before long I had copies of the novels of Flaubert and the complete works of Shelley. I ranged across time periods and the shelves in my thefts—from *Lolita* to *Tom Jones.* In one week I grabbed *Portrait of a Lady, The Decline and Fall of the Roman Empire, Middlemarch, Youngblood Hawke, On the Road, Stuart Little,* and the *Selected Poems of William Butler Yeats.* I got bleary-eyed from reading. When I looked up from the page, the air in my apartment had turned white. My imagination burned, and everything around me was hazy and quiet. I felt as if I were dreaming, and no matter how much I rubbed my sleep-filled eyes with the heels of my hands, the haze remained.

I stole a few books on magic just so that I could master sleight-of-hand. I got so good that I could pocket a Macintosh apple from the fruit stand while the grocer was standing right in front of me talking about the lousy weather. If I wore the right coat, I could steal anything—eggs, milk, loaves of bread, cans of soda—a full week's shopping in one afternoon. Of course, that meant I had to steal a few good coats and jackets from Barney's and Alexander's on Fordham Road, but I must have been born with an innocent face because nobody did anything but smile at me as I walked out of the store with two light-weights tucked under an oversized pea coat.

I stole money, too—from Drewsen's, out of customer's purses, from the poor box at St. Mary's Church—but the steadiest source of cash came from the golf courses in Riverdale and White Plains. I dressed like a caddy—that is, in tan pants and a crewneck sweater—and found ways to get into the locker rooms. There was always plenty of money lying around. I never could figure out how those guys could have so much money and still wear those orange shirts and plaid shorts. I felt guilty about the poor box at St. Mary's and stopped taking anything from it after a few times, but I never felt bad about those golfers. It actually felt good taking their money. There's something about golfers that makes you want to steal from them. All that grass. All that time with nothing better to do than pay attention to that little white ball. It didn't seem to me that they needed all that money too. For what? More plaid pants?

I never thought too much about stealing in general, about its being wrong or how my mother would have been upset if she knew what I was doing. For me it was just a job, but one with an adrenaline rush. When I was stealing things, I imagined myself as somebody else, someone like Jesse James or Clyde Barrow.

When I was in the supermarket, strolling the aisles, slipping a package of chopped meat or Swiss cheese down my pants or palming a can of diced peaches, a gust of fear would strike me. It felt a lot like that icy sense of sadness I used to know at night when I was at home by myself. But the fear, even though it had the same numbing coldness to it as the sadness had, was sharp and swift. It made me stand up straight rather than slump over. It felt good in a way. It was like being so awake that I could see and hear everything around me, and as much as it scared me, it made me feel connected to the world and separate from it at the very same time.

I spent the better part of the year stealing and reading and, when I was in school, daydreaming. I even stole *Crime and Punishment* from the school library one day during lunch hour, but I was too superstitious to read it, I mean because all that talk about crime and punishment. It made me feel guilty just holding it. I used it as a doorstop.

I read *The Great Gatsby* and envied Meyer Wolfsheim his cufflinks made of human molars. In *Moby Dick* I was hypnotized by Queequeg, but I was still young enough to think I understood Captain Ahab. I read Steinbeck and Hemingway and Chaucer and Tolstoy. I was so busy reading that I barely had time to pay any attention to my schoolwork. I barely had time to remember my sadness. I read so much that I began to dream of fictional characters rather than real ones. My days were stitched together by the stories I read.

I might never have gotten caught if it hadn't been for Mark Twain. But you could also say that later he saved my life. It's all in my great-great-grandfather's journal. But I'm getting ahead of myself again. And I'm convinced that the only way to tell this story and have a chance of getting at the truth is to tell it as it happened to me. That way you can make up your own mind about what it all means because it's likely, I suppose, that my view of things is not everyone's.

I was reading *Adventures of Huckleberry Finn* in chemistry class one day. As the teacher talked about the chart of elements, I was reading the chapter toward the end of the book where Huck has lost Jim, ditched the Duke and Dauphin, and come to the Phelps's farm. Mrs. Phelps thinks that he is Tom Sawyer, and Huck is so happy that he says, "It was like being born again, I was so glad to find out who I was." I remember thinking then that having someone hand you a new name like that, as Mrs. Phelps did Huck, was a wonderful piece of luck, like finding out that you were really not your old, half-miserable self but actually someone else altogether—someone who you happened to envy and admire a lot besides. Maybe you were a prince when you thought you were a pauper—Twain had thought of that one too.

Well, right as I finished reading that sentence, Mr. Snyder's shadow darkened my desk, and his open hand pushed down my notebook and revealed the copy of *Huckleberry Finn* beneath. He gave a short speech about "everything in its place," like the elements on the chemical chart, "and this was *not* the place for *Huckleberry Finn*." He made a squeaking sound that came from his nose. It was a noise he always made when he disciplined somebody. Then he took up the book, to be locked in his cabinet with issues of *Playboy,* packages of gum, and other contraband. That locker was more interesting to most of us than any mystery of science he could solve with a piece of chalk or a heated beaker.

I had to steal another copy of the novel that afternoon to see what happened to Huck. It was a weekday, and I didn't want to take the train all the way into Manhattan—so I jumped onto the back of a bus, balancing on the bumper while I gripped the metal strip that held the advertisement for Lavoris below the grimy back window. I hopped off at Fordham Road, startling a woman with a baby carriage as I landed next to her on the sidewalk. She let out a little screech as I ran past her.

The bookstore was down the hill near Webster Avenue, a dark, dusty store with high shelves and not much alphabetical order. A bald-headed Englishman ran it with his honey-haired wife. He always seemed to be on the verge of yelling, and she always appeared to be scooping up some fallen books. He wore a stained green apron, and not even his English accent helped him seem to be anything but a butcher who had wandered into the wrong establishment. My intuition warned me that this was not the place to steal a book. It was simply too unorganized. In a well-run bookstore I became part of the order of the place. But here there was no order that I could see. Everything seemed out of the ordinary.

The books of Mark Twain, which should have been on a lower shelf that people could reach, were balancing precariously near the cobwebs on the ceiling. I needed a stepladder to reach them. Once I went to the trouble of climbing the ladder and stretching on my tiptoes to grab *Huckleberry Finn*, I decided I might as well take *Roughing It* and *A Connecticut Yankee in King Arthur's Court*, too. I got down off the ladder and slid the books under my

Columbia sweatshirt (an extra large stolen from the Columbia University bookstore in April). Of course, I had no idea then about how important Mark Twain was going to be in my own life, but as I look back on it, those high bookshelves seem part of the way things were meant to turn out. It's not so much that I believe in fate any more than I believe every writer has a theme in mind for a story. But just as you can see a meaning in any story if you look at it the right way, you can see a design in the events of your life if you look at each moment steadily enough. Of course, you have to be looking backward, too. That's the trick. It hardly ever works looking forward.

I shouldn't have taken the owner for granted, that's for sure. The bald-headed Englishman in the greasy apron was a surprise, and, for that matter, so was his wife with her teased honey-colored hair. I heard someone call them Mr. and Mrs. Levy, which didn't sound like an English name to me. I expected Montague or Bartholomew or something like that. *Levy* sounded like the Jewish tailor who had a little shop on Hunt's Point Avenue that smelled of steam and starch and the river that ran nearby. Levy was moon-faced and had glasses with lenses so thick that they made me dizzy to look at him. Short and squat, he waddled around the store, I mean really waddled, up one aisle and down another. He didn't look sharp enough to catch anyone as practiced as I was. He looked like a guy who was meant to be weighing pigs' feet. I underestimated him. That old saying about a book and its cover holds true for bookstore owners too, I found out. I should have walked out of the store right then and there, but I really wanted to finish the novel.

He not only saw me put the books under my sweatshirt, but he also moved like an athlete and had a grip so strong that I couldn't even think about trying to break free. He looked over at his wife. Her teased hair reflected light in a way that made it seem to have a life of its own apart from her. She stood protectively by the cash register. "Mrs. Levy, call the police," he said. Instead of being scared, I recall being amused and puzzled by his speaking to his wife in such a formal manner. I wondered if all Englishmen spoke to their wives in that way or only when something to do with the law was at stake.

Two cops came within minutes, as if this were an important case. One of them, a big black cop with coal for eyes and breath that smelled like salami, handcuffed me. He seemed to hate me as much as my father would have hated him. He asked me a few questions that he didn't expect to get any answers to, I could tell, and then he shoved me into the back of the patrol car. For a moment I wished that my father were there to call him a nigger. If I'd had the guts, I would have done it myself. I thought maybe my father had gotten it exactly right. It was all turning to shit because they were taking over everything, the neighborhood, even the police department. Right then, I was my father's son, and the goddamn niggers were making a mess of my life. I didn't dwell too much on the fact that I had been robbing someone else's stuff. It was just one more injustice, as far as I could reason at the time.

A few people walked by and looked in the police car window to get a peek at what kind of criminal they had in there. It wasn't long, though, before they took me to the station house and called my home. Once they realized that the phone had been disconnected they sent a patrol car around to speak with my father. I knew they were going to find out the truth eventually, but I saw no reason to make their work go faster or easier by telling them about the past year. Besides, I thought something might come up—a fire in the precinct, or maybe my father had returned— and I'd be sent back home with a JD card. Of course, those kinds of things happen only in certain kinds of novels, and the only thing that happened to me was that time passed. I felt about as lonely as Huck Finn and not nearly as smart. And then, as my father used to say, the shit hit the fan back and front and sideways.

The officer found the apartment filled with the things I had stolen—books and coats, dress shoes, a radio, jars of caviar, six pairs of Chuck Taylor Converse All Stars, records, tools, and too much other stuff to list now. He didn't know right away that it was stolen, but it didn't take him long to figure it out. Then the rest became clear fast. I won't go into the gruesome details. Just let me say that I ended up for a while in the detention center on Spofford Avenue, a six-story building that could have been apartments except for the bars on the windows and the barbed wire on the fence that went around the whole place. All the beds were in a dormitory, and there was a big community room with a ping-pong table and a worn orange sofa. The place really wasn't that bad. The worst part about the whole situation was that there was never any real privacy or silence. We were forced to meet for group sessions, and it seemed that we went everywhere in groups. We were never left on our own.

They didn't let me stay long at Spofford Juvenile Center. One day they took me down to the Bronx Courthouse, a building with large marble columns. From the outside it looked like a museum. I used to pass it all the time when I was on the bus going down the Grand Concourse and wondered what it was like inside. But now, even though I was pretty tired of making choices about things and was willing to let someone else tell me exactly what to do, I wished that I wasn't seeing the inside of the place. There was something about it that made my throat go dry and my palms sweat. The courtroom was all gray. The rugs were gray, and so were most of the walls. Only the paneling behind the judge's bench was beige, but for some reason even that looked gray to me. Other than a flag on each side of the judge's bench, there wasn't anything on the walls. All you could hear was the hum of the air conditioning and the sound of a baby crying outside of the heavy wooden doors.

The judge looked about my father's age, but he had a stupid half-grin playing on his thin lips and a tuft of curly dark hair standing in the front of his shiny skull like some kind of misplaced cowlick. He reminded me of the priest who used to substitute sometimes for Father McGrath at our church, soft-spoken and nearly as shy as a little kid. I could tell that the judge felt sorry for me. He asked me about my mother's death and when the last time was that I saw my father. He said that the child welfare department had been unable to find any of my relatives, pausing for a few seconds as if he hoped I could tell him about a forgotten uncle or grandmother. He also asked me about the envelope that the officer had found on the kitchen table, the one with the thousand dollars in it.

"Son, why didn't you just use that money to buy food and books, to buy all those stolen items the police found in your home?"

I didn't want to tell him the truth. I'm not even certain that I knew the truth then—so I just said that I had decided to save it for a rainy day. I would have told a magnificent lie if I could have come up with one, but I couldn't. He looked down at me and sighed, "Well, son, it's pouring now. But we'll make sure that it gets put in an account for you to use when all this is cleared away." Then he told me how sorry he was that things had turned out the way that they had for me, but that really wasn't any excuse for stealing. He went into what was definitely a pat speech for him about the paths of destruction that all began with taking someone else's stuff. He thought it was best, he said, to get me out of the neighborhood, as far away from Hunt's Point as he could. "Therefore, the court has determined," he said in a voice made to read the Magna Carta out loud, "that you will be sent to the Washington Lake Boys' Home until your eighteenth birthday." As I was turning to leave the courtroom, he asked me, "You're a Catholic, son, right? Well, you should feel at home there." He said it as if he meant to be kind and encouraging, but it sent a chill into me anyway.

So, on a humid day in June I found myself in Penn Station waiting for the train to Port Jervis, New York. In Port Jervis, one of the people who worked at the Boys' Home was going to pick me up in a car and drive me the remaining twenty miles. It was a three-hour train ride and then another half hour by car into what looked like the wilderness on the map I had snatched. I didn't really care how long the ride took because I had lifted a copy of *Huckleberry Finn* from a bookstore on Seventh Avenue when the guard was buying a newspaper, and I was eager to have the time to find out what happened to old Huck.

SHOHOLA FALLS

5

It was about eight o'clock at night when the train pulled into the station in Port Jervis. As it clanked to a stop, I was thinking that I had escaped just as my father had. None of my friends would know where I was. If my father returned, he wouldn't know where I had disappeared. I was gone in a puff of smoke. There wasn't even a puff of smoke. There was nothing.

Dusk made the Victorian houses look dark and the whole town depressed. Two scrawny kids with scabs on their knees leaned against rusted bikes and tossed stones at a gray cat that stood with its back arched under the steps of the train station. The kids looked bored enough to do some real harm if only given half a chance. As long as they stayed close to the station, though, they were probably able to believe that there had to be another world beyond the one that fell like a heaviness against them. And maybe, they could tell themselves, that other world waited for them to enter it. But I'm not sure if the possibility of that other world reined in their cruelty or stimulated it. I guess the whole idea of possibility can make a person feel desperate or tingling with hope. They seemed caught somewhere in between, tossing rocks but not taking careful aim.

It wasn't much of a train station, just an open platform with a roof over it. About ten yards from the tracks stood a building no bigger than a shed. Some old guy with white whiskers and a tattered suitcase was arguing about the price of a ticket to Hoboken. There weren't many people on the streets near the tracks, and those that I saw didn't seem happy to be in the neighborhood. I had gotten out of the Bronx, but this wasn't the kind of place that made me feel that I had gotten very far away.

We waited about fifteen minutes in the cool night air, the guard shifting his weight from right leg to left as he looked into the distance for my ride. I could tell that he was anxious to make the next train back to the city. It was easy enough to see that he didn't want to be left standing there as night fell upon the town. The guard and I were both looking off in the wrong direction as the truck clattered across the tracks and sprayed dust and small rocks into the air. The driver was only around twenty-five, but he looked middle-aged. His dark brown hair was brushed straight back and glistened in the lamplight as he stuck his head out the window, smiled, and said, "You must be Blanks. I'm Mr. Calabria. Your ride."

I watched him as he talked to the guard, who kept glancing over Mr. Calabria's shoulder at the train which was scheduled to depart for New York City at any minute. The guard handed over a sheaf of papers as if he were getting rid of a live grenade and took off without turning to look one last time at what he was leaving behind. Mr. Calabria spun toward me, for the first time his face completely visible in the shaft of light coming from the lamppost a few feet away. His face shone like a moon—literally. It was pocked and cratered from the acne he must have had as a teenager. But there wasn't anything hard or harsh about his face. The craters weren't bad to look at. They seemed to give shape and dimension to what would have otherwise looked too round and happy. The pockmarks probably made people take his face seriously.

The train howled twice and slowly began to move out of the station. I listened to the wheels click and watched the windows, looking for the face of the guard. I had forgotten what he looked like already and wanted one more view of him so that I could be sure that he was real and that I hadn't been standing on the platform forever imagining my life. I felt something hard tap against the top of my head, and I looked up to see Mr. Calabria's hand, a red-jeweled college ring with a thick gold band on one of his fingers, drifting away toward the few stars that had appeared in the darkening sky. "C'mon, kid, time to wake up and head for the wilderness. Right after we stop for a hamburger, that is. You eat hamburgers in the Bronx, right?" He didn't wait for a reply but turned toward the truck with me behind him.

A few blocks from the station we stopped at a diner called Homer's. Mr. Calabria ordered us each a hamburger and a vanilla milkshake. He didn't ask me any questions, not even if I wanted chocolate instead of vanilla. He just ordered and then talked, about the food at Homer's, about how much snow they had seen last winter, about a bear that he had found sitting in the back of his truck a few weeks back, eating a box of stale doughnuts. He didn't quiz me about anything—my mother, my father, how I came to be sent away—he just talked and talked as if he suspected that the sound of a voice was all I needed.

The ride to the "wilderness" wasn't far. About a quarter of a mile past Homer's on Route 97 the road rose into the curving darkness and away from the lights of the town in the valley below. "Hold on, kid," he said. "We're on the Hawk's Nest." There was still just enough light to see the river snaking along hundreds of feet below the road. A stone wall along the edge of the cliff was all that separated the truck from the blank space above the river. The road slithered and arched between the cliffs to the right and the precipice to the left. Most of the time Mr. Calabria drove on the left side of the road, leaning right and then left with the angle and sliding into the right lane only when car lights appeared around a bend. For the time it took us to go through the Hawk's Nest, it seemed likely that we would crash into some oncoming car or leap the stone embankment and float into the chilling blackness and become part of the dark scar at the bottom. From where I sat it didn't look like Huck's sun—and moon-soaked river at all but like death, like falling into death. We were going higher, away from the river, and upstream. And beneath my fear and my longing I knew that I wanted to be on the river, as dark as it was, drifting downstream and gazing up at the cliffs, away from any chance of falling. The river led toward Philadelphia and the Delaware Bay and then into the Atlantic Ocean. Its current would pull me away from myself and everything I knew into some other world than the one I was headed for now.

Descending from the Hawk's Nest was like finishing a roller coaster ride. My stomach rose and the air left my lungs in a rush. Then the darkness was complete and utter except for the twin beams of light coming from Mr. Calabria's truck. We went up and down the hills but saw nothing except pine trees and occasionally a house off in the woods. At the peak of one hill there was a billboard that said "Reber's Motel," and then a long decline toward an intersection with a blinking light.

"This is Barryville, kid. Don't sneeze or you'll miss it."

Reber's Motel was on the left side of the road, next to a bridge that ran across the Delaware River into Shohola, Pennsylvania. On the right was a real estate office, and through the intersection on the left was a grocery store. Mr. Calabria glanced at it, saying, "That's Otto's, the center of culture and communication for miles around. This isn't the Bronx." He looked sideways at me. "But, hey, that's not necessarily bad now, is it?"

The road between Barryville and Yulan, about five miles, was one long hill, and Mr. Calabria's truck sputtered and bounced its way to the blinking light at the Yulan Four Corners. The truck lurched to a rolling stop, and then we drove past a store on the left and a gas station on the right. And then we were out of the town. About half a mile up was a wooden sign with faded black letters nailed to a pine tree. It had an arrow pointing to the right and a sign that said "Washington Lake Boys' Home." I had never been to camp, but I had gone to a Boy Scout meeting right after my mother got sick. I lasted less than an hour, though. Something about it gave me the creeps. Maybe I felt too old to be a scout. The Washington Lake Boys' Home made me uneasy in the same way. It was like a Boy Scout camp for delinquents.

The dirt road that led down to the Boys' Home and to Washington Lake twisted and turned past a cemetery, and the rutted path got steeper as we descended. The holes in the road made the truck groan and squeak and made us rise and fall from the right to the left. When we reached the bottom of the road, three big houses lit up the darkness and the lake was flung out before us as wide and sparkling as the night sky.

Mr. Calabria looked at the lake and said, "It's two miles across and seven miles long. And in the daytime you'll see how clear it is. Pure enough to drink when you're swimming in it. I'm not recommending that you drink it, though. I've got to be careful what I tell you city boys, especially ones from the Bronx. You might do all sorts of strange things, I've heard."

He glanced over at me without turning his head. "Let's get over to the Lodge and settle you in."

He nodded in the direction of a rambling, old Victorian house, three stories of turrets and varying rooflines and two screened-in porches that hung out over the rocky shoreline. The water lapping against the rocks and the rhythmic whine of the crickets were the only sounds I heard, and I remember thinking *I'm about as far from the Bronx as I could ever get.* This seemed a different world from Port Jervis and so far from the Bronx that it was hard to believe that New York City really existed anymore.

The wooden steps creaked under Mr. Calabria's weight as he led me to the back door. The screen door swung open with a squeal, and just as we entered the kitchen a thick-armed woman with dark-gray hair and bushy black eyebrows looked up from something she was mixing on the stove. "So this is the new one, eh, Richard? He's too skinny. How do they get that skinny? This young man needs some of my cooking."

"Yes, Mama, a new food taster. You'll fix that problem. Thomas, this is Mrs. Frazier, the chef and the real chief executive around here."

Whatever she was cooking smelled good, but I told her that I had just eaten when she asked me if I wanted to try some of tomorrow night's dinner in advance.

"Okay, then," Mr. Calabria said, "let me take you inside to meet Father Boyd. He's the director of the program."

Double doors opened from the kitchen into a room that was bigger, it seemed to me, than my high school auditorium in the Bronx. But there was nothing cold about it. A fireplace stood at each end of the room, and comfortable-looking old chairs and sofas surrounded scratched tables in between.

"Wait here a minute," Mr. Calabria said. "Let me see if Father Boyd is free."

When Mr. Calabria disappeared behind the heavy wooden doors at the far end of the room, six boys stepped into it from the porch as if they had been waiting for his exit. None of them said anything. They just edged into the room slowly as if they didn't want to get their fingerprints on the furniture. They seemed to glide past the tables and the chairs until they were in a half circle that separated me from everything but the worn sofa behind me.

Most of them seemed to be about my age, sixteen or seventeen. One of them, his dark hair slicked straight back with Vitalis, smelled of aftershave and baby powder, but I could tell he was a mean bastard and intended to use me to break the monotony of his existence. There are times you can just see it in a person's eyes, your whole future with them. He leaned down and whispered something to the smaller boy next to him and then turned toward me and laughed. He looked straight into my eyes but addressed the boys around him, "Look at the new girl in class. Ain't she cute?"

I knew right then and there that I was going to have a miserable time and that this guy with the slick-backed hair was going to cause it. So I decided that I might as well get the misery started and then maybe it would end sooner.

I hadn't been in a fight since the seventh grade, and that fight hadn't turned out well. I had ended up with the right side of my face pressed into dogshit as a crowd of boys and girls stood around watching and feeling, I'm sure, the wonderful satisfaction of not being me. This Puerto Rican kid had one knee on my shoulder and the other on my face. All I could see were sneakers and, across the street, a bum lying near the gutter, using a copy of the Sunday *New York Times* as a pillow. His eyes were wide open, and he was smiling at me in pity or empathy, I couldn't tell which. We were just two guys lying in the gutter—or near it. He seemed happy to have some company. The sad thing is that even with my face in dogshit, I felt superior to that guy, but it should have been the other way around, I guess.

So it wasn't as if I had a good fight record or anything like that. I didn't do what I did because I had any illusions about being tough. I just couldn't stand all the posturing and feinting. It was all too stagy, and I didn't want to be in the middle of things but on the outside looking in. I figured that if I broke the silence right then and there, I might have a chance of getting my solitude back right away, or at least soon, but if I let him control things, then I would be dealing with him in one way or another as long as I was there. In order to unveil my new self, I took a half step forward with my left foot, turned in the direction of the darkened porch and the moonlit water beyond it, and punched him as hard as I could on the left side of the face. He fell backward into the chair behind him and landed with his arms dangling and his head tilted back against the cushions as if he were a little drunk and fast asleep.

The boys all stepped back at the same time, uncertain what was to come next. There were murmurs of "Hey, shit" and "What the fuck." But no one moved to step in for their fallen leader. No one seemed to want to test just how crazy I might be. I felt exactly as I had when I was eleven years old and in my first Little League baseball game. I had signed up one afternoon and taken the bus to Van Cortlandt Park, been given a baggy, ill-fitting uniform by a skeptical coach, sent to right field and placed ninth in the batting order. In the third inning, when it came my turn to hit, I swung at the first pitch and the law of averages kicked in. I grazed the ball, swinging with my eyes closed and out of fear, but it caught enough of the bat to send it soaring to right field, over the surprised fielder's head. I got a triple, and the coach smiled with the conviction that he had discovered a natural. Of course, he had only witnessed a case of dumb luck. But it took him three more games, ten strikeouts, and seven errors to face the truth. He sagged in disappointment the rest of the season and didn't even pay the slightest attention to me in right field or when I got up to bat after the pitcher.

I found out the next day at the Home that it was Adam Delano that I had hit. I was never sorry that I did it. He turned out to be a merciless bully, and for a good long time my punch kept him away from me—that and a piece of good luck, that is. Everything seemed to slow down enough for me to day-dream about Little League baseball and even to wonder about how long it might reasonably take the guy I had punched and those around him to figure out, as the baseball coach had years before, that I wasn't what I appeared to be. I was just what the circumstances had momentarily made me and nothing more.

Delano was just opening his eyes and rubbing his reddened cheek when Mr. Calabria stuck his oversized head into the doorway and asked, "How's everything out here, boys?" Calabria had a look on his face of someone who knows that an important scene has just been enacted but he's not going to ask any questions about it because it would only make things more complicated. So when everyone nodded and a few mumbled, "Okay, Mr. Calabria," he turned to me like a man shaking off an unwanted notion that's crept into his mind and said, "Father Boyd wants to see you."

Father Boyd reminded me of Delano as soon as I saw him sitting behind his wide wooden desk. His hair was black and combed back from his high forehead. He had the same smell that Delano had—Vitalis, aftershave, and baby powder. His eyes were wide and dark and as unyielding as the headlights of a bus on Marion Avenue in the Bronx. His glasses didn't soften his appearance at all, especially when they slid down away from his eyes and he tilted his head slightly upward and looked down at me over the line of his straight nose.

"Richard, why don't you leave Mr. Blanks and me alone for a while so that we can have a little chat?"

Once Mr. Calabria left the office, Father Boyd showed me a smile as white as bones drying in the desert sun, a line of teeth straight and big, almost too large for his mouth.

"Well now, Mr. Blanks," he said, "welcome to your new home."

I didn't like the way he said home, but I did my best to produce a half-smile and nod. "There are one hundred and twenty-four boys here, Mr. Blanks, and they're here for a variety of reasons. Their parents have died or they can't handle them—or they don't want them. We're here, the Brothers, myself, Mr. Calabria, and the other teachers, to inculcate Catholic values, to shape you into the young Christian man that you were meant to be, that you started out being before something went wrong. Our job is to teach. Your task is to obey. We are your home now. Is there anything unclear about that, Mr. Blanks, anything at all that you don't understand?"

Although there was plenty that was unclear right then, I knew that he wasn't really asking me a question but making a statement that he had made plenty of times before, so I just said, "No, sir."

"Well, that's a good start, son, but remember the correct response is 'No, Father.' I've seen your records. You are a smart boy. You won't have any difficulty here as long as you remember the motto of our school—Serviam. We serve the Lord here. Not our selfish desires but the Lord. As you do your work, keep that in mind and you won't get into any trouble."

I wish that I had been able to tell him: *I'm your man. I'm the last person who wants trouble. I'll be happy if you'd forget I even existed.*

He lowered his voice a scratch above a whisper, "And you don't want to get into trouble here, son. Be certain about that. You don't want any trouble with me."

After saying that, he smiled and stood up. It was the kind of smile that made my stomach tighten. It was a smile that seemed to have a hiss of breath behind it, a curse. The smile hung there, naked and veiled at the same time. He took off his glasses to clean them against the sleeve of his cassock, and when he did, his eyes looked vulnerable and old. He put the glasses back on right away, and behind them once again his eyes glinted like polished metal. He walked over to the office door, opened it with a flourish, and held his arm out, flapping like a black wing in the draft. "Mr. Calabria will show you where your room is."

Delano and the other boys were gone. Mr. Calabria looked around the empty room and scratched his cratered chin. "It won't take you long to figure out who to stay away from around here. But until you know for certain, be awake, kid. Just keep your eyes open and you'll be okay."

My room was on the second floor. It was so narrow that if I stretched my arms out as far as I could my fingertips just about touched both walls. On the right side two beds lay in a line, pillow to pillow. On the left were two small dressers that served as desks, two metal chairs, and a closet. The window had no curtains and looked out onto a pine-covered path that led into the woods. On the bed closer to the window lay a young man who looked to be older than I was. He twisted his head around lazily as we came into the room, and

Mr. Calabria said, "Take care of him, Fitzy. This is your new roommate, Tommy Blanks." As Mr. Calabria turned to leave the room, he said, "And try not to make his life any more miserable than it has to be in the first few days, eh?"

"No, sir," Fitzy said, turning onto his stomach and looking up at me, "I'll treat him as if he was my own little brother."

Even though it sounded like sarcasm at the time and he fell asleep without another word or even a second glance at me, that's exactly what he did.

6

The next morning I woke up before there was any movement in the house. The sun had just risen, and a whippoorwill's repeated cry was the only break in the silence. I went downstairs and onto the screened-in porch. The morning air was chilly, and the sky to the east was layer upon layer of clouds rising from thin to thick. Orange bled through the lowest layer and streamed into the horizon line of water. The lake was glassy, a gray-blue mirror with steam rising from it. It was quiet enough to be the beginning of time and seemed so far from the streets and sounds of my old neighborhood that I had to blink to see if the lake and trees were real.

For a moment I felt a strange catch in my breathing. Then a dizziness, as if I were dreaming and had fallen into a heart-stopping wakefulness. How had I gotten so far from the Bronx? So far from anything I knew? I felt both scared and excited at the same time. Both lost and free. In some way I felt as if I didn't have any idea who I was, as if I had to make myself up from nothing into a new person, but it also felt good to have the chance to start over again. The glistening lake flung out in front of me like an affront to the past erased all those apartment buildings and subway stations in the Bronx. It left nothing but the present and the future.

The wind began to pick up and the water started to lap against the shore-line. Whitecaps flicked up and down the middle of the lake. I walked down to the waterfront and opened the door to a boathouse on the property that reached on pilings out onto the windswept water. A boat with an inboard motor was tethered to the front and side walkways, and it rolled gently against the wooden frame of the house. I angled toward the door that opened wide onto a view of Washington Lake. The walkway was gritty with sand, and I heard it scrape against the soles of my sneakers as I lost balance and fell into the water. I was surprised at how deep and cold the water was, at how quickly I got used to the idea that even though it was barely sunrise I was lying in five feet of chilly water fully clothed and the world around me was a complete mystery.

I slogged through the water to the dock alongside the boathouse and climbed up the ladder, my clothes heavy and dripping. The way I remember it, I didn't swim but walked under the water. A better delusion, I suppose, than remembering that I walked on top of it. I expected to be alone with my embarrassment, but Mr. Calabria was standing there along the shore smiling. He didn't seem surprised at all to see me stepping out of the water into the perfectly silent morning. He bit down on his lower lip and shook his head.

"You haven't even been here half a day and you've already baptized yourself. You better get upstairs and put on some dry clothes before the other boys wake up and you acquire a new name that you don't particularly like. Names are very easy to come by in a place like this. And they tend to stick longer than you would think. If you can manage it, you want to get stuck with a name that you feel comfortable with."

Saying that, he walked off toward his truck, once again shaking his head and leaving me to rub the water from my hair and wring some of the weight from my shirt and pants.

I took off my socks and sneakers and tiptoed up the stairs. I felt pretty lucky until I saw my new roommate look up and observe me with amused detachment as I squeaked into the room, leaving dark, wet footprints in my path. The skin around his green eyes narrowed into fine lines of concentration.

"Good morning. You can call me Fitz."

He turned his head back so that he was looking up at the ceiling.

"And by the way, I don't know how you guys in the South Bronx take baths, but up here among us mountain folk it's the custom to take your clothes off first."

Fitz never said another word about my swim in the lake, but later he did talk to me about my first meeting with Adam Delano.

"You did a good thing there, Tommy," he said later. "For a couple of reasons. First of all, Delano is an asshole. The supreme asshole of Washington Lake. Maybe of all Sullivan County, who knows? But, shit, I could have kicked his ass a dozen times. I didn't because it was more trouble than it was worth, I thought. I don't want to fuck around in any way with Father Boyd. I'm convinced he's one sick fuck. I don't give a shit about his sweet smile. There's something not right there. He gets a hard-on controlling people. He may even get one over pretty young boys—so watch out. All I know is that, generally, I do whatever I have to to stay out of his way. He'd love any excuse to piss on me, I'm pretty sure of that. So I stay as far away from him as I can, and stay away from trouble, too—and that means not kicking the shit out of Delano. But, blessed soul that you are, innocent among wolves, it worked out for you in every possible way. Delano deserved it, but that's not the best part of the whole fucking thing. The best part is that he thinks you're absofuckinglutely crazy and so do his jerkoff friends. Of course, I knew from the first time Calabria brought you in here that you weren't crazy at all, actually probably not crazy enough for your own good, but it's a nice idea to have people think you might be."

A lot of people liked Fitz, but a lot of people thought he was crazy, too. He had a round face and a big-toothed grin that swung into a room like a moon rising unexpectedly around a bend in a country road. He seemed to possess the kind of innocence that could be turned into fury with the flip of a switch. He was probably a shade under six feet tall, but he had forearms and biceps like my father's. He wasn't really good-looking, but he always wore an ironic expression that convinced people he was handsome in some way that was difficult to define. Girls got all giggly around him and didn't seem to mind the unusual smell. I don't mean that he smelled bad, just that his smell was unusual. He loved hamburger pickles and always kept a jar under his bed. He also liked strong aftershave. So to me he always smelled of pickles and cologne, salty, sour, and sweet all at the same time. But it only appeared to make the girls love him more.

That first day, after I dried off, we had breakfast in the dining hall in a building next to the Lodge. We sat at big round tables. A few minutes after we got into our seats, Mr. Calabria came over and said, "Stay put, fellas, today is group therapy for you lucky souls. Your chance to find your true self." He winked. "This could be scary to watch. Very scary, indeed."

I wasn't certain if I had a true self. But even if I did, I was pretty sure I didn't want to find it. I noticed then that there were place cards on the table. The one in front of me had my name printed on both sides. For some reason, I couldn't stop focusing on the side of the card that faced me, on the letters of my own name. I had the strange sensation that I was seeing a new word, a name that wasn't attached to me. A foreign language. The letters swam together, and I felt a cold stream flash down my chest and into my stomach. It was as if I didn't really recognize my own name—or that I recognized it but it didn't refer to me at all. It was like looking at a photograph of yourself from the distant past. Those twelve letters—Thomas Blanks—were not me. They didn't name me. I had to concentrate hard to make those letters come back into clear focus. That was me—Thomas Blanks—and I was in Yulan, New York, and would be for the next year and a half. There wasn't a Tommy Blanks of the Bronx any more. He was gone, along with my mother and father.

The card next to me read "Francis Fitzpatrick." Around the circle were other cards with other names and a variety of faces behind them—Vincent Tosti, Jimmy Knecht, John O'Malley, Anthony Bufano, and Stephen Brown. It was an unusual group, each boy dramatically different from the others, the only common feature a look of carefully shaped indifference. Every one of them looked as if he had just stepped into the dining room to check things out. Each one had an expression on his face that said *I'm not fucked up like the rest of you shitheads—I'm here because of some cosmic mistake but I'll play along with the joke for now. Just don't get the idea that I'm in any way like you.*

Knecht had on a stained white T-shirt with the sleeves rolled up, the bottom of a package of unfiltered Camels peeking out from one sleeve like a growth upon his stick-thin bicep. His sandy hair looked as if a brush had never touched it. His dirty fingernails, fingertips a brownish-yellow from smoking, drummed on the table, and he moved his head to some internal music. Every now and again he parted his lips into a half smile, a brief flash of yellow and brown. Vincent Tosti was as dark as one of the Bedouin traders in my old geography book. His black eyebrows stretched across the bridge of his nose and shaded his already hooded eyes. And he barely ever looked up but instead watched his hand tap against the tabletop in a rhythm that unconsciously and perfectly imitated Knecht's beat. Directly across from me John O'Malley sat between Anthony Bufano and Stephen Brown. O'Malley had a pleasant, shapeless Irish face, oval and red-cheeked. His curly red hair twisted around his ears and rolled down over his collar. He seemed ready to be jovial if anyone gave him a decent chance to be, but between Bufano, whose eyes looked like layers of obsidian, dark and cold, and Brown, whose thin lips were pursed together so hard that they looked purple, it didn't seem likely.

Fitz explained to me that we were all waiting for Father Boyd, who ran all the group therapy sessions because in addition to being the director of Washington Lake Boys' Home and a Jesuit priest he was also a certified counselor, a Ph.D. in psychology, and had even written a book titled *Deviant Behavior in Urban Adolescents*.

When he walked up to our table, Boyd's dark hair was oiled back into stiff, glistening furrows, and he smiled in a way that made me tighten the muscles in my legs and arms. It was like preparing for a race. I was just waiting for the starter's pistol.

Boyd sat down at the table, folded his hands together in a way that reminded me of a guy about to say the Lord's Prayer, and slowly allowed his eyes to fall on each boy's face, lingering for a few seconds before moving on to the next one. For each of us, he had the same smile stitched into his face—a look suggesting he knew a well-kept secret about every one of us.

"Mr. O'Malley," he said, "Let's go back to where we left off last week, shall we?"

It sounded like a question, but it wasn't. O'Malley didn't say anything. He just sat there, smiling dumbly like someone from another country who is hoping that the words he is hearing will become clear and mean good things to him if he just sits still long enough, if he concentrates with enough care.

"Do you recall saying that in terms of doing your homework, you just didn't feel ready to wet when you meant to say *yet?*"

O'Malley turned red to the very roots of his red hair.

"Do you think, perhaps, that there is a connection between your lack of initiative and your . . . um . . . any other problem?"

O'Malley was a rust color now, as if anger had oxidized his blood in a matter of a few seconds. All the other boys were looking hard at the tabletop in front of them. It wasn't until later that Fitz told me the story about O'Malley, a sweet kid with an innocent, easy smile who was sent to Washington Lake for chronic truancy and then stealing some pocketbooks at the Wednesday night bingo sessions at St. Philip Neri Church in his neighborhood in the North Bronx. Twice in his freshman year he had been given paddlings in front of his class, and both times he had gotten so nervous that he had peed on the floor.

Father Boyd moved on around the room, asking Tosti why he felt so nervous and Knecht what he thought his plans for the future were. No one had much to say, and when they did, they spoke in low tones as if there were a dead body in the room. By the time Father Boyd got to Fitz, the clock read a few minutes before nine o'clock, and that meant the session was about to end and I had escaped until next week.

"I'd like to talk about a dream that I had last night, Father," Fitz said.

I hoped that it was a long, intricate story, but it turned out that it didn't have to be. Everyone looked up, wondering what this could mean, Fitz volunteering a story in such a meeting. Maybe he was crazy after all. You could see them wondering, even Father Boyd. Fitz paused long enough for everyone to register their surprise.

Then he went on, "It's a little embarrassing, though. It's kind of private, you know? Because it's about . . . Knecht's sister." And with the sound of the syllable "tuh" the bell rang, Knecht started to rise in anger, his skinny arms flailing like a clown getting ready for a comic bout in a circus ring, and Father Boyd tightened his jaw all in the same instant of sound. For a moment it seemed as if the bell had caused all the confusion, and Fitz's words disappeared into the ringing and were lost in the metallic echo.

"Well, I guess I'll try to remember it for next week, Father," Fitz said as he pushed back his chair and elbowed me to rise.

Back in our room, Fitz and I stretched out in opposite directions in our beds. The tops of our heads were nearly touching. We were close enough, it seemed, to exchange thoughts without speaking. We stared at the ceiling silently. I lay there trying to remember my mother's face. I pressed my eyes shut tight and looked into the darkness that rose around me. Her face was there, on the edge of it, ready to appear, about to appear, but it wouldn't. I got an empty feeling in my chest when I realized that no matter what I did, I couldn't make her face come out of the darkness. I lay there, awake, my eyes shut hard and straining to see, for about thirty minutes. Then, finally, I saw her face clearly. It was her face in a photograph. I saw it for a moment in exact detail. I remember feeling a great sense of relief that I was able to recall her face from the emptiness all around me, and then almost immediately I felt a pang of failure again because the only image I could come up with was a photograph, an artifact and not the person. It seemed shameful somehow not to be able to bring her back to life, to reimagine her vividly enough for her to be in the room with me. It felt like a failure of love and the imagination at the very same time. I felt as tired as I had ever been and fell into a dreamless sleep.

Some time in the middle of the night I woke up and sensed Fitz awake behind me. We spent the hours before sunrise talking about our lives in the Bronx. He came from Briggs Avenue, a block of two—and three-family houses squeezed between squat apartment buildings that bordered Mosholu Park. His father had died when Fitz was too young to care, and his mother had remarried, this husband a narrow-faced man five years younger than she and just off the boat from the Dingle Coast of Ireland. His stepfather was an O'Hanlon, a man used to the windswept spaces of the southwest coast of Ireland, and he never made sense of the buildings and buses that blocked his view each day in America. To make matters worse for him, he became a superintendent of an apartment building on Briggs Avenue, and the family moved into the coal-coated bowels of the place. No light at all seemed to find its way into their apartment. By the time he was thirteen, Fitz was bigger than his shrunken stepfather and hated his every small gesture.

The only time his father was not banging pipes or clanging the furnace door shut was when he was at the Jolly Tinker Bar on Webster Avenue, a place as dark and cavernous as his basement home. The elevated trains ran outside the bar with a rattling regularity that was almost like breathing. Fitz sought the light and ways to avoid his father, but often he was not successful. They argued but never, until Fitz was sixteen, came to blows. He couldn't remember exactly what he had fought with his father about. Maybe it was the car Fitz had bought for a hundred dollars from a friend. The day after he bought the car Fitz parked it by the schoolyard, borrowed a saw, and cut off the top. He made himself a convertible and then drilled seven holes in the floorboards so that the water would leak out when it rained. He wore a plastic garbage bag with the eyes and mouth cut out during rainy weather. The car lasted the spring and half of the summer and became a common sight sailing up Bainbridge and Valentine Avenues or along the Grand Concourse. In the rain, Fitz's plastic mask, tied to his chest by two book straps, fluttered in the wind. Fitz knew that his stepfather would hate his buying the car and then hate his cutting it up even more, but Fitz didn't care. He didn't buy it or saw off the top to make his stepfather angry. He just didn't care if his stepfather got angry. And that indifference infuriated his stepfather and made him hate the car and Fitz even more.

"You and that goddamned plastic bag and sawed-off car," he'd mutter whenever Fitz walked into the basement.

Fitz had sawed off the roof in such a way that when he made a sharp left turn, the door often flew open. "I decided to fix it," he said to me, "after Joey Paglia fell out one Sunday night near the church steps. He was getting a piper in the back seat from Anne Marie O'Brien when the door flew open and she bit down in surprise. Lucky for him he ended up getting nothing more than a few teeth marks—he kept his dick. But he never rode with me again. And he never got another blowjob from Anne Marie, either. I think the experience transformed her, too. She went into the convent, I heard. It's almost too good to be true, though, isn't it? A nun who enters the convent because she nearly bit off some guy's dick?"

Fitz fixed the door after Paglia landed on the steps of the church, his pants down around his ankles and Mother Concepta searching desperately to find her glasses to see who it was as he raced down the alleyway, struggling to pull his pants over his white ass. For the rest of the summer, passengers in Fitz's car had to hop over the jagged metal to get into the backseat because the doors were tied together with a clothesline that was pulled taut across the backseat from one window handle to the other.

But Fitz couldn't be certain that it was the car that caused the explosion with his stepfather. There were simply too many things between them, and all of them were part of what happened. But even if he couldn't explain all the causes, he remembered every detail of the fight itself.

His stepfather had pushed him, two callused and coal-stained hands against his chest, into the door that led into the hallway of the basement. Everything seemed to slow down for Fitz so that he could actually see himself lifting his arm, making a fist, and reaching back to hit his stepfather squarely on the nose. Blood spurted onto Fitz's white T-shirt in a red hieroglyphic of dots and stray lines almost before he heard the crunch of the broken nose. His stepfather moaned like an injured animal and rammed into Fitz, both of them crashing into bikes and sleds and boxes of toys stored in the next room. A tricycle was flung against the rectangle of glass that served as a street-level window, shattering it and spraying pieces on the square-toed shoes of two women who stood outside the apartment building leaning against their laundry carts.

The women shrieked and, below, her voice echoing along the basement walls, Fitz's mother screamed, "Stop it! Stop it, you two!" But they continued to swing at each other, knocking into the furnace, rolling in a hill of coal, and burning their forearms against the hot-water pipe. As they banged bone against furnace and pipe, the sounds echoed up to the pavement like the clangings of doom from the underworld. Blood mixed with dirt, and coal dust coated their faces and arms. By the time they rolled out into the alleyway, tenants had their heads stuck out the windows and some had come out of their apartments and into the street and were peering into the alley to see the battle. In the cold light of the October afternoon, both Fitz and his stepfather looked like characters in a silent film comedy, in torn T-shirts when everyone else had jackets on, and begrimed like blackface vaudevillians while the onlookers were clean and rosy-cheeked.

It wasn't long before the cops showed up, and within a week Fitz found himself at the Washington Lake Boys' Home marked as an uncontrollable adolescent. Fitz was certain that when any of the neighbors asked him about his stepson, his stepfather simply said, "What a bleedin' idjit, eh? They'll be screwing his head on straight up there, that's for sure."

Instead of telling Fitz how I got sent to Washington Lake for stealing a copy of *Huckleberry Finn*, which was only half true, of course, I told him about what happened right after my mother died. She had said that she wanted to be cremated and what was saved on the burial for us to spend on flowers. She wanted lots of flowers.

My father made it clear that the urn had to be buried in consecrated ground and that now that she was gone the flowers weren't important any more. "It won't matter to her now that she can't see them," he said. The money he would have spent on flowers went to the church—a donation—but it seemed to me more a way of getting them to forget that she had been cremated than anything else. I knew that my mother really cared more about the flowers than she did about any idea the Catholic Church had about holy ground.

Her favorite place in the world was the Botanical Gardens up past Fordham Road, right next to the zoo and across the road from Fordham University. Before she got sick, she loved to walk around on the flowering paths on a Sunday afternoon after church. I decided that I'd spread her ashes in one of the gardens so that she could have flowers near her all the time.

I went to the store, bought a big bag of potting soil, and took it home when my father was at work. The hard part was prying open the urn. It wasn't exactly an urn. It was really a black plastic box. I was afraid to look, and to tell the truth, I didn't. I just poured the ashes into an old gym bag and then scooped handful after handful of potting soil back into the box until it was filled up and about the same weight it originally was. I sealed the cover on the box. Then I zipped up the gym bag and took the subway to the Fordham Road and Decatur Avenue station. The bag sat next to me until the train got so full that I had to place it on my lap. It was an odd sensation carrying a dead person's ashes on the subway. I couldn't get it straight in mind that those ashes had once been my mother, so I didn't think about it. There are some things it's impossible to think too much about. You'll never make sense of them. They'll just drive you crazy.

Of course, no one on the subway suspected a thing, but I had the sense that those subway passengers might have been equally indifferent to a dead body sitting propped up next to me. You can do pretty much anything you want in the subway as long as you leave everyone else alone. If you never look anyone in the eyes, you'll never have a problem.

It was a long walk to the Botanical Gardens from the station, and by the time I got there it was getting close to dusk. The sky was a dark gray and the air was turning cool and purple. I found a perfect spot in one of the garden trails for her. It was quiet and lush with plants and flowers, and you could tell that even in the winter something would be growing there or in the hothouse that was clearly visible nearby. I dug out a little hole and turned the gym bag upside down into it. I still didn't look at the ashes, not even when I covered it up with dirt. I was happy she was there and not in some cemetery. It didn't even feel like the Bronx there but like some place the Bronx once was a long, long time ago and never would be again. I dropped the gym bag in a garbage can on Fordham Road and took the subway home.

I guess it was cruel for me to just stand by as my father and the neighbors and the priest all looked mournful when the urn was placed in the ground as if there were anything but low-grade potting soil in it. But I did anyway. I just stood there thinking about my mother surrounded by plants and flowers all the time. I didn't want to speak to any of them even if I could have or if they would have asked me to.

So there was no Mildred Blanks buried in Woodlawn Cemetery. The name etched in marble was a lie. My mother, like me, had escaped. She was somewhere else, had become someone else and could choose any name that suited her in her new surroundings. It was as if she had the whole cemetery to herself and all around her were the things she loved. I'm sure what I did was a sin and a sacrilege, but it didn't matter because I had given up believing in God anyway and long before that I had given up believing in the Church.

7

Winter and good luck came to the mountains early. Adam Delano was gone from the Boys' Home. There were all kinds of rumors—sent back to live with an aunt, shipped to a juvenile detention center, reached his eighteenth birthday—but all that mattered to me was that he was gone, for I knew that as long as we were in the same place together, it was just a question of when we would have had to finish what had been started. His departure made me begin to believe that I might be able to spend the next year without the world catching me off guard.

By late October Washington Lake was frozen solid enough for fishermen to cut circles into it. The sun made a bright path along the center of the lake, dark holes of water staring wide-eyed into the sky and shades of gray and white lying like an abstract painting framed by the leaf-covered shoreline. Behind the Boys' Home a narrow creek raced over slick rock, slicing through a landscape of pine needles and leaves, moss-covered granite outcroppings, and seedlings of various heights. The large trees rose high into the cloudy sky, some bowed by the memory of past winds. The snows came on the last day of the month.

I had never seen so much snow. The flakes were as big as my hand and the whiteness blotted out everything—cars, trees, water, houses. It even smothered sound. Engines ceased sputtering, birds went silent, people and cars stopped moving. It snowed for two days, and the whiteness seemed intent on changing the world back to something I had once imagined it to be. By the third day, the sky cleared but it was still so cold that the air—like the ground—was white and brittle. Snow blanketed the whole world. It was silent as death.

Right after lunch that third day Father Boyd canceled our classes and told us to get ready to pay back the community for being gracious enough to have us in their midst. We were going to shovel the snow off Irishtown Road, he said, and we were going to make the Home proud of how hard we worked.

"Gratitude, boys," he said, "it's all about gratitude. You have so much to be grateful for. Your heads should be bowed with the weight of what you owe. You owe every person, man, woman, and child in this town, for permitting you to be part of their community."

A fragile line of drool hung along the left corner of his mouth as he said all of this. I couldn't tell if it was some liquid left from his lunch or just the saliva produced by an undefined pleasure. I watched the spittle lengthen its course down his chin as he spoke, looking sadly at us from the warmth of the door-frame as we began to trudge up the hill toward town.

It started to snow again before we got to Irishtown Road. A hand-painted sign with green lettering was barely visible as we hiked off the main street onto the hard-packed dirt road, now white, that stretched up the white mountainside. It was a world transformed, it seemed, by magic whiteness. Every detail of the landscape had become something new, what it had not been the day before.

A wooden sign with the name *Souther* on it was nailed to a pine tree and pointing toward a farmhouse on a rise a few hundred yards away. Fitz looked over at me through the swirling snow and nodded at the sign.

"Old man Souther gives a donation each year to Father Boyd. We keep his road clear all winter. It's called gratitude, I think."

It was so cold I didn't believe it would be possible to sweat, but I was wrong. After about two hours, the shirt beneath my jacket was damp. It was only four o'clock in the afternoon, but it was already turning dark in the shad-ows of the pine trees when she came out of the woods in a funnel of wind and snow like an apparition. I was standing there halfheartedly lifting my shovel and thinking about my mother's ashes in her Bronx garden and whether the snow was covering the ground there, daydreaming about the whiteness of the earth in the Botanical Gardens, and she just appeared at the top of the road. For an instant the warm air stopped coming from my mouth. The space be-tween my eyes and her face was a cold, clear page with nothing written on it.

Her eyes were a dark gray that cut through the whiteness all around us, a gray that seemed to turn blue as you looked more deeply into them. Against the snow, the image of her skin hung like a falling leaf. It was the color of a flash of sunlight on dark marble. She smiled at me as she passed by, I'm pretty certain. Her skin was dark lightning against a white sky. I looked over at Fitz

to see if he saw what I did, and he shot me the kind of grin he had shown me
a number of times during the past few months.

"Son, you look thunderstruck."

I didn't answer him, just turned to watch her disappear like some dream
into the snow and oncoming night. And as she went out of sight, I heard the
ice-coated branches creak and sigh in the dark wind that made me shiver.

Her face stayed in my dreams for the rest of the winter, even though I tried
hard to think of other things. Of course, there were always Delano's friends to
think about. They'd let me alone for months, but I assumed it was only a matter of time before one of them came at me. They were eyeing me more and
more each day—and more directly. But without Delano there, they circled my
quietness as if it were a ticking bomb about to go off. As I watched them out
of the corner of my eye, waiting for them to see my ordinariness beneath the
mask of craziness, I dreamed about the girl in the snow. It didn't seem like a
good idea to be thinking about some nameless girl who had floated past me in
a storm, but I couldn't help it. The more you try to keep an idea out of your
head, the more it finds its way in. It was like daydreaming about Natalie
Wood—something I'd done my share of in the past after falling in love with
her image in *Splendor in the Grass*. I realized that daydreaming about the girl
in the snowstorm was ridiculous, but it was a secret foolishness, and I fell into
those dreams effortlessly, without ever trying to shake my head clear. What
would any of us do without the undiscriminating pleasures of the imagination? Even our nightmares can help make us whole, I guess, allowing us a
chance to prepare for the worst. But our dreams may give us the opportunity
to get ready to face the kind of good fortune that we spend our lives wishing
for but that has the power to destroy us. It seemed to me then that such daydreams were safe, anyway. They couldn't be taken away by anything or anyone
but the real girl. And what were the chances of that happening?

I hadn't seen anything but her face, her brown skin framed by a white
world. Her head had been covered in a fur-trimmed hood. Her green jacket
came down to the mid-thigh, and her boots rose up to the middle of her calf.
She was hidden from my view, a mystery except for her face, and that seemed
an even greater mystery for being there, a beautiful question in the midst of
such a white silence.

Eventually, I found out that her name was Nadine, although she called herself Nada, the long a sound drifting into the short. I was studying Spanish then, so it seemed to me a strange name for anyone to carry, especially someone with a smile like hers. It took me a while to realize that a name can be an invocation and can make the world shape itself around it. A name can make its own meaning.

Each day I walked to the post office at the Four Corners to get the mail for the Boys' Home, and I looked for her—along the road or in the town, even though I didn't admit to myself that I was on the lookout for her. I didn't think too much about what I would say if I actually saw her. My dreams never got past just seeing her one more time. When I didn't see her, I was disappointed but happy, too. Who needed the confusion and complication knowing her would surely bring? It seemed to me that Fitz had it right—a crooked smile that kept the world at bay. Who wanted the hazards that such a girl would have to carry with her? My life had a delicate balance, a perfect equilibrium of silence and separation, and even a racing heartbeat could make that all collapse. The truth is, though, that I always lingered for a few minutes in the post office, hoping she would come in to pick up her mail. In the mornings when I went to town, I would first glance into the store next to the restaurant, the Blue Ribbon. The restaurant was always closed, waiting to open its doors at five o'clock for the few cars that would slip into the sloped parking area. Outside the gas station, the owner was always rolling a half-flat tire toward a barrel of murky water. Across the road, the woods lay flat like the edge of the world that led into an unmapped territory.

As the months went by and I didn't see her, her face didn't fade in my memory, as it logically should have done. It got clearer. It was like watching a photograph being developed, the features getting sharper, the colors brighter on the paper in the tray, as the seconds pulsed away. And I couldn't take my eyes off that image. There was something about the idea of her that made me want to believe in the good intentions of chance. The way she glided out of the snowstorm into my view—her eyes alight and her smile as personal and suggestive as a dream—made me determined to believe that certain people were destined to meet one another, that there were many lives anyone could live but only one that would make true sense, that there was someone each of us was supposed to meet and if we did we would know it, and if we didn't we'd know that too.

I guess you could say that I was a kid and she was beautiful and leave it at that. I wondered about my own foolishness in thinking such thoughts, and I wondered if the idea of her was what interested me—not the complication and danger of the real person. Maybe I really didn't want to get to know her. That way I could keep her safe in my head. I didn't know then, perhaps, that even that can be lost—dreams can slip away as easily as people. Our imagination can place us in as much jeopardy as the world can. It can save us too.

When the weather got warm enough, I'd lie in my bed at night, the window open, the hum of insects becoming just another form of silence, and wish to hear the sound of her voice. But I knew that if the wish became real there was always the possibility that something could destroy it. Anticipation has a perfection to it, I guess, that realization can rarely have—and anticipation never loses its shine either.

I carried my daydreams of her into the slow beginning of spring. I carried them as we worked on the roads or cut wood for the Boys' Home to sell. I heard her name in the anonymous song of the ice expanding and contracting in the ponds. Her image appeared to me in science class and in the complicated branches of diagramed sentences on the blackboard in English. I tried not to think of her too much in school, though, because it was important to be on guard in most classes. More often than not, my daydreams and the natural silences that they produced kept me out of trouble because not much attention came to me in the private world I was in. My silence made Delano's friends and most of the people I didn't know think I was worth staying away from. With all of the teachers, except for Mr. Calabria, my silence made me invisible. Other than Mr. Calabria, who taught us world history, most of the teachers were Marist Brothers who appeared to take more pleasure in confirming their worst suspicions about the human race than they did in teaching anything. Brother Boniface was a good example. He taught calculus as if it pained him to see anyone discover the answers.

One thing was even more certain than the fact that there was only one right answer in Boniface's class: that each week someone would have to march up to the front of the room and get paddled. Everyone called it shots, probably because the crack of oak paddle against the flesh and bone of the backside sounded to us like a gunshot echoing against the classroom walls. The only time Boniface appeared happy to me was at those moments in the front of the classroom when he was winging his right arm back, the black robe billowing out in the breeze he created, and he was a split second from feeling the shock wave run through his hand and hearing the thwack and the rush of breath from the boy bent over in front of him. You could see a sort of spark of pleasure flicker across his eyes, and then all his features squeezed behind his black-rimmed glasses as if he didn't want the emotion he was feeling to escape.

Some of the boys, like John O'Malley, were a lot bigger than Boniface, but few would have thought to stand up to him because we all knew that to be thrown out of Washington Lake Boys' Home meant some brand of reformatory that most of us desperately wanted to avoid. Who knew where Delano had been sent? Who wanted to imagine what his life had been like for the past few months? So when Boniface told O'Malley to come to the front of the room to show him how carefully he had done his homework, he walked up to the blackboard knowing, as we all did, that nothing was to be learned that day but the inevitability of humiliation. It was a ritual we had all come to know well.

"Mr. O'Malley," he began in such a sweet tone that it seemed for a second that we must be wrong about the ultimate outcome, "if you had done your homework, if you ever did your homework, you might be able to get beyond the level of the multiplication tables."

Boniface paused, pinched the features of his face together, and then said, "And I'm not certain you even know those."

"Yes, Brother," O'Malley said, fear and resignation fighting for control of his voice.

"You mean you don't know the multiplication tables yet, Mr. O'Malley?"

"Yes, I mean, no, Brother, I mean you're right about the homework. I tried, but I just couldn't get it."

"But you will get it, Mr. O'Malley." He paused again and smiled. "Bend over."

The paddle itself was austere in its simplicity. It looked to me like something a monk might have in his living quarters. It was a rectangle of oiled oak, an inch and a half thick and about eighteen inches long and five inches wide, narrowed at the handle. It looked humorless and efficient. The first shot cracked through the silence and then the second and the third. On the fourth, the tears welled up in O'Malley's eyes. On the fifth, there was a puddle at his feet.

"Sit down there, Mr. O'Malley," Boniface said and he pointed toward the wet ground. And that's where he left him for the remainder of the class, sitting in his own piss as we tried to figure out the value of *x*.

Most of the other teachers weren't that bad. How could they be, I suppose? A few were even fun, like Mr. Calabria, with his chiseled grin, his lips pressed together as if he were suppressing a laugh whenever he looked at us. His eyes would roll in comic exasperation at every wrong answer we made. He made me feel safe to be wrong, to make a mistake. But usually when one of the teachers was funny, it was despite himself, not because he intended to be.

Brother Eden's class came right after Boniface's, and for that reason I felt a little sorry for him. Everything that built up in Boniface's class leaked out in Eden's. He was in his late fifties or early sixties, but most of us would have sworn he was ancient, older than time itself. His glasses were so thick he seemed to be looking at us from another era, a past so distant that we all must have looked blurred to him. And that's the way he looked to us, I'm certain, *blurred*. He taught geography but seemed to be concerned only with the complexities of the dairy farm industry in New York State. He spent weeks, months even, talking about cows and feed and types of milking machines and milk cans. Truck routes from the Catskills to the stores in New York City were more exciting to him than the news story about the seventeen-mile-long bridge that had just been built to span the Chesapeake Bay. It was as if even in terms of geography, he couldn't see beyond a few feet in front of him.

Each class with him was a dance choreographed on the spot. One day half of us would disappear into the clothes closet in the back of the room, led by Fitz, who had a deck of cards and a flashlight so that we could play stud poker until the bell rang and we all walked past Brother Eden as he squinted at us, at the dim, hairy shapes that floated by him into the hall. On another day we would maneuver all of our desks into the far back of the classroom as soon as he turned to put notes on the board. When he looked back at us, we were at a great distance from him. He would take off his glasses, rub them with a stained handkerchief that he rolled up in the sleeve of his robe, and turn back to the board. When he looked at us again, we were squeezed into the front of the classroom, with barely enough room for him to turn around.

He reminded me of the comic figures in the Shakespeare tragedies we read in English class, our Polonius there to make sure that we didn't take ourselves too seriously. In his class once a week Patrick Duffy took a sneezing fit. "Ah

. . . ah . . . bullshit," he'd say until a few guys would laugh. Brother Eden would twist his face into a sorrowful expression and say, "Now, now, gentlemen, it's reprehensible to make fun of someone in distress." And Duffy would look gratefully at Brother Eden, cover his mouth with his hands, and sneeze again—"ah, ah, ah, booshit."

Brother Eden also taught us English—and with the same dreamy dullness that he taught geography. Most of my reading came outside of the class assignments, but every now and again he gave us something to read that made him seem like the dull-witted bearer of the truth, the messenger who, despite his own inability to hear, brings news of great value to anyone within earshot. He would stand before us, squinting as if we were seated on an island hundreds of yards from him.

"Now, gentlemen," he would say, "Milton's *Paradise Lost* illuminates the ancient tradition of *felix culpa,* the fortunate fall. It is a necessary doctrine for any Catholic to accept if he is committed to the knowledge that God has the universe in His benevolent control. Without a belief in *felix culpa,* man has to see an error on God's part. Something went terribly wrong. Something is terribly wrong.

"And that is not the case and not what Milton says. What does he say? He says, 'O goodness infinite, goodness immense! / That all this good of evil shall produce / And evil turn to good.' "

Then Brother Eden would slide into Latin—*"O certe necessarium Adae peccatum, quad Christie morte deletum est! O felix culpa, quae talem ac tantum meruit habere redemptorem"*—as if we all understood his every word. But it was all sound to most of us, like his talk of milk cans and milking machines. So when he did say something that made me pay attention, when a sentence or two came out of the fog of Latin and repeated details, it sounded like a brick dropping in a silent auditorium.

"Look at the last lines of the poem, gentlemen. What of the fall of Adam and Eve? What of their expulsion from paradise? Is there not something fortunate in it for them, for us, some hope to overshadow any sorrow? Look at the lines: 'Some natural tears they dropped but wiped them soon; / The world was all before them where to choose / Their place of rest, and providence their guide; / They hand in hand with wandering steps and slow, / Through Eden took their solitary way.' " He slowed down a fraction and smiled shyly over "Eden" and then continued, "Even with the burden of their regret, they have each other and the exhilarating prospect of the world before them, no?"

That day the bell rang, catching Brother Eden in mid-thought, it seemed. "Is it desolation or redemption. . . ?" The words just hung there as if he didn't know how to end the sentence or what he was asking—or even if he were asking a question at all.

The words meant something to me even though I wasn't sure then why. They seemed a message in a bottle, a whisper directed toward me alone. It took time—meeting Nada, finding my great great grandfather's journal, taking to the road—to recognize that Brother Eden was speaking to me, even if he didn't know it himself. Usually that's the way we understand the nature of events in our lives, words transform themselves into messages years after we first hear them, we make sense of the meaning of our fall long after the thud of the crash echoes in our ears.

Brother Eden took us on a field trip one spring afternoon to some of the dairy farms in the area. A few of the boys leaned against a fence railing and teased Julio, a Puerto Rican kid from the Inwood section of upper Manhattan, calling him Felix Culpa.

"Hey, Felix, ain't it fortunate you with us today, man? Hey, Felix, watch out for the culvert, don't fall. Hey, Felix. Hey, Felix."

Finally, he snapped back at them—"Shut the fuck up, willya, man"—and threw a plate-size piece of cow dung toward them.

I looked in the direction of his toss, and that's when I saw Nada for the second time. A dozen of us stood behind Brother Eden and Nada's uncle at the entrance to the milking barn, feigning interest as they talked about the shining new equipment used on the farm. It was a warm spring day, and Nada came up the dirt road that led to the house, carrying her schoolbooks. For a moment, I didn't recognize her from the snowstorm. All I had really noticed was her face, her eyes, like ebony against the snow-covered oaks and pines. The rest had been covered by the hood and coat. Now she was wearing white shorts and T-shirt. Her legs and arms were slim and dark. She was thin, but her hips and breasts curved slightly against the light fabric and made my skin tighten. Her brown hair fell thick and twisting in cords below her shoulders, spreading like a flood of dark water against her white shirt.

As I watched her walk up the path, I separated myself from the group and angled toward her. Her eyes were a deeper gray than my dreams of them from that winter afternoon. She smiled, and I know I mumbled something, although even when she laughed and said, "Me too," I had no idea what words I had actually spoken. But once the silence was broken, it seemed as if it had never existed.

I couldn't remember why I had been satisfied with the dream of her. The dark wind that sailed through me at that moment felt good and clean. Her voice sounded as strange and familiar to me as my own.

8

I saw Nada every chance I got after that afternoon. Her parents had died when she was just an infant, and she had lived with her aunt and uncle, her father's family, for as long as she could remember. She couldn't recall anything about her mother or father that someone else hadn't told her. The photographs of them in her bedroom were her only proof that they were flesh and blood, and not just characters in an elaborate children's story that others had created for her benefit. The photograph showed a blond-haired, blue-eyed young man who had a smile on his face that suggested he had just been released from military service and found his way back to the woman he had thought about the whole time he was away. The woman looked like a Tahitian girl in a painting by Gauguin. Shoeless, in a soft summery dress, she smiled into the eye of the camera in a way that seemed not to discount sadness. Her hair, like Nada's, fell thick and dark against her bare shoulders. Her features were delicate and her skin the color of the sky at the beginning of nightfall.

At first, neither Nada nor I talked about the color of her skin, and in a sense it wasn't because either of us was avoiding it. Her aunt and uncle, who were good people and kind to her in their somber way, had been shocked by Nada's father's choice of a wife. They had found a way to face it for the short time the marriage lasted, but it had not made them openhearted to pieces of the world they didn't know and didn't want to understand. As far as I could tell, they didn't think about Nada's mixed blood. They didn't acknowledge it at all. For them, her skin color was like a birthmark, a queer business of chance that had nothing to do with race. And nothing to do with them. They were just a country family, and Nada was, as they saw things, like a niece born with a limp or a harelip. It was a little embarrassing but it could happen to anyone.

They never would have allowed her to see a boy housed at the Washington Lake Boys' Home. The mark on me had nothing to do with race, but for them the mark was there and was not something they could avoid seeing. Maybe they hoped she would marry a young man from Bermuda who was studying law at Columbia University, someone whose family had money but whose skin had been darkened by the tropical sun.

It was easy enough, though, for us to keep out of their sight. The woods were all around us and gave us plenty of places to see each other. Our meetings, then, were separated from the world, outside of family and school and history and color. Each of our meetings seemed outside of time itself, and for this reason, it took us a long while to acknowledge the topic that would have naturally consumed most of our attention on an ordinary first date. It was as if our relationship had nothing to do with the world as we had come to know it. The shadings of our skin meant no more to us than the color of our clothing.

I volunteered for any jobs that would send me away from the Boys' Home and into town. After a few months they trusted me to drive the rust-eaten van on the place and gave me the job of picking up two-by-fours or groceries. Nobody else cared much to go. What was there in the town anyway? Most of the boys preferred not to do any extra work. Usually I met Nada in Shohola, Pennsylvania, a town a few miles to the west of Yulan, on the other side of the Delaware River. I'd park the truck off the road on a lumber trail and hike back a mile to Shohola Falls. Or what Nada called Shohola Falls. Our meeting place was really just a section of Shohola Brook, a place where the canyon narrowed and the water throbbed down from the high ground and pooled up to about ten feet deep in one tree-shadowed circle. The actual Shohola Falls was about seven miles to the west. A reservoir and a dam with a gradually tiered falls stretched for a hundred yards and then dropped sharply into a knob of the river that flowed toward us in the brook. The real falls were the source of things, but too many people gathered there. We needed a place that no one else knew about or at least a place where no one else was willing to go.

It's difficult to describe the section of the stream that Nada and I called Shohola Falls without sounding like I'm making things up. About halfway along a twisting path with tree limbs and rocks of various sizes blocking the way, you come into sight of the Weiry brothers' place, which hangs like a loopy cartoon cabin off the side of the mountain. The cabin has a front porch filled with tires and rusted metal. The porch is actually buckling under the weight of junk—pieces of tricycles, wheelbarrows without wheels, velvet paintings of Elvis and Jesus Christ, refrigerators without doors, bottles and cans and stacks of tires. The place looks like it hasn't been painted in twenty years. The roof over the porch sags, and the tiles on the main roof are chipped and discolored. In spots the torn tarpaper shows through. A spavined horse usually stands pawing the dirt by a ramshackle barn, and on most days an equally swollen-limbed dog with patches of fur and flesh quilted to its rib cage droops over a fallen tree trunk.

Most people saw the Weiry brothers only once a year, during the St. Patrick's Day parade. Dressed in black tuxedos, they came riding through town in their 1937 Chevy. They were always unshaven, but their hair was brushed back wet and their teeth, except for those that were brown or missing, were glistening with tooth polish. They always followed the Barryville fire engine through the Four Corners, keeping their eyes straight ahead, grim and serious as if they were part of a funeral cortege.

Other than St. Patrick's Day, they could just as well have been ghosts. In all the times I passed within view of their cabin dangling off the side of the mountain, I never saw them around the place or heard any movement inside. I'd glance in the direction of the cabin and keep on going down the path toward the falls. A half a mile beyond the Weiry brothers' house, the narrow path ended in the creek itself, as if the trail were coming to the end of the world. The water was always cold there, even in the middle of the hottest part of the summer. It ran swift and shallow over slippery rocks. Balancing carefully, I stepped from one rock to another until I sat on the flat top of a boulder in the center of the creek. A few yards in front of the boulder, the water welled up darker and as deep as ten feet.

There was a small waterfall about fifty yards beyond the pool of dark green water. You could see it through the cliffs that were once connected before the creek had cut a swath through the mountains centuries before. The sun fell into the ravine like broken glass spraying the spaces left by the big trees that stood above the cliffs. On one side, the cliffs themselves hung in levels like a gallery, rising from ten feet high to fifteen and then to a twenty-five-foot plateau near the top. Each level was a few feet back from the one below it. I had heard that many years before I first saw the place some people had jumped

off the different levels into the pool of water directly below, but each jump required more nerve, not because of the height but because the higher leap demanded a jump outward as well as downward. If you didn't jump far enough
out, you landed on the rocky level beneath. If you jumped too far, you
smashed against the flat cliffs on the other side. And there was a rumor that
somebody had done just that, flown arms outspread into the wall of rock and
dropped like a broken bird into the water below. No one followed the brook
back to the cliffs anymore. For most people who lived in the area, the cliffs
were a legend, some mysterious place back in the woods where a wild kid had
once fallen to his death. For them, this hidden part of the brook was just another story, a tale parents told their young children to frighten them, and the
dead kid just another myth no more real than the story of Dedalus.

Shohola Falls felt separated from everything. It was like finding a part of
the world that nobody else had ever seen before. Even the sunlight could get
in only in certain places during particular times of the morning and afternoon.
Beds of dried leaves and moss-covered rocks led to the stream. Even in August
the water was icy cold. Diving into it was a jolt to the senses. With a shock,
every part of your body came alive. The water in the stream was never deep
enough to cover the boulders strewn around like dead bodies after some
tremendous battle. So the rocks stood out from the rippling current, a great
puzzle of sizes and shapes. Those rocks in the water had a sheen to them, polished by the stream over time. The sound that the water made as it slid over
the rocks, uninterrupted, was like a new kind of silence, as soft as a breeze
swimming through the branches and leaves. It was a sound so repeated that it
was like no sound at all. Even in a drought the water ran, gurgling, so that the
presence of the running brook was more difficult to notice than your own
heartbeat.

The shoreline was thick with ferns and vines. Mosquitoes skimmed across
the water, and birds flew from a cantilevered tree trunk out of the canyon, angling straight up, parallel to the sheer cliffs, and into the daylight that you
could only imagine beyond the Falls. On the ridges above the streambed,
fallen and decayed trees lay close to the mouths of a dozen shallow caves.

By late spring, even though the water was so cold it made us shout with
surprise, Nada and I held hands and jumped from the first level and eventually
the second. The third seemed too risky, though it was clear to me that Nada
was willing to jump from it if I wanted to. I was satisfied with the exhilaration
I felt, our hands locked, as we struck the water with a crashing silence and mo-

mentary blindness. We lay on the boulder in the middle of the stream, positioning our bodies so that we moved like the hands of a clock, touching each other and a piece of the sunlight as the afternoons drifted by.

Nada knew the country better than I could ever have hoped to know the Bronx. She knew it well enough not to seem afraid of anything.

"Don't step on that rock," she said one day in a matter-of-fact tone that I would not have been able to match. "Snakes like to sun themselves on warm rocks." She looked into my eyes and smiled. "That's not a stick on that boulder."

We never saw a bear near those caves, but I knew that there were times that they would be there, and I knew that Nada had seen them in the woods. I was certain that if she saw a brown bear, she would be able to make herself look down at the ground to avoid eye contact so that the animal would not feel threatened. She'd be able, I was sure, to make her heart and mind behave as she wanted them to. I wished that I had the confidence that mine would as well.

Over the next few weeks, no matter how long we were able to spend at Shohola Falls, and often it was only about an hour or even less because I had to go back to the Home, time seemed suspended. The place itself felt as if it were outside the realm of clocks and watches. It had a kind of quiet that was unlike any I had ever known. The silence left by my mother was an ache. The silences that my father and I had created made the air feel weighted. The silences in the classroom at the Boy's Home were laced with tension, the anticipation of punishment. At Shohola Falls, with Nada, the silence was lighter than air itself. Every silence was filled with a different sort of anticipation— with possibility and a simple lazy contentment. Our voices slid along the quiet like dust motes on a breeze. Nada's voice was soft and silky and as warm as sunlight on my chest.

Shohola Falls could have been an island. It seemed as separate as a triangle of land surrounded by the sea, except when we were there, it surrounded us. The rocks and trees enclosed us. Only a few feet of sky peeked through the canopy of leaves and branches. The outside world could not get in, not the sound of a car or another human voice. The silences between Nada and me were not like silence at all, but like the sound of the ocean rolling against the shore, soft and constant, or like the whispering of the stream nearby us. Once the weather got warm enough, I'd spend the afternoons lying on a rock, my fingers tracing the curve of her arm, and breathe in the scent of her skin and hair. She smelled like the world that surrounded us—limpid water, sunlight and pine needles, moss-covered rocks. One afternoon when I said that I had to go back to the Boys' Home, she turned dreamily in my direction and smiled at me as if I spoke a strange language, as if I had uttered a word that made no sense in this world where we were. But she opened her gray eyes wide in mock despair, propped herself on her elbows, and said, "One day let's never leave."

I rose up and pulled her to her feet.

"C'mon, I'll give you a ride to the Four Corners."

But I was already thinking of my memory of the place, my dreams of the future, and both hoping and afraid that she had spoken with absolute seriousness.

9

I kept pretty much to myself at the Boys' Home. Most of the boys were friendly in a careful way, but when I wasn't in class or working on one of Father Boyd's crews, I stayed in my room, reading or talking to Fitz. Or daydreaming about Nada.

As the months passed, some of Delano's friends seemed to suspect that my silences were not a prelude to another burst of craziness, that maybe my punching him without any preliminaries or announcement was not a true indication of who I was. They still had a reasonable doubt, though, and that's all I needed. In front of them, I continued to use my silence as a disguise. It was better than a foreign accent or dressing in drag. I was playing a part and hoping that I wouldn't forget any of the lines. Of course, there weren't any lines—that's what I had to remember. Around that time I was reading *One Flew Over the Cuckoo's Nest* and I felt a little like Chief Bromden, faking like I was deaf and dumb in order to protect the life I had. My silence made me invisible to most people. To Delano's friends, it just reconfirmed my mystery. I knew that if any of his friends came to believe that I was not waiting, even eager, to snap at any moment, I would have to face a form of misery that would be worse than anything Brother Boniface or Father Boyd had to offer.

But I was too focused on Nada to be as watchful as I should have been. In my happiness, I began to forget my silence and invisibility the way someone can forget to carry a phony draft card. With a phony identification, you remember it only when you get to the door of the bar. With invisibility, it's the same thing. You can remember to be wary when it's too late to do anything about your mistake. I guess I started to believe in my own good luck. I began to think that falling in love with Nada was enough to protect me from disaster.

On the night of my seventeenth birthday, the moon hung outside my window, a pockmarked orange circle bigger than common sense would imagine possible. It appeared to take up the entire horizon. It filled my eyes, took my breath away. I could feel the heat coming in waves on the faint breeze. Fitz stretched and said, "It's too hot to move."

Then he turned his head and looked at me lying on my bed.

"You look like you're dressed to go out, son. But I wouldn't advise getting caught by Boyd or one of his boys."

He scratched his bare stomach.

"Not many girls would be worth that trouble. And—if I'm not mistaken—the one you're after brings a special brand of trouble in the kind of world we live in. She's a pretty girl, no doubt, but her skin is too dark for your white ass. No that I give a shit, of course, or that it's anybody's business, but that's the way the world is and it ain't going to change soon. No, buddy, not many girls—even lighter-skinned—would be worth that kind of trouble."

"She would."

"I can see that you've lost all power to reason. But try to keep your dick in your pants until you get off the grounds. Nobody wants to see that little worm in the moonlight. And watch out for Boyd. I don't want to have to break in another dumbshit roommate."

About a half an hour later, I was on the road to Shohola Falls. It took me about an hour to walk there, cutting over the mountain and through the fields and woods. I was thankful for the moonlight. When I got to the falls, the light of the moon was shifting from orange to yellow, and it hung like a Japanese lantern above the cliffs. Then Nada's shadow fell across it, a momentary image on a blank screen. The light illuminated her face and spread flames along the edges of her dark hair.

"I'll be right down," she said.

A shaft of icy air swept into the heavy heat, a shocking runnel of cold that passed through and was gone like an uncertain memory before I even had time to fully feel the chill. But I thought I saw her shiver as she pulled off her T-shirt, stepped out of her jeans, and leaped from the moonlight into the darkness, a spark of dark flesh in a world turned upside down, flickering downward to disappear with a quick sizzle into the black water.

"Happy birthday," she whispered as she slipped her moonlit arms around my neck and pressed her breasts against my chest. I couldn't tell whose heart I felt beating wildly, hers or mine, as I kissed her, and we sank into the stream, into a mysterious, new world.

And the next day the world was different. Not perfect or simple or less threatening but changed somehow, as if the place I inhabited were much larger than I had ever imagined. It's hard to describe. In an odd way it felt like the day John F. Kennedy had been assassinated, without the sadness, of course, although there was some sadness in it too in a strange way that I didn't understand then.

Back in 1963, it had felt as if someone had given me a pair of polished glasses and shown me that the world I had been seeing only dimly for thirteen years had become, in an instant, clear. All of a sudden, I felt, I saw the world as it was, and how I had not seen it before that moment. Later, when my mother got sick, and especially when she died, I noticed the same sudden clarity that came on me in the form of a dull pain. It was like realizing that everything I'd been seeing for years had been blurred, and I had gotten so used to it that I just assumed all things had a colorless haze around them. Now, it was not just that every image seemed in sharper focus but that the very margins of the world were extended and I could see those distances close at hand. It was the kind of clarity that made me feel wobbly.

After the night of my birthday at Shohola Falls, I felt so good that I began to get nervous. I felt too lucky and sensed that something had to go wrong. There were so many things that could happen. Nada's aunt and uncle would find us walking along the road. Or a fight with one of Delano's friends would keep me locked up at the Boys' Home or, worse, a fight would get me thrown out, separated from her when I had less than a year before I was eighteen and free to choose where I wanted to be. I guess it was odd that I didn't even think about the color of her skin or mine and what that would mean any place outside of Shohola Falls. Because I think I sensed that Shohola Falls was no more real than a place in a book. At times it seemed less real than Huck Finn's Jackson's Island. It was as if I had imagined Shohola Falls, even when I was sitting right there with Nada.

I was afraid to think too far ahead. Afraid that everything would disappear on me—Shohola Falls, Nada, my own new identity. I started to get a hollow nervous feeling that stayed with me all of the time, and that made me find Nada even more mysterious. She didn't seem to be afraid of anything. She seemed able to believe that things would always turn out all right or as they were meant to be and that she could discover a way to face whatever happened. I never admitted it to myself back then, but I think my deepest fear was that I didn't have the courage that Nada did, the simple strength to live each day inside or outside of Shohola Falls. I also had this suspicion that I was more like my father than I dared acknowledge, that the color of Nada's skin added just enough vulnerability to make me doubt myself. Was I my father's son?

The day after my birthday Fitz and I sat on the porch and watched the whitecaps on the lake gather under a gray sky that seemed to mirror the turbulent water. On the table in front of us the *New York Times* was opened and someone had drawn a pencil line around a story about seven crewmembers of a cargo plane who were killed after a midair collision with an Air Force Phantom jet the night before near Saigon. Lying there, circled, the story seemed another message to me. The war lay in wait. It was on the other side of the world from Shohola Falls, but it too was a dreamscape, no more real than my dreams of Shohola Falls but maybe less forgiving in its unreality. The war didn't need to make sense any more than the plot of a nightmare did. It had only to be possible to be true. I was afraid I'd close my eyes and find myself there, sleepwalking through the jungles and rice paddies. And then Shohola Falls would be as real and no more real than Vietnam.

Things drifted along that summer—with me feeling an equal sense of dread and heart-racing anticipation, separately and, sometimes it seemed, simultaneously. Nada and I met every chance we got at Shohola Falls—sometimes twice in one day if we could invent the right excuses for the Boys' Home and her aunt and uncle. We met whether it was sunny or cloudy. It was like being on the edge of sleep and willing yourself back into a dream from which you hadn't fully awakened. One day merged into the next, always the same, always different, when we were at Shohola Falls. I didn't want my dream of Shohola Falls to end. And for a while it seemed as if it might not end but take us both to my eighteenth birthday and graduation and a new life.

By mid-October I had worn a visible path through the woods to the falls. The forest had exploded with color, and going to meet Nada I often felt dizzy as the sun streaked through the orange and red leaves, spinning and flashing like prisms in the light. I'd stop occasionally to get my balance and squint into the sunlight to watch the yellow oak leaves float down around me with every exhalation of wind. They were like dancers twisting gracefully in the breeze, like flakes of sunlight broken free from the sun, like letters of a lost language. They were to me signs of good fortune. I feared such good fortune, though, because I couldn't help wondering what would follow such luck to take it away, had to come to destroy it. Finally, I realized, of course, that they were only fall leaves and probably meant no more than that, but bad luck caught up with me anyway—as it always seemed to in those days if I gave it enough time.

Often we create our own luck, of course. Even at seventeen I sensed that was true, but knowing it didn't make it any easier for me to make the luck I needed for myself then. I lived much of my life during those months like someone who is watching himself in a play. I was both actor and director, but most of the time I couldn't do anything about the director's voice except hear it inside of my head.

In the middle of the autumn, Indian summer made Shohola Falls as comfortable as it was in June. The sun warmed the rocks, and birds fluttered from one branch to another, moved mindlessly, it seemed, by the wind. Nada and I met there each day for two weeks, even Sundays. At the end of those two weeks, I began to forget that I had once had a life without her and before her. At times there seemed to be nothing more than the moment I lived in—no past, no future. I'm not even sure what day of the week it was when we sat upon the bank of the stream and she touched my arm.

"Let's get married," she said.

I didn't say anything. I just looked at her. I knew what I wanted to say, but I couldn't make the words come. I was thinking about all of the hours we had spent at the falls, how much I wanted that time to go on, and I wanted to tease her, say *you'd be too much trouble to marry, too fearless for any sane man.* I wanted to say it the way Fitz would have said it to me, as if he meant it when he meant powerfully the opposite. And she would have taken the flesh of her lower lip beneath her top teeth and shaken her head in mock sadness. *You need some trouble in your life,* she would say. *You'll get bored and fat and lazy if you don't watch out.*

Instead of saying anything, though, I found another voice rising up inside my head, a voice that wasn't mine at all, or one that I didn't want to be mine.

"Don't look so nervous," she said. "I don't mean now, today, or even next year. I mean let's get married one day. Let's be together long enough for that and everything else to happen to us."

I knew that I wanted just that. Or maybe I didn't want *everything else to happen to us.* I might have understood that to mean something different from what she meant by it, or she may have been able to face what that meant better than I could. I know I wanted to say what would make her keep loving me.

So I don't understand why I said, "It's not easy to think about a month from now, let alone forever. Besides, getting married is so complicated, so public. Sometimes I think it's better to feel married in private."

I heard that foreign sound in my voice. It was exactly like listening to my father speak, as if the words were his and fell directly into a silence. I started to wonder if I was afraid of what she said because to acknowledge *forever* meant acknowledging it could be cut short. Or was I like my father in other ways and did the color of her skin make me a coward, afraid of what was deep inside of me?

"It's not hard for me to think about forever. It seems natural to think about it," she said.

"Thinking about it doesn't necessarily make it real." I was listening to the sound of my own voice again, standing outside of myself, observing the mystery of my own behavior. I was saying things I didn't want to say, but I couldn't do anything but listen to my own voice.

"It only becomes real if you begin to imagine it. Are you afraid to imagine it?"

"What's that supposed to mean?" Although I was pretty certain I knew. "I'm just being realistic. Things change. People leave. They die. How long is forever anyway?"

"You know sometimes there's a sadder form of cowardice than being afraid to die or even see other people die."

"Maybe that's true. And maybe you think I'm someone that I'm really not. Maybe I'm not as brave as you are. Or maybe I know more than you do."

Nada moved her hand from my forearm and turned her gray eyes toward the opening in the trees where the sun was sinking in the west. "Or maybe you don't know enough."

There was the knowledge that lay between Nada and me after that conversation. It was something we both knew and left unnamed—perhaps out of wariness or maybe because we truly couldn't give a name to it. I liked myself less for knowing it, for even unnamed it told me that I was not the person that I thought I was and made me doubt that I could ever become that person.

That's when I started my own bad luck. And I would make it worse a few days later. I'm not sure we can ever say that something is really bad luck until we see it from quite a distance because I've learned over the last few years that even bad luck might turn into something good if we have enough patience or look at it in a certain way. We usually can't see far enough to know where things will lead. And, besides, maybe what we think of as bad luck is actually a lot better than what could have happened and surely did happen to someone else. But at that time in my life I thought that Nada might have gotten it backward. She didn't seem to understand—even dying, perhaps, was a better fate than living at times—it could be a way out of all the bad twists of fate.

But what happened to me at the end of October seemed like bad luck at the time. Back then I couldn't see it any other way. Because I wanted things to stay the way they were, for me to be able to sneak off and see Nada every day and to see her in the same way we had seen each other for the past year, I started to get very cautious. I began to imagine all the ways in which things could and probably would break into pieces. I became so watchful that my hours at the Boys' Home were like a chess match in which I tried to anticipate every move by my opponent before it happened.

This pleased Father Boyd and a number of the other teachers, I'm certain. Boyd didn't even seem to see me when he spoke, you could tell, and, of course, that was a good thing for me. I didn't want anyone to notice that the Boys' Home wasn't my real life. My real life was at Shohola Falls and the dreams of it I had as I walked through the necessary details of each day. It was a life that I lived in my imagination as much as I did with the books I read. But this imagined world at Shohola Falls was real, too. It was like being able to make a novel that I loved come to life each afternoon. I wanted that world of Shohola Falls to be the only truth—at least, I wanted my dreams of the place to be real and true in a way that made the rest of my life a daydream.

Nada was quieter than usual in the days after our conversation, but she never became anything for me other than what she was. Her voice never changed into someone else's as mine had. Her smile was always there, rising from her lips into her eyes as unconsciously as an inhalation of breath. She was always willing to be who she was and, even more surprisingly maybe, able to know. She made loving someone seem so effortless that I got angry not being able to do the same. And as unreasonable as it was, I felt angry with her for not allowing me not to care.

It's nearly impossible to explain why you fall in love with someone. What is it about that person that makes you love her? At first, it might be that she's beautiful or that she loves you, but I believe it's more than that. I think you recognize something in that person, something of yourself. I'm not talking about vanity here, like being entranced by your own image in a mirror. I mean that when you meet the right person, it's like meeting a part of yourself that you didn't know existed. It's surprising and familiar all at the same time. If you're fortunate, you discover some part of yourself that's better than you expected—generous and daring and spirited. I understand that sometimes that gets lost, but as long as someone is in love, that surprise and familiarity are there, I think. That's the way Nada made me feel, and she made me feel that it could last forever. It scared me to be that lucky. I didn't want to jeopardize it by changing anything in any way. The world just seemed jealous of good luck. Good fortune always brought a curse with it.

So I did my best to keep quiet about my happiness so that no jealous fate would want to even things out. I wanted to remain unnoticed and, for the most part, for the time I had spent at the Boys' Home I had managed it. As the weeks had turned to months, I had faded like the H. G. Wells hero, little by little, until I was no longer there for anyone but Mr. Calabria and Fitz. My life was with Nada at Shohola Falls, even though I hadn't quite figured out how to make that perfectly true or to be there as unwarily as she was. The rest was an act. I was Tommy Blanks, a name and nothing else for Father Boyd and Brother Boniface, and for Delano's friends I was a lit fuse attached to something hidden in the darkness.

Each day I waited to leave for the falls. If it rained, I went anyway, and Nada and I sat under the lip of the mountain, the drops accumulating until a waterfall made a glistening screen between us and the rest of the world. In the sunshine we lay on the moss-covered rocks. We didn't talk about what we were going to do when it got too cold to sit in the shadows of the forest any more than we talked about the shades of difference in our skins that in Shohola Falls still seemed as inconsequential as how we might live on another planet. As it turned out, we didn't have to talk about how we would face the cold weather. At first, we didn't talk about it because there was a chill between us, before the weather turned cold anyway. We both knew I was holding a part of myself away from her as if she were the edge of something and I didn't want to see over that border, get dizzy, and fall. Eventually, though, I knew we would have to face the weather, if not ourselves. What was unspoken would have to be put into words. But the weather did not have to be faced and those unsaid words were not spoken. Delano took care of all of that.

He returned one day in the middle of the week toward the end of October. I was standing in front of the main house with Fitz. We were raking leaves into a pile, and each pile would be carted back in a big cardboard box to the burning pit behind the house. Along with the leaves, tree limbs and broken chairs, anything that had satisfied its usefulness and could be burned was tossed onto the pyre. It all seemed perfectly Catholic to me—all that Boniface and Boyd needed was a stake and a human victim.

Both Fitz and I looked up at the same time, lifting our heads from the monotony of raking, and saw a Sullivan County sheriff's car bouncing down the pitted road toward us. The driver opened the rear door on the passenger's side, and Delano stepped out, raising his hand against the sunlight. It was a gesture that seemed sad and childlike to me. For a moment, he looked like a kid crouching in fear against a parent's cruelty. As much as it made me sick to see him return, in that instant I felt sorry for him. Right then, as he stepped out of the police car, his palm facing the sky like an acknowledgment of defeat, I saw myself in him. He was back because, as with me, there seemed no place else for him to go. Maybe his mother had died and his father had fallen into the emptiness that death creates. Maybe Delano, as I did, wanted no more to do with mourning, but where I chose stillness and silence to ward off the treachery of the world, he may have chosen treachery itself, like setting a blaze against a fire which has gone out of control. Delano may have determined that the way to combat the unfairness of the world was to bully it into submission or to simply beat it at its own game of unaccountable cruelty.

I was on the verge of reaching out my hand to shake with him. *Welcome back. All's forgotten, eh?* Like some suave movie actor playing a British commander in a prison camp during World War II. *I can make peace with my unheroic fellow prisoner.*

The county sheriff led Delano by the elbow past Fitz and me. Delano never slowed his gait as he passed us but looked directly into my eyes and hissed, "Now it begins."

Fitz turned to me. "What did that cocksucker say?"

I just shrugged, but we both knew—I'm certain—that whatever Delano's sorrowful tale of growing up, he was back with us now as if the malicious universe had been given a face and a name, if not an explanation. And it really wouldn't have mattered if we had been twin brothers because it was clear that there was no chance we would find a way to see any kinship or ever discover a common language to speak to one another.

No one at the Boys' Home made an official announcement about Delano's return, of course, but that day the entire atmosphere changed as if a front had suddenly come through. What had made me safe with Father Boyd and many of the other teachers at the Boys' Home created a problem in a short space of time for me after Delano returned. It wasn't long before I could see that Delano had begun to look at me as if he were solving a curious puzzle. A smile sometimes crept across his face when he looked at me in the cafeteria or the classroom. At times he seemed to know something that only the two of us understood. Soon, I was conscious of the effort I made to avoid his company and when in his company to avoid eye contact with him. I could tell by the way he squinted at me and his lips pressed together and flattened into a smirk that he was wondering if I were a fake. I began to feel like a coward. Maybe Nada was right. And if she was right, I wasn't sure the form my cowardice would take, and I couldn't pinpoint exactly what I was afraid of.

I knew I was afraid to lose her and didn't want to live away from her. Away from Shohola Falls, I felt panicky. Without any specific reasons, my stomach shaped itself into a cold knot, and I had to breathe slowly and deeply to uncoil the fear. The love I felt at Shohola Falls was wild and boundless, I thought, but maybe it wasn't strong enough or was really just a weakness because at the Boys' Home it made me prudent instead of daring. Each breath at the Boys' Home was a tiny flame of fear—fear that I would see Nada slip away, that the world or some stupid mistake I'd make would take her from me. Fear is like anger. It makes you become the object of your emotion, and in the process you lose yourself. All you can see is what you want deeply to avoid.

Delano was like some sort of inescapable fate. I suppose I shouldn't have been surprised that he held the memory of our fight as long as he did—over a year—that he had left as if he had never been there and returned as if he had never been gone. At first I hoped he might have forgotten all about me in the sure nightmare the circumstances of his leaving must have meant for him, but wherever he had been seemed only to sharpen his memory of me. He came back as if he had been at the Boys' Home the whole time, waiting for the right moment to finish what had been started, watching me to see if I was who I had told him I was on that first day at the Boys' Home.

It started to become obvious that he wasn't going to let me slip by unnoticed. At first, he angled toward me slowly, almost silently. His smile—hard and malicious—found me in the dining hall or the classroom. His teeth appeared preternaturally white contrasted with his glistening black hair. His teeth shone like tombstones in my dreams. His eyes seemed to be everywhere.

He began to sweep by me with a group of his friends, his cologne and my name exhaled as part of the breeze he left behind. When I didn't respond, he clearly gained enthusiasm for the game he was playing. He would say, "How're ya doing, Blanks?" But he said it in such a way that it was a challenge and a threat, never a real question. He seemed to be telling me and everyone around us that he knew quite well how I was doing. He knew who I was better than I knew myself.

At night sometimes I would lie in bed, not thinking of anything in particular, and apprehension would grab my chest like a gloved hand and my breathing would tighten. On those nights my dreams would turn crazy. Nada and I would be walking along Irishtown Road holding hands and without any warning the ground beneath her feet would open up and I'd feel her hand slip slowly out of my grasp. She was gone before I could see anything but her hair, her raised arm, the creases of skin at her elbow, her dark freckled forearm, her hand disappearing into the ground. I'd wake up with a start and reach into the absolute blackness, not sure for a few seconds whether I was awake or asleep or if the blinding darkness all around me was the hole she had slipped into before either of us could speak. I'd wake up not knowing if I were my dream self or not, awake in the darkness or asleep in the light.

Delano gave flesh and reality to my nightmares. I knew that eventually I would have to face him and in facing him my life would be transformed again. I didn't want another change in my life. I wanted it to remain as it was—with Nada at least—as it had been in the months before at Shohola Falls. But after a few weeks of seeing Delano's smile, like a glimpse of an unsympathetic future, I began to want to fight him just to get it over with—to hear the bad news that I knew would come and maybe to show Nada and myself that I had been right all along about holding some part of myself away from the world, keeping it secret from everyone—even from myself.

What was to happen started in Mr. Calabria's history class on a Wednesday afternoon. Wednesday afternoons were the worst. Anyone who was bored felt the boredom more on that day, it seemed. I loved Mr. Calabria's class, though, even on Wednesdays, and it was never boring to me. Mr. Calabria might not have known how much I enjoyed his class because I kept pretty quiet. I'd answer a question if he asked me directly, and once in a while my enthusiasm overcame my instinct to be careful, and I contributed my voice to a discussion, but generally I kept my mouth shut. Words were dangerous and could get you in trouble. They could upset the equilibrium, and there was a delicate balance I didn't want to disrupt. I didn't want to call too much attention to myself even in his class where I felt relatively safe in the company of his gentle teasing and rough-edged smile.

On this day, Delano looked bored, and he seemed to want to make something happen to change the atmosphere. He was slouched in his seat, which was next to mine, his eyes half closed, his head canted slightly to the right, looking at the side of my face through the slits of his eyelids. The class period was nearly over when I sensed his shifting his gaze toward me. For forty minutes, Mr. Calabria had glided from one side of the room to the other, rolling his eyes and grimacing like a slick-haired silent film star, asking questions about the Louisiana Purchase and Sacagawea and snapping his middle finger against the lowered skull of any student who appeared to be drifting away from his excitement about Lewis and Clark's journey into the West.

When Calabria turned his back and walked up to the map in the front of the room, tracing with his thick index finger the route that the Corps of Discovery took to the West Coast, Delano turned his face fully in my direction, opening his eyes slightly, but not enough to suggest that he had any enthusiasm about anything that might happen in the near future.

"Who's the girl I saw you with last week?"

My chest went a little cold, and I felt my mouth go dry. "You must have seen someone else."

"No, no, man, it was you—and some light chocolate piece of ass. I think I could be persuaded to fuck her myself on a day like today. Maybe you should arrange a date for me. I'm not prejudiced. I'll fuck a nigger—or whatever she is—quick as the next guy."

He eyed me carefully, calculating after all those months he had been gone, I think, just how far he should go and if he had already made a bad mistake.

"I guess we can talk about it in Jocko's class," he said and turned his profile to me.

I didn't say anything, just looked long and hard at him, in part because silence was the only answer I could readily come up with but also because I wanted to play for some time, to let him wonder what would happen next and to give me that same time to think what that response would have to be. My mind was racing ahead of any clear thoughts I might have held onto, but I knew already what had to happen next. I had the sense that Delano had seen Nada and me together on a few occasions or he wouldn't have said anything. For him to know about Nada and to mention her meant that my life had changed abruptly but irrevocably, and I would have to face that in Jocko's class the next period.

If there were a part of me that wanted the complication and hazard of happiness swept away, then Delano was my twin self, there to help me escape, waiting for me, a few ticks of the clock away, in my next class.

10

Jocko—the boys called him Jack Strap—was Mr. McIntyre, the gym teacher. He was tall and thin, red hair edging his bald head like the retreating flames of a forest fire. His trimmed moustache was flecked with gray. His cheeks too were red, just a slightly pinker shade than his hair. He had been a Navy SEAL and looked as if he could have been an athlete as well a long time ago, but it was his first name—Jack—and his obsession with whether or not students were wearing jockstraps during physical education class that got him his name. He made spot checks, pulling down a person's shorts as he walked behind the line of students doing deep-knee bends. No jock and you would have to run laps around the gym while everyone watched. Discovering a naked ass or expressing his heartfelt disdain for any kid's troubles always brought a flush of pleasure to his already rosy cheeks. His favorite expression was "I don't give a rat's ass" and I was convinced he didn't.

He was saying just that to Vincent Tosti as I walked into the gym that morning.

"Tosti, I don't give a rat's ass how you feel. We're all going to march over to the auditorium and listen to Herr Schmerler, or whoever he is, tell us about writing novels. You have a stomachache? A stomachache, for Christsakes! Ask me if I care."

Tosti opened his wide, innocent eyes even wider, about to speak.

"No, no, noooo—don't ask me anything, Tosti. Just move your skinny butt into the auditorium."

I avoided Delano in the lecture hall. I looked for him and sat on the other side of the room. I knew this lecture gave me a day to think about what I was to do, but for a moment I didn't want to think about anything but the room I was in and what the speaker had to say. The auditorium had a cathedral ceiling, and the acoustics made sound resonate in such a way that everything a speaker said was clear but seemed to come from a distance. A narrow rectangle of light stained one wall and a wider shaft lay directly across from it, but it was impossible to tell where the light came from in the windowless room.

The stage was raised a few feet above our seats, and a podium stood in the center of it. The novelist, a hollow-cheeked man with stringy blond hair, sat in a chair on the right side of the stage. He looked as if he had nothing to do with the performance that was about to begin. He just happened to be sitting there, waiting to see what would occur next in his life. When Father Boyd came onto the stage and walked up to the podium for the introduction, the novelist looked over at him with an expression that suggested he was surprised even a little annoyed, to have company. The shadows danced across Boyd's face, darkening his cheeks, making him appear to be unshaven. The shadows separated his face into parts—eyes, teeth, chin—floating free above the podium. The smile appeared to be too big, the eyes too wide, the chin too pointed. I could imagine him standing there, making a conscious effort to hold all the pieces together, to present the face of the holy man, whole, held tightly together, for public viewing.

After Father Boyd made his speech and stepped aside for the "highly regarded novelist Otto Schmerler," the blond-haired man rose from his own lethargy, it seemed, and walked toward the center of the stage. He was thin, I knew, but I was shocked by how small he was—he couldn't have been more than five feet two inches tall. I noticed then that two phone books had been placed to the side of the podium. He slid them over with his right foot and stepped up to the microphone.

It was like being in chapel. The more I thought about Delano or even Nada the more tired I became. My eyelids got heavy, and my chin began to fall toward my chest. Things started to go out of focus. There were two Schmerlers, two stringy-haired heads blending into one and then sliding farther and farther apart in the stuttering light until my own head snapped up and the graduating darkness broke once again into precise images and clear sound.

I began to listen to the hum of Schmerler's voice as he read from his story about a confused young boy in post-Holocaust Germany. The boy was "bwave" but he couldn't come to "gwips" with the "elabowate" plot of the Nazis. It had been a "howibble deecade" for the boy. At the end of the story Schmerler described the young boy standing by the "wiver" watching a "wainbow" form. His lisp seemed as sad as the Holocaust to me, and I was able to suppress any inclination to laugh until he began talking about how many Hollywood producers were interested in the movie "wights" for the story. I tried to think of those millions of dead bodies, the piles of skeletons, the children being herded into gas chambers, something horrible enough to stop me from laughing. All I could see, though, was Schmerler dressed like a Nazi version of Captain Kangaroo, ushering me into camp, saying over and over again, "I'm your fwend. Remember, I'm your fwend."

To erase the image, I finally bit into the flesh on the side of the index finger of my right hand, bit until the blood beaded up along the edges of the teeth marks. I watched the blood bulge like a red eye, and the Holocaust and Schmerler's voice disappeared. The red seemed beautiful to me. And I closed my eyes knowing that I wouldn't see Adam Delano until tomorrow.

Early that night Mr. Calabria came up to my room and asked me to take a ride with him to pick up some classroom supplies in Milford. We crossed the bridge into Pennsylvania before he spoke.

"See that opening in the woods up ahead?" he asked. "It reminds me of an entrance into the woods outside the town where I spent my early boyhood in Italy."

He stopped the car near where I usually entered the woods to get to

Shohola Falls. I got the strange sensation that he knew all about the falls, about Nada, and Delano, about everything I had been thinking since I got there. He pulled up the emergency brake but let the car engine idle. For a few moments he just sat there, staring at the woods without speaking. When he did speak, he didn't turn toward me but kept looking in the direction of the shadowy opening in the treeline.

I knew Calabria was an Italian name, of course, but I was surprised anyway that he had been born and lived some years in Italy. Everything about him seemed American, the way he canted his head to the left and rolled his eyes, the manner in which he smiled—lips pressed tightly together and lifted to the right—the sort of irony that appeared to have become part of every angle of his body. And he had more of a New York City accent than I did. There was nothing of the immigrant about his speech. Like most Americans, he didn't seem to carry the weight of some considerable past, just the light burden of the present, something that could be joked about and tossed off when it was necessary to do so. He had the eyes of a man who believed the future was new territory. A promised land, but he wasn't going to jinx himself by being senti- mental about it. Outwardly, it seemed, he wasn't going to take anything too seriously, but I could tell he was a dreamer, a believer in the generosity of time and most people, as well. Behind his mocking lightheartedness lay a man who took everything seriously.

"I was born in Taormina, on the coast of Sicily. You probably thought I was born in Newark, eh?"

He looked off at the shadow line leading into the woods.

"This place was like nothing I've ever seen in America, though. Perched on a cliff overlooking the Mediterranean."

As we sat there in the gathering darkness, he told me what he remembered of Taormina, the jagged cliffs and the rocky path leading to the hem of beach below the town. He recalled the flat black mountains that framed the town against the sea and the old women in scarves and shawls streaming in on mar- ket days. He described the men driving mule-drawn two-wheeled carts deco- rated with paintings and wrought iron, and the plaintive sound of the church bell on Sunday mornings.

"I remember the town," he said, "the way you would recall a fairy tale that you were told over and over again by your grandmother. In every one of its details Taormina seems precisely clear and unreal to me, a foreign land, an- other person's story. So when I talk about it, it's like remembering a book that

I once read and summarizing it. It seems like it's something I experienced but second hand or only in my imagination."

He turned off the car engine and the sounds of crickets swelled like background music.

"A fairy tale," he said. "My mother and father were like a king and queen, it seemed to me as a child. They were both beautiful and happy. No story in any book I read seemed to match their lives. The shopkeepers all knew my father and smiled at him when he strolled down the street holding my mother's tiny hand. That's what they did then, by the way, they strolled. I don't think anybody does it any more. We're in too much of a hurry.

"The streets seemed ancient to me then and still do as I remember them. Our home was on a hill overlooking the main street of Taormina. The house was filled with dark red armchairs and dome-shaped porcelain lampshades with pastoral landscapes of shepherds with flutes painted on them and illuminated by an amber light. A square of beveled glass in our front door flung the morning light into the house like flashes of lightning. Lightning to a child, at any rate. A lightning that brought no threat or danger. The parlor smelled of roses and cat fur. It makes my nose itch to even talk about it. From my second-floor bedroom window, I could hear my mother each day humming Verdi in the kitchen, and I could smell tomato sauce and garlic on the stove.

"I loved going to my father's tailor shop. It was just off the main street in the center of town. Somehow, being a tailor still seems to be a romantic profession to me. I don't tell my dates this, of course. So, remember that I'll deny any hint of my own silliness if you repeat this anywhere.

"I would sit for hours on end in the back of the store playing chess against my father. He'd walk away from the front counter and the customers who were there to see what move I had made and to counter it. He never took more than half a minute to decide what I had done and what he should do in response. Then he left me to think about my strategy. Sitting there, gazing out the window at the sun sparking off the sea three hundred feet below me, I felt like a prince in some story peering from a castle tower. It's odd, isn't it, kid, that you can feel like a prince in the back of a tailor shop where you're surrounded by the smell of steam and damp clothes? But it's true. It seemed a princely smell to me.

"When the war came, at first nothing changed for us. The fairy tale remained exactly the same. It was as if the war were just another story. It was as distant as a Greek or Roman legend. There were still the smiling shopkeepers, my mother's warm hand, chess with my father in the afternoons, and the window that framed the Ionian Sea and my daydreams.

"But after a while, I noticed that fewer and fewer young men walked the streets day or night, and the young women rarely gathered together near the fountain in the square and never laughed aloud when they did. For years, my father had made uniforms, but I didn't think much about the war until he too was taken into the army. Then Taormina seemed to become a prison instead of a kingdom by the sea.

"The war didn't last long for my father. He returned a few months later, shortly after the Americans landed in Sicily. He returned dressed in a uniform that he made with his own hands in his shop. The day he got back he surrendered his rifle, ammunition, and the military clothing to an American soldier he met on the outskirts of town. It was less a surrender, I guess, than it was an exchange of goods, though, because the American gave him a pair of old pants and a white shirt so that he wouldn't have to march back into town in his underwear. As quickly as my father had been transformed into a soldier, he became a tailor again. That's how fast things happen sometimes.

"I saw him walking down the street the day he returned from the war, looking as if he was coming home from work for the midday meal. When I saw him, it was hard for me to remember what it had been like when he was gone.

"But, somehow, even with him back, Taormina wasn't the same, and when I was nine years old, in 1946, my family left for America. Like thousands before us, we sailed past the Statue of Liberty and the dizzying skyline of New York City. It was like sailing from one fable into another.

"My father opened a little tailor shop in Brooklyn on Fulton Street, and our lives returned to something like what they had been in Sicily. The streets were wider and far more crowded, but it wasn't long before I recognized most of the faces I saw on the street near our brownstone and my father's shop. The three blocks that made up most of my life—home, school, my father's work—were like a small town, and they were as familiar and soothing to me as Taormina had been. It was as if my father had transported the fairy tale of Taormina to a new world."

Mr. Calabria rolled down the windows of his truck and the smell of pine came floating in on the dewy air, and the smell of Shohola Falls, too, it seemed to me, the cool, sweet scent of the river. He still hadn't turned to look at me. His eyes focused on the edge of the woods as if he expected someone to emerge into the half-light of the stars in the scrap of meadow in front of the treeline.

"Well, this is a longer story than I expected to tell," he said, turning now to look at me. "But you're a pretty good listener for someone who's not Italian. Come to think of it, Italians aren't very good listeners at all. Talking's our strong suit. I think I inherited my inclination to tell a story from my father.

"I'm not sure where this story is leading me," he said, gazing once again at the opening in the treeline that led to the falls. "But I know the facts. My mother died two years after we moved to New York City. Everything seemed to change then. What the war hadn't been able to change, her death had. Soon after she passed away, my father began to lose his eyesight. I was just a kid in grade school, but even then I remembered thinking that he was somehow willing his own blindness, not just accepting it but also relishing it as if it separated him from the past and the future. It left him with the things he could touch—a needle, thread, a piece of cloth—but kept him safe from what he didn't want to see.

"I think I was a little jealous of his blindness. It seemed to me for a while that it made him invisible, that the blind could hide in the darkness. When my father went deeper and deeper into his private world, I became more American than any kid in my school. I played American sports and learned how to make American jokes. I already knew the language, but I learned the gestures, the way to walk and to lean against a parked car. It wasn't long before my accent was more American than anyone on my street.

"Eventually, my father was legally blind, seeing only shadows, silhouettes against the light and flashes of movement in the dark. I walked with him before supper each night, holding his hand and describing for him everything I saw—the streets and chestnut trees, the new signs in the storefronts or a plump pigeon wobbling along the ledge of an apartment building. Other than asking me how my day at school had gone, he was silent. I explained everything to him as if he was the child and I the adult. After a while I began occasionally to notice a smile growing on his face as we'd walk along past the houses and the shops, me naming the world around us. He was like a child who starts to understand that words name things in a way that make them the speaker's own to keep. He was beginning, slowly, over those months, to get the world back. I didn't know that then. I just knew that he was becoming who he had always been for me in Taormina.

"It was like he was seeing the world all over again, believing in the names that I was giving to things he couldn't see. It was a sort of faith in my eyes, you see, Tommy, a faith in me, but in himself, too."

He paused again as if he were trying to figure out what this story, his own life, meant to him.

"There's no romantic Hollywood ending to this. He didn't learn to play the violin or anything like that. There was no beautiful woman off a boat from Palermo whose kiss brought his sight back. He just kept on being a tailor, seven days a week, and he stayed blind. He was a very successful tailor—blindness didn't change that at all—even more successful than he had been in Taormina. He made clothes for bank presidents and even the mayor of New York.

"My father and I continued to take our afternoon walks, and he started to tell me what was around us, a mother pushing a baby stroller, a cat sniffing around some garbage cans, a young woman in a hurry to get home from work. He began to see more clearly than I could, even though he was blind. He could see things that I never would have been able to see, never would have noticed—and neither would he before he had gone blind. I hadn't brought him back to life by holding his hand and naming things around us. He had brought me back, but I didn't fully realize that until he began to show me the world as if it were all Taormina. Blind, my mother gone, he seemed to be content with the strange blessings of Fulton Street."

Mr. Calabria turned on the car lights, and I was confused momentarily by his adult face. The light fractured the picture in my mind of a dark-skinned boy with wide eyes. In that instant the face of the child dissolved and he changed from boy to man, from immigrant to American again, his expression went from pensive to softly ironic.

"I'm not sure what I'm getting at here, son, are you? By the way, that's one of the things I've always loved about being a teacher. You can give an elaborate lecture and then ask one of your students to explain what you just said, to make some sense of the lesson.

"But I'll let you off the hook tonight, kid. I'll tell you what I think my own story means. Maybe the whole point is that you have to be willing to be lucky. Otherwise, life is just a matter of waiting for the worst to happen. The way my father figured out his blindness, it always seemed to me, was to find meaning in the darkness itself, to enter the chance and possibility of it fully. I think he came to believe that the very riskiness of the absolute dark was exciting, that it was even more interesting to see once he realized that than it had been before he went blind."

When I walked into the gym the next morning, one of the boys went over to Jocko and said, "Mr. McIntyre, I have a headache. . . . Could I . . ."

But Jocko cut him off and said what I expected him to say. That's one of the things I loved about Jocko: he never disappointed you. "Ask me this, son: do I care? I'll tell you the answer: I don't give a rat's ass. Now get back in line with the rest of the ladies."

I watched the kid find a place in line two spaces from Delano, and when I saw Delano's face I knew for certain that before this class was over things were going to happen that would change my life. I tried to think of Mr. Calabria's father and hope that maybe that wouldn't be a bad thing, but I knew it didn't matter much what I thought. Things were going to happen anyway, and, as usual, I'd figure them out only after they had done their work. Delano wasn't going to go away, and there probably wasn't a much better place to face him than in the open belligerence of Jocko's class.

I was rubbing my thumb along the ridges of my scarred index finger—the blood had hardened and changed from bright red to a deep brown—when Delano snaked up next to me in the gym line. At about the same time, Father Boyd and Brother Boniface walked into the gymnasium and started heading around the perimeter to get to the exit on the far side of the room. It seemed the right time then—with Boyd and Boniface and McIntyre in the same room as Delano—to do something. It was like all the bad luck I could imagine had been given a personality and put into the same room with me. It was a chance to do something with it all.

Delano positioned himself right next to me as if he were was reading my mind and trying to be accommodating. He turned to me and said in a whisper, "That chick, Blanks, is she a nigger or a spic or . . ."

I did the same thing that I had done on my first day at the Boys' Home. I hit him hard on the jaw. This time, though, he was expecting it because he turned away from the punch quickly so that it didn't catch him squarely at all. I felt my fist glance off of his cheekbone at the same time that I felt his body sweep into me. Then it was hard to tell what was happening. I heard Jocko say, "Hey, you little motherfuckers," just as a chair crashed down on his exposed head, a bald target in a sea of hair. It seemed then that everyone was fighting. Father Boyd and Brother Boniface ran toward the center of the gym, their black robes instantly disappearing, two ravens in a dust storm.

I saw Delano heading toward me again, shoving aside the few boys who stood between us. I tried to root myself in the spot where I stood, getting ready for him. But two steps before he reached me, a hand sprang out from the crowd and tapped him, almost courteously, on the left shoulder. When Delano turned, the hand formed again as a fist and hit him flat in the forehead.

His knees buckled, he knelt on the hardwood floor, and then he appeared to slide into a fetal position, a drowsy teenager taking a nap. Fitz took a step forward, looked at Delano on the floor, and then turned, smiling broadly, to look at me. He started to open his mouth, but before he could say anything, two boys crashed into him and knocked him back into the center of the melee. As I backed away from the swirling bodies, I saw Jocko stagger to his feet and, with a wild swing, hit Brother Boniface, who went over slowly but irreversibly like a felled tree. I assumed that the punch was unintentional, but perhaps it wasn't, and if not, Jocko was a much more interesting man than I had suspected. A medicine ball came hurtling across the gym and slapped Jocko in the back of the head. He crumpled and passed out before I could discover a look on his face that might have revealed something deeper than the dumb shock that was pictured there when he disappeared toward the floor and into the crowd.

I headed toward the door. It was a bit like walking on one of those air cushions in an amusement park. The floor seemed to be moving up and down as I tried to get across it to the exit. I kept getting bumped and shoved, occasionally getting banged to the gym floor. One boy glided out of the mob of bodies, flying past as he neatly clipped me in the back of the legs and spun me around. Another body seemed to come from above, falling full weight against my back. Each time I was knocked to the floor, and each time I got up a bit dizzier. Bodies and sound swirled around me.

The whole gymnasium looked like some kind of insane party was going on, people spinning around the room, people falling and rising, dance partners reaching for a hand, twisting in midair, shouts bouncing and echoing off the walls, a hallucination that was real. It was the kind of situation in which it was easy to feel as if you were looking at yourself the whole time you were swept up in the untidy business all around you.

Boyd caught my eye when I was near the gym door. He raised his right arm and pointed his index finger at me. Twice his lips pursed to form the word *you*. Then he seemed to be about to tell me something important, some message that only he could deliver, but he never got to say a word because Fitz headbutted him so hard that they both crashed to the hardwood floor. From the floor, Fitz raised his hand. A gesture of victory or a wave of farewell? I couldn't tell.

I knew I would miss Fitz and Mr. Calabria, but I knew I had to go even though I wasn't sure where I was heading. For a moment I thought of Nada and wondered if I were running toward her or away from her. When the gym door swung shut behind me, it sounded like wings flapping against a wild wind. The sound turned to a whisper as I ran from the building and into the sun-streaked world that waited for me.

11

After the fight, I didn't have a chance to think about anything besides getting away from the Boys' Home as fast as I could. I assumed that I would be blamed for the fight, that Boyd held me responsible for the whole thing, which was true, in a way, of course. As I look back on it, if I hadn't run, I might have been able to explain some things, and I think Mr. Calabria would have supported me. The blame might have been spread out a bit. But it was a good excuse, I suppose, to get away, to leave everything—including Nada, especially Nada, maybe—behind. This all sounds crazy, I know. As I look back on it, it's hard for me to understand why I ran from my own happiness. But sometimes and for some people, I guess, happiness is scarier than misery. And sometimes, as Brother Eden said, a fall from paradise can be just what a person needs. At any rate, the fight gave me a reason to run. So I ran from the Boys' Home and the consequences of the fight and the war in Vietnam and Nada and myself. And I didn't stop to think about what I was running toward at all.

I took off down the path behind the dorms and headed for Shohola Falls, the sun's rays knifing through the branches as I raced along. I couldn't hear anything but my own quick breathing. I thought about Nada for an instant again, and then I just concentrated on listening to the air rush in and out of my lungs and seeing the fragments of sunlight burst against the trees as I sped by them.

When I came to the Delaware River, I ran along its left bank for about half a mile. A few hundred yards from the bridge that led to the Pennsylvania side, I slipped into the water and lost a New York Yankees cap I was wearing. I saw it drift into the dark current. Later, I discovered I had lost my wallet in the fall, too.

Sweat and river water soaked my shirt by the time I reached the path that led to the falls. When I slowed down to get a footing on the slippery rocks, a sound stopped me in midstep. It was like the grunt that a weightlifter would make as he jerked a barbell over his head. I came around a bend in the path and saw one of the Weiry brothers, dragging himself up the hill, a chainsaw tied to his ankle by the shoelaces of one of his boots.

"Damn, boy, it's good to see you," he said. He spoke as if we were old friends. His voice was soft and pleasant, not what I expected at all from what I had seen in the parades or the pictures drawn of him in townspeople's stories at the post office or Otto's store. He stretched out his vowels like someone who had spent his boyhood in western Massachusetts. His voice seemed capable of a slow-tuned facetiousness, of a language that was mulled over until it came out like a feather floating on a light breeze. I liked him right away, and trusted him, too, in the way that you can like and trust certain people before you really know anything about them at all. I had assumed that he was either crude and gruff or ignorant and mute. He was neither. His beard was grizzly and his teeth were bad, but his eyes were kind and playful in a way that suggested intelligence and even what might be seen as some brand of wisdom.

It took me fifteen minutes to untangle the chainsaw from his boot and lug him up the slope. Then I went back for the chainsaw. He smiled at me when I reached him.

"My back's gone out on me," he said. "It does it every now and again. But I'd be damned, for sure, if I was going to leave that chainsaw down there to rust in the next rain."

"Why didn't your brother bring it up for you?"

"I don't have a brother."

I learned a lot about Andrew Weiry that night. He was younger by twenty years than I would have thought. The man that everyone in Yulan assumed was his brother, the man everyone saw with him in the St. Patrick's Day parade, was a guy he had served with in the Army in Korea. The two of them had made a deal in 1952 to get together every St. Patrick's Day to prove to each other that the war had not killed them on March 17. Because it nearly had. Mr. Weiry didn't know where his army buddy lived. He didn't seem to live anywhere. But he found his way back from wherever he was to Yulan for that day each year, and then he was gone the next morning without a word of farewell.

I learned that Mr. Weiry wasn't ignorant. He'd grown up in Holyoke, Massachusetts, had gone to the University of Vermont, and had graduated with a degree in history. He had even taught for a few years after the Korean War, but whatever the war had done to him, it made him seek solitude as if it were as necessary as oxygen. When his father died and left him a little money, he bought the land near Shohola Falls, built a cabin, and listened to the rhythms of his own breathing. He was like a man who has gone off to a room in the library to think things over and decide what to do next. More than a decade later he was still thinking things over.

He didn't ask me anything about myself. He seemed to know a lot already—that I was a resident (or had been) of the Boys' Home, that I should talk to Nada but couldn't right now, that I knew every inch of Shohola Falls as if it were my real home. We sat on his porch. Night had just begun to fall, and our words opened up in the darkness. He looked at me more directly than he had before, as if he were appraising something about me.

"I knew your great grandfather," he said. "As a matter of fact, I've been expecting you to come along one of these days. He expected it himself before he died. He has it in his will that I should take care of his place. I take much better care of it than I do my own—the way he took care of it himself. I go there once a week to keep things up. I'll take you there next week."

I knew then that he had invited me to stay and that for some reason it was a place where I was supposed to be.

For most of that night I thought of Nada. Delano was not the only person who would call her nigger, especially if she were with me. From some kinds of people our relationship would always demand attention. I didn't want to see her hurt, but if I had been able to be honest then, I might have seen that I was looking to protect myself, not so much from the sort of pain that shades of skin color can produce but simply from the ordinary jeopardies of love.

If I hadn't hit Delano, perhaps everything could have remained just as it had been. I began to wonder at that moment if I had hit him so that everything would fall apart, so that I wouldn't have to wait for something bad to happen to her or me or us.

There was something about Nada's bravery that scared me. Not her physical bravery—although she had that too—but her courage in the face of a world that seemed to me to lie in wait, crouched, ready to spring at us. Something about her seemed too bold, too open to what each breath would bring.

I was afraid that she might be crushed by her own innocence. Her intuition that love or happiness or beauty could last, or at least last as long as they were meant to last, made me nervous, worried that some hard fate would see her faith as shameless pride. Maybe I was just afraid for myself, though. Afraid that I didn't have the courage to lose her, that I wasn't the person she thought I was. Maybe she was just too openhearted for me. She had the kind of generous spirit that seemed possible in the very young or the old, in those who didn't know enough or those who knew a great deal. She had a way of looking at the world that culminated in her laughter. She laughed more readily than she cried, but either rose naturally from her, and she made no effort to hold them in check.

Nada invented herself, and she knew it. She made the world fit her imagination.

"And why not," she once said to me as we lay on the rocks of Shohola Falls, "the world is just a story we tell ourselves. Why let someone else make it up for us?"

Then she rolled over, kissed me, and pulled me into the cold stream as if she had planned to do so in her dreams.

Like Mr. Calabria's story, Nada's was almost as simple as a child's fable. She had lived in Yulan for all but a few months of her seventeen years. She didn't even know how her parents died until she started elementary school. Up until that time she just accepted her aunt and uncle's statement, "They died when you were a baby." Perhaps she would have accepted that story forever, but her uncle felt that once she started school she needed to know the details. So, on that night at supper after she told her aunt and uncle about her teacher, Mrs. Happy, a name that, even at six years old, Nada probably sensed was an impossible responsibility for an adult in charge of children to shoulder, her uncle recited the story of her parents' death.

Her mother and father had married after the war, two people from different worlds, her uncle said to her many times. It wasn't until a few years later, looking hard at the photograph near her bed, that Nada understood what he meant by different worlds and why she was different, too. Staring at the photograph of her parents, Nada saw her own face truly and accurately for the first time in her bedroom mirror. The story of Nada's mother and father was like the tale of Cinderella and the prince—except there was no castle, just a second-floor walkup in Riverdale.

They lived in a studio apartment on the second floor of a three-story house just north of the bridge that separated Manhattan from the Bronx. Her father was still in his postal uniform when he came home from the late shift and saw flames leaping from the top two floors of the house. The windows were red with fire. He pushed past the ring of onlookers and ran into the building. It was minutes before he emerged, the baby wrapped in a blanket, and smoke rising from him like steam in the bitter night. He placed Nada in a neighbor's arms and leapt the front steps three at a time. The windows and the door glowed a dark red by then, like entry points into hell, and neither Nada's father nor her mother came out of the building.

After her uncle told her the story, Nada knew for certain what she suspected throughout her childhood—that she had been saved from death and that each day for her was stolen from the fire. She was already living a second life, and the older she got, it permitted her to live unafraid, it seemed to me. It was as if the second death was not to be feared. As a child she thought she had been saved like a fairy-tale princess for something wonderful, and as she got older she still believed that might be possible—but if not, she had seen the worst anyway before she even knew how to see.

At Shohola Falls she told me that she had been waiting for me to come along for years. She hadn't known it, of course, she said, until she saw me that day in the snowstorm.

"It was the way you looked at me," she said, "as if you knew me, as if you'd been looking for me a long time and had finally found me. But it's not really the way you looked at me but the way I felt myself looking at you." She laughed. "I know it sounds stupid, but it's not, is it?"

It may have been stupid, I realized, but it was true, anyway. I just wasn't sure if it was better to stumble upon what you didn't even know you were looking for or never know the thing existed at all. After all, you couldn't lose it if you didn't know it existed. Or could you?

For the last two months before the fight at the Boys' Home, every afternoon we were able to meet, we spent at Shohola Falls. Sometimes we slid cool and naked onto the leaves, the only heat we had from our bodies and what remained of the warmth the sun left on the ground. The only sounds were those made by our flesh and our breath against the murmur of the wind. It was like making love at the end of the world. We were the last two people on earth, or the first. The color of our skins meant no more than the color of our eyes. There was nothing outside of our desire for each other. Nothing that we wanted outside of where we were. No past. No future. Just our tongues, wordless, our bodies removed from any calendar. She seemed so willing to be naked but shy about it at the same time. Every time she opened the buttons of her blouse or lifted her T-shirt, it made my heart race as if she were doing it for the first time in front of me. In the cool air, her skin was ridged with goosebumps, but once she moved toward me, her soft breasts pressed against my chest, she felt warm, and the friction of our skin made the world disappear.

I lived from one meeting with Nada to the next as if the rest of time was a deep chasm to jump across. I didn't want to fall into it, just get to the other side, to another hour with her at Shohola Falls. Sometimes we just lay there on the bank of the stream, her legs draped over mine, talking like a long-married couple about the past. I don't remember either of us ever wearing a watch. We had only the graduating darkness to measure time. The unchanging lilt of the stream made the minutes seem to flow backward until every word was a memory of the last one, one gesture a conscious repetition of one before it.

Some afternoons, Nada's voice flowed as effortlessly as the water that flowed an arm's length away from us.

"The first day I saw you," she said, "I went home, and my aunt and uncle asked me if anything was the matter. They could tell something had happened. I just smiled and told them that I had the flu. Even if I'd wanted to tell them, I wouldn't have known what to say. I remember feeling very tired that night, barely able to eat supper. I couldn't wait to get into my bed, and as soon as my head touched the pillow I was asleep. I dreamed of you by a river. You kissed me and walked into the water and swam toward the other side. It took forever even though the river wasn't that wide. Then you were there and we were separated by the water and you stood there without speaking. I kept talking to you but you didn't speak at all."

I turned over so that my body lay on top of hers and looked carefully into her gray eyes.

"Why am I always a bad guy in your dreams? Always silent or drifting away? You're always sexy and beautiful in mine."

"You're always sexy, too, just on the other side of the river, that's all."

We kissed until she remembered another dream and another, our dream life merging indistinguishably with our waking moments, all a story that she was reciting as I listened with all my heart.

The morning after the fight I sat on Andrew Weiry's front porch. He walked up the path and nodded to me as if we were old roommates, and as he opened the front door to enter the house, he tossed the local newspaper, *The River Reporter*, into my lap without turning his head. The headline on the bottom of the front page told the story of my Yankees cap and lost wallet in the river. "Boy From Washington Lake Home Feared Drowned."

Without reading the rest, I wrote a letter to Nada. I didn't know when I could safely see her or how much blame I'd get for the riot at the Boys' Home. As I look back on that time, I'm not certain I was concerned about that at all. Simply, I had become the man of her dreams, the man on the other side of the river. I could stand there, silent, invisible, outside the hazards of loving her too much or too little.

In the letter I wrote to her I told her to give me some time before I saw her. I gave the note to Andrew, and he left it in her post office box in town. Being dead to the world seemed all right to me. I felt as if I had gotten rid of some burdensome weight and was able to sit quietly and still as the world drifted by me.

The next afternoon there was a note from Nada tacked to a tree at Shohola Falls. The message must have been placed there early in the morning because it was damp with the day's moisture.

"Thomas, I don't know where you are, but I know you must be close by. Whatever happened at the Boys' Home or afterwards—or before—it can't change anything for us. Or between us. We can change with the world in any way that we have to so that we can be together. Come to the Falls. Believe that I'll be there and I will. I just need for you to believe that I am there, waiting for you. I need for you to believe it for it to be the truth."

I didn't write back. I wanted to, but I didn't. I told myself each day that I would write that day, and then I told myself it would be the following morning and then that night. One day turned itself into the next until enough days passed and I just let the days and the silence surround me at Andrew's place, where it felt safe from loss and where there was nothing much for a dead man to lose anyway.

12

For a few days I worked around Andrew's house. I raked the lawn and helped mend a stone wall. I didn't ask him about any news of the Boys' Home, and he didn't ask me about what happened there. Each night we sat on his front porch and looked at a patch of sky that sparkled through the tree-tops. Then one night, as he got up to go to bed, he said, "Tomorrow morning we'll get up at the crack of dawn and go see your granddad's old place. I'll wake you at first light."

The next day I was dressed before Andrew knocked on the door. The trip to my great grandfather's house was about ten miles up Route 97, a road that curved gently alongside the dark waters of the Delaware River, waters that churned white in places against the outcroppings of polished rocks. At Min-isink, we crossed the Roebling Bridge, a miniature version of the Brooklyn Bridge, and drove into Lackawaxen, Pennsylvania. The road to my great grandfather's house twisted like a spiral until it came to a quarter-mile stretch that ran straight along the river where it was wide and seemed to have no cur-rent. Another road, a one-lane dirt path really, slashed off to the left, cutting across the belly of the mountain. The road passed near a pond that had over-flowed its banks. We sloshed through the wet field that bordered the road. The road ended on the other side of the mountain, like a diameter line in a high school geometry text. Before we got there, we turned right into a switch-back and edged our way up the mountainside.

His house was perched on a piece of hill overlooking the river, next to an ancient burial ground and in the shadow of a weeping willow tree. The wind hissed all around us. Crickets ticked faster and faster until their sound turned into a whirr, a whine. It reminded me of the sound that a playing card attached to a bicycle tire made as some boy on Garrison Avenue in the Bronx pumped the pedals with increasing fury. The few stones in the graveyard were tilted by the wind and the years, and they were nearly smooth, worn anonymous by time, blank marble, deeper mysteries than they would have been with clear names and dates on them. Train tracks ran along the ridgeline above the house, and the mournful howl of the whistle in the distance signaled an en-gine pulling a line of freight cars had just passed.

My great grandfather's place was a narrow two-story frame house, painted white only a couple of years ago, it looked to me. The front porch was screened-in, and even that was in good repair. From the front yard it was possible to see the Roebling Bridge, the water racing under it. Inside, the house smelled of pine needles and mildew, and it was smaller than even its narrow frame suggested. The kitchen and dining room were one room and formed an ell with the living room. A small bedroom and a bathroom right next to the stairway led up to the second floor. The stairs went directly to the first bedroom, which was separated from the other bedroom by a pine door with a beam above it. There was no wall above the beam, just an opening that showed the ceiling of the other bedroom. It was one big room that had been fashioned, somewhere along the line, into two sleeping quarters.

In the second bedroom, a rolltop desk, too big for the space, took up half the wall below the one window in the room. It wasn't much of a window and allowed only a square of light to squeeze through. In the shadows of that light was a leatherbound journal. It fit into the palm of my right hand, and I could smell the distant odor of animal skin and desire, sharp and sweet. The journal lay in one of the cubbyholes as if it had been placed there a few hours before, as if my great-grandfather had left it in precisely that spot for me, had known that one day I would find my way to it, would need to read it. Its smooth cover was scarred and dappled with age. The leather was shadowed by spots of mildew and cracked like old skin. The gilt-edged pages glinted in the light as I held it up to the window. A white silk ribbon marked the opening page and slanted across the small, faded script: *The Journal of Thomas Blankenship.* As I read the first page, I realized that I was reading a message from my great-great-grandfather, and I had to shake my head to get the rattle of my own voice out of my mind and hear his instead. The words started to swim into one another on the page until only one stayed clear—*betrayal.*

It was hard for me to believe that Thomas Blankenship, a man related to me, had met Mark Twain when he was just a young boy, a little freckle-faced red-haired kid. My great-great-grandfather had been in Twain's father's store, had met his mother, had lived in a house across the road from the Clemens family. He was different from Twain, he said, but I didn't know how or if being different was something to be ashamed of or merely a statement of fact.

They had something in common, my great-great-grandfather had written, and their lives were to be intertwined like brothers. That meant Mark Twain had something to do with my life too. I was related to him in the same way that my great-great-grandfather was. I wanted to know and at the same time I didn't want to know too much. I was afraid, I suppose, of knowing too much, finding out more than was good for the fragile hold I had on my self at present. This journal even put my very name into question. I wasn't sure if I was ready for new answers or any other questions at that moment.

I remembered reading a story about Twain's early life in one of the books I didn't steal from the library. It was simply too big to get under my coat. So I sat in the Bainbridge Avenue Library in the Bronx and read the pages amid the kids coughing and whispering and the librarians hissing "shhh." When Sam Clemens was four years old, his sister Margaret lay feverish and desperately ill in her bed. Sam walked in his sleep into her room, stood at the foot of her bed, and pulled the coverlet off. When his parents came into the room, they were horrified to see him standing there, coverlet at his feet. Their superstitions told them that removing a coverlet was an omen of death. A few days later, Margaret did die. Sam's parents were certain that he had foreseen the death. Sam seemed to think that he might have had something to do with causing it. After that he had an inclination to take on the guilt for any death near to him. And maybe that made him especially jittery around death, I don't know, but it would have made me that way.

I was curious about my great-great-grandfather, and equally so about Mark Twain. I couldn't help but wonder if Twain and I had something good and magnificent in common or if it had to do with death. I have to admit—I was a little afraid to find out which it was.

It was a strange experience to see my name written out in full, not Blanks but Blankenship. It was as if those other letters were a piece of me that had been lost. I was no longer Tommy Blanks of the Bronx but someone else with a different name and maybe a whole different destiny from the one I thought I had. I had died in the newspaper, and now I was someone else in this old journal. I felt as if I had discovered a new history that made for the possibility of a different future. A history that included Mark Twain some way in my life.

I can't explain why I didn't read every word of the journal right then and there or why I didn't read it immediately when I got back to Andrew Weiry's place that night after we cleaned up my great-grandfather's house. I guess it was because I wanted the suspense to last, to keep things in the realm of pure and thus protected possibility. Or it may have been that I suspected that reading the journal would change my life, and I'd had more changes than I wanted already—even the chance of a change for the good made me feel tired. Or maybe I simply sensed that, perhaps like Twain, I had had enough of death. Whatever my reasons, I let it sit for a while. It stayed with me unopened. And I thought of Nada.

I spent my time trying to think about all the reasons why my exit made sense. Delano, the fight at the Boys' Home, the draft—all of those dark clouds told me to get out, to disappear. But my focus kept drifting to Nada. Most of the time we had spent together we had been alone, and I learned quickly that she could talk for hours on end about school and teachers and classmates or she could be absolutely still and silent. Neither talk nor silence seemed forced for her.

The few times we had gotten into the larger world together—to Port Jervis and once to Newburgh—a playful, teasing part of her emerged. In a Woolworth's in Newburgh, she asked the manager if he could help her find a denim shirt for her brother and pointed to me. When he led us to the shelf with work clothes, she picked out one, held it up to my chest, and said, "This matches your blue eyes perfectly." Then she gave me a slow, passionate kiss that made the manager confused and inert.

I had the suspicion that our future lives in the outside world together would be a surprise each day. Her skin color was dark enough to make people look twice when we were together but light enough to make them doubt, perhaps, that we were an interracial couple. The surprises in our future, I suspected, would come not from the difference in the shades of our skin but from her—from a silliness in her that came from an appreciation of any discrepancy the world had to offer. Her gray eyes lit blue-black with amusement whenever she had a funny story to tell. And the fire in them made her more beautiful. About her own beauty she was unselfconscious and without vanity. She wasn't without knowledge of it, though. There would have been no credit in that. She just accepted her beauty gracefully the way some people are able to take unexpected gifts.

She understood gift giving because she was the most generous person I ever met. It made her happy to buy presents for people. She enjoyed seeing other people smile with pleasure. I would say that she was like a child with gifts except that as much as she liked getting them as a child would, she liked giving them far more. In a way, though, she was as innocent as a child, but her innocence was strangely mixed with a tough, clear-headed way of being in the world that made her seem old enough to be my mother.

When I thought about losing her, I saw her floating away on the stream, her naked body just out of reach, her dark hair coiled into wet cords, her eyes wide in sorrow. I felt a cold regret and longing. How would I live without the touch of her—her lips and hands and breasts? How would I live without her body against mine? How did one make a life in the absence of such friendship and desire?

I waited with the journal in my pocket. I waited for something to happen to me, for something to tell me what I was to do. I waited for some story that showed me how to act. I had time, I thought. At seventeen, you think there is always time. There is more time than you can use. Time seemed to stretch all around me. Andrew Weiry didn't look like he was going anywhere. He didn't appear to be the type to make drastic changes, even though he let me stay at his house without asking any questions. So I decided to put the journal in my coat pocket for a while, put Nada out of my mind, if I could, and take leave of the world with Andrew until I figured things out a bit.

I wondered if my great-grandfather had left the journal, like a message in a bottle, for the next Blankenship to come along. I wondered if Andrew Weiry knew about the journal, but I never said anything to him about it, and he never even hinted to me that he might be aware of its existence. I had a sense that he was well aware of it, but I had no proof that he was, and we talked of other things the next two weeks on his porch each night. As I sat there listening to him, my fingers touched the bruised leather of the journal in my coat pocket, and I waited for the right time to open it again or maybe a reason not to open it at all. I concentrated on his stories, listening for my own name, and waiting for an answer to a question that I hadn't even asked.

13

Winter came upon us completely as Andrew told his stories. The cold enveloped us in a chill silence. There were no sounds but his voice, it seemed. I wrote to Nada once during that time, telling her that I was all right and would make sense of things soon. I wasn't sure I believed that, of course, but I couldn't bear the thought of losing her, and I couldn't face the complication and responsibility of being with her either. This doesn't mean that I spent a lot of time trying hard to figure out my own life. I wanted to stand outside of myself, to forget for a time that I existed, that life was a choice, forget the mysteries of chance and consequence. So instead of living my own life, I listened to Andrew tell of his. Instead of thinking about the war that waited for me to enter it, I listened to him tell of his war. I fell into his past as if it were a dream I was having.

We sat on his front porch, blankets around us, the heat from the wood stove pulsing out the opened front door, and he talked in stops and starts over the next two weeks. The pieces of his story stitched themselves together this way:

"By the end of October in 1950, around the time you were born, I guess, most of us thought we had the goddamn war won. And it was a war, not some military action. Somehow it seems to have gotten lost, forgotten, between World War II and what's happening in Vietnam now. But it seemed real enough to us back then. In early November rumors started to spread about how many Chinese soldiers had crossed the border, but MacArthur told us that the whole lousy thing would be over by Christmas. We could count on it, he said. We could put it in the bank. And we believed him. Or wanted to. And sometimes wanting is stronger than believing.

"Our Thanksgiving dinner was like a Girl Scout meeting. We ate canned turkey and pumpkin pie in an apple orchard by a stream. The cooks made up everything in the lights from two trucks parked across from one another on hills to the north and the south of our camp. It was a strange kind of light like some sort of bridge between nothing and nowhere. The next morning the temperature dropped to five degrees below zero, and most of us had the runs. Goddamned MacArthur, the turkey had been bad.

"I stepped out of the foxhole that morning because of the cramps, and just about got my ass shot off. I could feel the bullets cut through the air near me. My hands were so damn numb I could barely get my pants back up. Even with the adrenaline shooting through me like some sort of liquid heat, I couldn't come near to buttoning the layers I had on. When I started to return fire, my carbine jammed with the cold. I remember thinking, *This is a hell of a way to die. I never expected to die this way. My pants half buttoned and shit stains on my shorts.*

"Before I could even take a half step backward, a mortar exploded. Shrapnel sizzled all around. It was like white-hot snow everywhere I looked. The lieutenant stepped out of a foxhole and a grenade dropped him. Machine gun fire rang out from our line, and in a few minutes everything was quiet again. It was eerie, as if nothing had happened at all. The smoke smelled like rotten eggs. When it cleared, on the ridge above us and not more than forty feet away a line of Chinese soldiers stood. For a second, nothing moved at all. I could hear our guys breathing. The Chinese had their hands raised.

"A young kid in our company named Jankowitz, we called him Jinx, yelled back to the Chinese. The kid couldn't have been more than sixteen or seventeen. He had gotten his parents to sign his enlistment papers for him. That was his first mistake. Believing all those war movies he had spent every Saturday afternoon watching in Iowa or Idaho or wherever the hell he came from. Yelling out was his last.

"He shouted up to them, 'Come down. If you want to give up, come down. We won't hurt you.'

"He was like a kid playing cowboys and Indians. Playing by some rules he had learned in the schoolyard. More Chinese floated into the line, hands raised. Looking like the goddamned Rockettes up there, like they were getting ready to kick up their legs. But instead their arms bent back behind their shoulders and fell forward together at exactly the same time. Come to think of it, it was a lot like the Rockettes. Except the sky turned black with grenades. Then the air turned white with explosions. Jinx's hand flew past my face, and I couldn't help thinking that he had finally and surely lived up to his nickname, finally gotten himself killed and some others along with him. Someone's leg, the boot still laced, came by next. The whole world turned upside down then, and parts of bodies floated on the air. It was like some magician's trick. I couldn't see anything after a while, but out of the blood and smoke I heard the captain's voice shouting, 'Take the goddamn hill. Take the fucking goddamn hill!'

"We inched from one rock to another. By the time I reached the top there were only two of us. Me and Hollingsworth, the guy who rides with me in the St. Paddy's Day parade. The Chongchon River was below us. I could see it through the smoke. It made some kind of groaning sound as the ice stretched and moved. The rice paddies behind us were red as blood. For all I know, they were filled with goddamned blood. There was plenty of blood to go around.

"We just lay there, Hollingsworth and me, for the rest of the day and the night, waiting for something to happen, waiting to die, I think. I didn't want to move. Why waste all that effort just to get killed? A few more shots here and there, but it was as if we had been lifted out of the battle. Everything was quiet. The next day was even colder than the last, colder than a witch's tit, and we made our way down the hill, moving from one boulder to another, keeping an eye out for anything even half alive and expecting to be blown up every time we breathed.

"After a while it was like we weren't in the war any more. We were two guys out for a walk who had gotten lost. I just kept my eyes on the river below us. It looked to be solid ice. About halfway down the hill we heard a noise that sounded like humming. I thought I was imagining things until I saw below us a dozen or so people in white clothing. I couldn't tell if they were men or women or children until we got a little closer and then I saw that it was a group of almond-skinned girls balancing packs on their heads. A bunch of goddamned teenage girls in the middle of a war as if it was a high school outing or something. They just came out of the mist like ghosts making this music that was beautiful and scared the hell out of me too. I could see the Chongchon River and the mouth of the Yellow Sea out beyond them. It could have all been a dream except I knew that it wasn't because of what happened next.

"The girls got to the edge of the water and they just about seemed to glide across the frozen surface. The snow began to fall just as a group of Chinese soldiers came out the north. At first, it looked like the soldiers were going to greet them in friendship, but one soldier sighted his rifle. Then another and another. The girls twisted onto the ice before I even heard the first shot fired. The soldiers seemed to move in slow motion, to take their time firing, watching the girls scatter and slide along the frozen river. Red cracks appeared in the ice wherever a girl fell. It looked like red writing on a white page, except the letters were not from any alphabet I knew. Or ever want to learn. I kept concentrating on those red marks as if I looked long and hard enough at them, I might be able to make some sense of what happened. When the last girl went down, the gunfire and screams hung in the air long after the soldiers walked away. They held their rifles down at their sides like they were carrying umbrellas and they just walked away.

"Hollingsworth and I just stayed put, behind a boulder midway up the hill. We hadn't made a sound, not moved. We'd just watched them, like we were frozen. We couldn't have done anything, but that didn't matter. The point was we hadn't done anything. We hadn't been able to do anything. We sat there for what seemed like hours not looking into each other's eyes. But when we got to the river, it was impossible not to see the eyes of the girls, dark moon eyes, wide with some kind of horror and sadness and a terrible sort of surprise. Their bodies had fallen in all sorts of angles like they'd dropped from the sky. Legs bent. Arms crossed. They were all dead. Except for one. And she looked at us, trying to speak. Instead of words, though, blood bubbled up on her lips. Like cartoon bubbles with the words inside. I knew what she wanted us to do. Hollingsworth looked at me and spoke. It was the first words we'd spoken in hours, and somehow it seemed shameful to say anything.

" 'They'd hear a rifle shot.'

"I knew that there were other ways, but I just stood there. So did Hollingsworth. It took fifteen minutes for her to die. Her eyes went from pleading to despair to plain disgust. Before we left, Hollingsworth closed them and we headed across the river.

"It took us a week to find the American camp. By that time we were both half starved and nearly out of our minds. On March 17 of the next year we both got shipped home. Hollingsworth comes back here every year to prove to himself and to me, I suppose, that we're alive, to make sure that it wasn't just a nightmare, the streaks of blood on the ice, the brown eyes, us unable to lift a hand, the whole goddamned thing. Or maybe he comes back hoping that it didn't happen. Maybe he's wishing that he'll show up one day and I won't be here and no one will remember having ever seen me. And then the Chong-chon River will disappear too.

"For me it's all a dream, no more real than what I'll experience tonight when I go to sleep. Being here in these woods makes the whole world outside this cabin and this creek seem like something that got put in my head after eating cheap Mexican food. I like the world out there left where it is. Leave it out there where maybe it doesn't know I exist. I don't want to care about anything that happens out there. How is it real anyway? How the hell is the past real? It's gone now, no more real than some story I can make up. So how's that any more real than a dream I'll have tonight?

"Even you, kid, I like you, I liked Jinx too, but you come and go as you please. It makes no difference to me. It's all the same thing. Stay here as long as you like, but leave the rest of that shit out there. I mean for that world never to touch me again. Why should it? People are no more real than our dreams anyhow. Are we going to live each day worrying about each dream we have at night?"

I took a good look at Andrew Weiry during those days on his porch. He was younger than I had at first thought, probably in his early forties, and his eyes were as clear and blue as mine. Most likely, he wasn't much older than I was now when he went to Korea. We all get old at different times and in different ways in our lives, but he was older than I ever wanted to get. I felt too old already. Besides I sensed that he had told me all that he ever would about himself or his war, that he had given me as much as he ever would give, and I was grateful to him and sorry for him at the same time. But whatever his story was it would not be mine if I could help it.

The next morning I got up and went to Shohola Falls. I could see the icicles through the pines as I headed toward the cliffs. The dead leaves lay in a three-inch cushion on the path. The water raced through eddies and over rocks. Walls of icicles hung from the mouths of the caves, and mountain laurel bushes were bent from the cold winds, their smooth leaves shining in the light. Moss carpeted the rocks, and ice capped the outcroppings where the brook had receded some. The water was higher than I had ever seen it in the summer or the fall, and when I came to the birch tree that Nada and I always held onto as we climbed down the cliffs to the dry rocks that bordered the stream, I realized that there was no path back to our spot. I could see the cliffs and the big boulder where we usually lay in the sun about two hundred yards away, but our path lay submerged under three feet of fast-running water. There was nothing to do but head back to Andrew's cabin.

Sitting on his porch that night, he had one more thing to tell me: "Life changes you, kid, remember that. At your age, you might think that it's impossible to change into someone like me. You assume that you can find some goddamned way to keep yourself intact, stay who you think you are right now. I remember thinking once that if I changed, it would be into some better self that I had spent my time as a kid dreaming about, that there were certain ways I could never be.

"But that's not how it works. All of a sudden, one day, you wake up and see that you've turned into a person you don't even know, can't even recognize. You look in the mirror and you're looking at a stranger. The oddest part of the whole thing is that you can remember pretty clearly who you were and what you thought you'd become but you can't find your way back. No matter how hard you try, you can't find your way back. So you just sit where you are and kind of sense the other you, the lost you, and at the same time, you watch this new guy, disappointed at how things turned out after all your fancy daydreams. But neither of you—the person you became or the person you wanted to be—are able to do a goddamned thing about it. You just can't do a thing about it."

Then he stood up and went in to bed.

That night I read my great-great-grandfather's journal.

14

*I*t wasn't until that summer, when I was about to turn thirteen, that Sammy, that's what we all called him then, and I became fast friends. For most boys in Hannibal, Missouri, in those times, the river was brimming with life and excitement, and it seemed to exist between two magnetic poles, Holliday's Hill to the north and McDowell's Cave in the opposite direction. To the south of town there was a bluff everyone called "Lover's Leap," a high ridge overlooking the dark brown waters of the Mississippi and the flat plains of Illinois across from it. The town spread out below that ridge like a fairy tale, all spires and idleness, it seemed to me then. One day Sammy and I came upon one another on the ridgeline not far from the mouth of McDowell's Cave, and as both of us wanted to go inside and neither of us relished the notion of doing it alone, we struck out together.

Every boy in town knew the story of Doctor Joseph Nash McDowell of St. Louis. Or at least we thought we knew it all. I guess we thought we knew a whole lot back *then. You come to learn as you get older not so much what you know for sure but how much you really don't know a thing about for a certainty. When his fourteen-year-old daughter died, the doctor placed her corpse in a glass-lined copper cylinder that he hung at the far end of one of the tunnels in the cave. Her body floated in a milky alcohol solution that gave her a dreamy look. It was like looking at someone through a fog. Rumor had it that the doctor hoped the corpse would get hard as marble in the limestone cave and if the experiment proved successful, he could sell space in the cave to those who would rather petrify their loved ones than bury them. I'm not sure if it was an effort to stop time or to make money. None of us were truly sure if Dr. McDowell's story was one of strange-hearted love or simple greed.*

Every boy in the village who had a thimbleful of adventure in him eventually found his way through the cave passageways to stand owl-eyed in the flickering darkness, candle in sweaty hand, to get a look at the girl. Her flesh was as white and foreign as the moon. A couple of years after he put her in there, Dr. McDowell discovered that the steamboats were laying over for a few hours longer in town so that interested passengers could go to the caves to see the girl's body. He took her away then.

But that was after Sammy and I walked into the cave that afternoon. That day the darkness was cool and moist, whispers echoed through it like the voices of the dead, and I was so glad to have company that I nearly grabbed Sammy's hand. I didn't, I made sure of that, but I did follow his every step as if they were my own feet. I stayed so close to his heels that a few times I bumped right into him and we just about tumbled into the darkness.

I followed Sammy as the passageway twisted and turned alongside a trickling stream. The stream flowed over a ledge that carried limestone sediment into the darkness and the perfect soundlessness below. I mean you could have dropped a stone in there in the morning and waited till afternoon to hear its sound.

We came to a spacious cavern filled with shining stalactites as long and thick as a man's leg. The roof seemed to be supported by a fantastic row of pillars, floor and ceiling knotted together like hourglasses created by the silent water-drip of the ages. Sammy stopped and held the candle above his head. The crystals glittered all around him like starlight, reflecting off the object that he stood before. Suspended from the roof of the cave was a copper and glass casket.

Sammy removed the top of the cylinder and, holding the corpse by the hair, dragged the head into view. There was a sucking sound as the alcohol spilled back and the head rose from the liquid as if it was gasping for breath. I suppose it was our gasps I heard. "Gosh, damn," one of us said. I heard the words but wasn't sure whose lips the words came from.

I don't remember Sammy letting the head slide back in or how long we stayed staring at the girl's body, trying to figure out how close she was to womanhood or how far from human. Once we got out of the cave and were under the cliffs near Lover's Leap, our eyes blinking in surprise that there still remained a place of bright daylight, I felt as if we had returned from the underworld, and we would have to be friends forever because we had gone down and come back together.

At first, it seemed as if we had nothing in common at all—except that we were boys, of course, and we looked something alike, like kin almost. A few said enough alike to be twins, but they meant the freckles and the curly hair mostly, I think. Sammy's father owned a store in town and became a judge as well. My father had an upstanding first name—Woodson—but he was drunk so much of the time I felt uneasy around him when he was sober. When he was sober, my father was as stern and quiet as Judge Clemens, only quicker to knock you sideways if he took the slightest notion to it. They didn't have much in common—the Judge and my father—they were as different as two men could be, I guess. My father had long greasy hair that hung like vines over his eyes and fell into his beard. His skin, what you could see of it, was so white that it could make a person's flesh crawl—a fish-belly white. His eyes were always streaked with red and his nose rose and swelled out in bumps that made it look like a cauliflower. Judge Clemens was a man of consequence, and he looked like one, too. His beard was always neatly trimmed, and his hair combed wet early in the morning. Even when Judge Clemens's store went bust and he had to move his family in over the pharmacist's shop, people always had respect for him—whether he had money or not. My father worked on the docks but only when he ran out of moonshine.

I guess you could say that our families were as different as two could be and still be living in the same country. Sammy's sister gave piano lessons to help out at home. I never asked any questions about how my sisters got the money they did to buy food. They just got it. They went out at night and the next day we had food on the table. My mother died before I was old enough to remember her voice. Sammy's mother was a firecracker. He had been sickly as a child and was still apt to sleepwalk when I knew him, and she was determined to cure him of anything that ailed him, even if she had to bring him to the brink of death to do it. She was the most enthusiastic woman I ever met for home remedies. She loved them all—purges and pills and poultices. She placed socks filled with hot ashes in his bed and fed him more teaspoons of castor oil than I've ever seen any boy take then or since. A light seemed to come into her eyes when she saw a sick child. Like she was thankful for any suffering because it gave her the chance to work a cure. And she worked a remedy with the same sort of narrow-eyed urgency that a fiddle player fingers the neck of his instrument.

But even though I didn't envy him all those potions and wet sheets and prying fingers, I suppose I did in a way—I missed having my mother around almost every time I saw Sammy's. I couldn't help but be jealous of all of his suffering and having a mother to add to it.

Mrs. Clemens had an easy laugh, and, despite the scoldings that came out of her as naturally as a boy's whistling, she was kind and gentle as any woman I've ever known. She loved animals so much that she wouldn't even trap rats. When she'd go into the back yard to hang the clothes on the line, half a dozen cats would trail behind her like she was a queen. Her eyes would sparkle and her red hair would catch fire in the light as her head shook when she laughed. She was inclined to tell a funny story or two herself, and she told them with the slowest drawl I've ever heard—except for Sammy's, that is. Even she was conscious of the theatrical slowness of his speech. More than once I heard her say to him, "Enough of your long talk now, Sammy. Just say it quick and forget the soul-butter and hogwash. I've got dinner to make before this week is done." But she seemed to love the surprise and expectation that rose and fell in the rhythms of his voice, and so did I. I have to admit it, so did I. All Sammy had to do was talk and people would laugh. Whatever he had to say, he could make it funny with that way he had of talking so calm and deliberate and slow.

He was his mother's son, all right. He wasn't big or strong, but you didn't want to exchange words with him. He always knew the right ones to get a laugh or to make a boy feel like a fool or a rapscallion. When he had a grudge against you, he kept it, that's for certain. Time never seemed to dull the point of his hatreds.

Sam liked to create surprises. He loved practical jokes, but he didn't appreciate being the butt of any. He didn't much like being surprised either. He liked being in control of what happened to him. Maybe that's part of what caused him to become a river pilot and then later on a writer. He was in control—as much as any man, even an artist, I suppose, can lay claim to that. I even think he was fascinated with all sorts of gadgets and machines when he was young and, from what I've heard, when he was older too, because he thought machines would help him control the world, keep it at a safer distance. Who wouldn't understand such a desire? But it's a foolish one, no doubt.

Like Sam, his mother had a temper, but unlike him, she seemed to shed her anger pretty quickly. She didn't hold a grudge. You could see a piece of her in each of her children—Orion, Pamela, Sam, and Henry. Mrs. Clemens didn't seem much matched to her husband, though. Rumor made it that she had married him in a pet when another fellow who was courting her had not proposed in a timely fashion. A Dr. Richard Barrett of St. Louis, I think. He was said to be tall and handsome and supposedly sent her a letter that was carried by an uncle saying he wanted to propose. Dr. Barrett wanted her uncle to bring her back to his family's farm so he could do the asking, but Mrs. Clemens was too high spirited or prideful for all that indirection, I guess, and she refused to go. The doctor disappeared soon after that and she married John Marshall Clemens just to spite her former suitor, some say.

Judge Clemens was altogether the most impressive man I had ever seen, though. He had only one form of relaxation that I ever discovered and that was reading "Hiawatha" aloud. I heard him once or twice in his study, reading it in the same unemotional voice I had heard him use in reading a charge to a jury of local farmers. I always half expected that when he opened his mouth to speak a roar would come out instead of words. He had the kind of face you might expect from a prophet in the Old Testament. I never saw him smile once. Generally, though, he was quiet spoken, or he didn't speak at all. Sammy told me that his father walked home nearly every night holding his temples and complaining to his wife about "sun pain." They were just headaches, I think, but they seemed to get worse after Judge Clemens's store closed down and the family had to move out of their house. None of Mrs. Clemens's cures seemed to help him at all.

Sammy's father didn't want him to associate with me, and I couldn't say that I blamed him much for that feeling. I didn't go to school but once or twice a month, and my clothes were a collection of rags. I had learned how to read and write (mostly from my sisters teaching me), and later I educated myself with as much passion as the Judge gave to his land deals in Tennessee, but that didn't mean a jot to him or anyone else then, and I understand why he couldn't stomach the thought of one of his own keeping company with the likes of me. At that time I was just one of the Blankenships. My sisters couldn't go to church and my father slept more often in empty hogsheads down by the wharf than he did in his own bed at home.

And there was my brother Benson. He loved to fish the islands near Hannibal. People made fun of him because he hardly ever spoke and he carried this dreamy look on his face all the time. He smelled of catfish most of the day and had big silver dollar eyes that shined like moonbeams. Most people in Hannibal thought he was slow witted. But he wasn't at all. He was just so sweet-natured that he didn't seem normal to most folks. I guess they were right—being that sweet-natured isn't normal. He didn't have much ambition, I guess, but he didn't have a mean bone in his entire body either.

Here's one example of how Benson was different from most in Hannibal. Not long after Sammy and I got to be friends there was a lot of excitement about a runaway slave who slipped away one night from John Robard's place on the out-skirts of town. I knew what happened and so did Sammy, I'm certain, and the rest of the town suspected probably, but no one had any real proof. Ben had found the slave hiding in some brush on Sny Island, and instead of turning him in for the money, which most people in town would have, he fed him and built a lean-to to protect him from the rain.

Ben took a skiff over every few days and brought food and news. Three months went by and Ben was still doing it and would have been doing it three months after that, I suppose, if some bounty hunters hadn't noticed smoke there one night and chased the slave into the swamp. They didn't catch him, but a few days later Sammy and I were fishing near Sny Island and a black head rose out of the water. The face looked like it had been pecked by birds. One eye socket was empty, half the teeth were missing, and the flesh around his cheekbones looked as if it was ready to peel off from the bone like old newspaper on a wet wall.

Nobody ever accused Ben of helping the runaway, but most people thought he might just be simple-minded enough to be an abolitionist. Sammy never said anything to me about Ben, but I could tell that he felt sorry for me that I had an older brother who might not even have enough sense not to help a runaway slave.

Sammy's older brother, Orion, didn't smell of fish, but I think he may have been as moonstruck as Ben in certain respects—and Sammy knew it too. He never said it exactly in so many words, but he knew. Orion always had a scheme that went bust, but he also believed that the very next one would make his fortune for certain. Like Judge Clemens, Orion had absolutely no sense of humor. In its place he had a morality as starched as his Sunday collar. He had the sort of optimism that was downright foolishness, the conviction that his next plan had to work out, that with the next idea he would strike it big. Like he was one of the elect and things had to turn out well for him. When Sammy wasn't disgusted by him, he found Orion funny. The older Sammy got, though, the harder he was on Orion, but even when we first met, Sammy seemed to know that he would have to take care of his brother one day. He seemed to be pleased with the idea and repulsed by it at the same time. He sometimes acted the sneering older brother, even though he was considerably younger, mocking Orion's deep, serious way of speaking and straight-backed posture. I knew that Ben wouldn't have an easy time of it on his own in the world in years to come, but I don't think I would have minded taking care of him. I think it would have been more of a comfort to me than it would have been for him. I never got the chance to take care of him, though, because soon after the slave was found near Sny Island, Ben disappeared. I searched for him for weeks, but he had vanished without a print. Not a trace. And things went on in Hannibal as if he had never existed.

Sammy felt sorry for me and, I think, envied my freedom. I had to make a life out of escaping—from school, my father, whatever the future could bring. Sammy seemed to like the idea of doing the same. That I didn't understand exactly. I think I might have run toward his life if I had the chance, not away from it. I couldn't get very close to his life, of course, during the times his father was around. Judge Clemens didn't want me—or any Blankenship, for that matter—near his family. "Never you mind that, Tom," Sammy would say as he slid down the lightning rod to meet me at night. "My father don't know everything in the world. And he don't have to know this."

Sometimes we would sneak around Wild-Cat Corner and slide like shadows along Bird Street past the old clapboard place where Judge Clemens had his office. He'd still be working there after supper, a bottle of Cook's Pills near his right hand and the oil lamp at his desk giving his long face the look of a skeleton. Once his father's office was out of sight, we ran past the blacksmith shops and tanyard and headed toward Bear Creek. If the pigs had been brought in by the drovers for slaughtering that day, the smell took your breath away—so sour it made the spit curdle and taste like acid in your mouth. We'd circle around toward the river, flushing a heron or some geese along the way. Or we'd head up to Holliday's Hill and watch the lights of the town below shine as pretty as the starlight above us. I felt like a god up there, above all those people and houses, like I couldn't be touched. I could see everything and no one could see me. Sammy and I would sit there for hours between heaven and earth and sometimes never say a word at all. At least once a week, we'd find ourselves sitting near the edge of Bear Creek or alongside the muddy slit of the Salt River and daydream about being somewhere else, about being someone else. Our two voices seemed to be one then, both wondering aloud if we would ever be content, if dissatisfaction was simply a part of being a resident of Hannibal or if it was some defect in our natures. We'd sit there in the dark, Sammy sucking on his pipe until it shimmered into a red glow that made his eyes shine like a cat's, and talk about slipping away and coming back one day bigger than life.

15

*T*hings started to change when Martha Wright moved into town with her mother. They took rooms next door to the house that Sam's family lived in. Martha's mother was a seamstress, and she mended and made dresses that she sold out of her home. She gave piano lessons as well. She was a quiet woman with a shy smile. If you didn't get to know her, you might think she was standoffish. But she wasn't—just careful like a puppy that's had its tail stepped on too many times. Martha and her mother had come from the outskirts of Louisville, Kentucky, where Mr. Wright had died some years back.

Martha wasn't like most of the other girls in town. Sammy and I saw that right away. She was prettier than any girl in Hannibal, but that's not what attracted us to her. She seemed to have a fire inside of her, one that burned steady and bright enough to keep her eyes warm and a little dangerous at the same time. She wasn't exactly a tomboy, but she didn't seem to worry about doing things or going places other girls wouldn't.

Sammy and I both fell in love with her, but neither of us said a word to each other about it. We just came together like three people shipwrecked on a desert island. And given that the first time the three of us were alone together was on Glasscock's Island, maybe we were like passengers tossed onto a sandy beach after a tempest. Glasscock's was only about a mile off the Mississippi shoreline, but it might as well have been another country altogether. To us it seemed far away and separate from everything in town.

The island was unpopulated except for beaver and some wild turkey and herons. There were no houses or churches. No schools or sawmills. "The only sound," as Sammy said, glancing over at Martha, "is the river riffling against the seams of fallen tree trunks." She looked back at him admiringly. He reddened a little and turned his eyes toward the sky, saying, "And not all that tears and flapdoodle the preacher gives out on Sunday, either." He wanted to impress her, and he did, but—just as I yearned to do—he wanted to do it in the right way.

From the very beginning, Martha seemed to understand Sammy in a way that I didn't. She said that he was a boy who wanted to rise in the world. He hated the poverty that his father had allowed his family to fall into. His father's hope that the hundreds of acres of Tennessee land he had purchased years before was *going to make the family rich was simply a pipe dream. Martha said to me that she could see the failure in Judge Clemens's eyes and the desire to escape that kind of a fate in Sammy's. Such a family story was a blessing and a curse and it couldn't be otherwise, she said.*

We had been to the island many times before, but never with a girl. In part, I think Sammy wanted her to come along because he sensed that she knew him better than anyone ever had, that he had something he couldn't put a name to in common with her. That summer our lives changed deeply, and that day on Glasscock's Island was the beginning of it all. Glasscock's Island lay over toward the Illinois shore, three miles below Hannibal, where the river was a little more than a mile wide. It was a narrow, wooded island about two and a half miles long with a shallow bar at its head. It was as close to nowhere else on earth as we could dream up as boys. It was hard for us then to imagine a place more cut off from the world.

Throughout the morning, we had gone exploring, digging for turtle eggs on the sandy bar and searching for snakes in the woods. Martha searched as eagerly as Sammy or me, and although we didn't find anything but an old bird's nest and a dead perch floating in the shallows, the anticipation was as good as any discovery, maybe better.

By noon, the sun was high in the sky and hot, and Sammy said, "Let's go swimming." As soon as he said it, we looked at each other in acknowledgment of the difficulty—Martha. But she didn't give us any time to mull over the problem of stripping down and diving into the river. She just said, "Turn your backs and give me a minute."

Sammy leaned toward me and whispered, "My mother wouldn't even change her clothes in her own bedroom until she took the portrait of President Jackson and faced it toward the wall. I bet Martha don't do it." But she was out of her clothes and in the water when we faced around. She turned and dove, the daylight sparkling off the water and her back, which seemed to be reddening already. She slipped away like the sun disappearing into the horizon.

We followed her in, dizzy in love with her daring. I kept my eyes above the waterline unless she turned her head, and then I gazed into the shadows beneath the muddy waters for a glimpse of her body. It was like looking at firelight in the heart of the river. I could tell that Sammy, like me, was straining hard not to look in her direction. Martha swam to the shallow bar at the head of the island and lay in the dark water, propped slightly on her elbows, letting her head fall now and then into the river. Her coarse brown hair braided with water and sunlight, and she smiled at us as if this was a normal adventure to be understood in the normal ways.

That afternoon, before we took the skiff back across the water to town, we lay there in the sun, our clothes drying on our backs, and watched the steamboats churn downstream. We didn't say much and although I can't say I knew for sure what Sammy was thinking, I know that I was dreaming of that afternoon already, before it was even done.

When we got back to town, we headed toward Sammy's house. We walked up the hill on one of the side streets so that no one would see us. When we got near enough to see Sammy's front door, we heard his father's voice as the door opened.

"You come with me! I'll teach you not to raise your hand to your mistress!"

Judge Clemens dragged Jennie, the family cook and housekeeper, outside by her hair. She was screaming, "No, please Massa Clemens. I didn't mean nothing by it. My hand just raised itself up. Like it wasn't part of me at all. I wouldn't have let it do no harm. Please, suh."

But Judge Clemens jerked her toward him and tied her hands with a bridle to a hitching post in front of the house. Then he whipped her until her screams were just soft whimperings. He left her there and walked away without a word. It was Martha who moved first. She went up to the hitching post and loosened Jennie's bindings so that she was able to slump to the ground. When I turned to ask Sammy if we should bring her into the house, he was gone.

The next week school let out for the year. For Sam and me it was a summer filled with death. We had seen the cholera and yellow fever hit Hannibal in years past, but in the summer of 1847 death seemed to stalk Sam and me everywhere we went. Even though I had Sam and Martha, I sometimes felt so lonesome that summer—because of the things that happened—that I almost wished I was dead. When I felt truly lonesome—with my brother gone, my father drunk and better off gone, and my sisters trying as hard as they could to hold the house together—I would walk down to the bank of the Mississippi and listen to the bullfrogs croaking and the currents of the river sliding along, and I'd gaze at the stars. Sometimes, I counted the drifting logs and rafts. If I counted the stars, it made me feel even lonelier somehow. But if I just stared up at the darkness, I felt better. It was so pretty—like an immense river and the stars floating jewels.

The summer started out pretty much the same as every other one. One night when it seemed too hot to breathe, Sam and I climbed the path to the top of Holliday's Hill, a bluff that looked down on the river and town from two hundred feet. The slave Jennie's son, little Mr. Bill, was with us, too. His name was Bill, but we called him little Mr. Bill because he was the oldest little boy, black or white, that any of us had ever seen. He had the eyes of an old man, and he never smiled, ever, that I can recall.

Little Mr. Bill trailed along behind us and stood off to the side when we got to the top of the hill. Sam said, "C'mon, Tom, help me move this boulder." I wasn't certain what he had in mind. With Sam you never did. I just lent a hand. We pried and pushed until it was about three feet from the edge of the hill. Then Sam sat down and pushed with his heels until the three-foot-wide stone appeared to will itself over the edge. The boulder crashed and bounced down the hill gaining speed all the way until it exploded through the tanner's shop, spraying wood and metal into the night air.

The next day the tanner accused little Mr. Bill of sending the boulder through his shop because he saw him in the vicinity that evening. The tanner was always accusing people of things, so we didn't pay it no mind. Sam and I never said a word to put a lie to the accusation and never gave it a second thought until the next month.

I was sitting on the docks watching them unload a steamboat when Sam came up to me slit-eyed with guilt, and said, "They sold Jennie and little Mr. Bill down the river. But it couldn't have had anything to do with the tanner's shop. They never even whipped him for that."

Sam never mentioned little Mr. Bill or Jennie again but the weekend of Independence day he said, "That boulder jinxed us, Tom. I wish I had never sent it down the hill. It feels like it started an avalanche."

Whether the boulder brought us bad luck or not, I'm not sure, but bad things surely multiplied that summer. And July Fourth was when it started, when, as Sam said, "the boulder began its work."

Sam and I were sitting with Martha in the shade of an alley off Main Street, just trying to while away the time before the fireworks that evening, when we heard a man's voice raised in anger, the kind of voice that means something bad's going to happen soon. We got to the corner of Main just in time to see a white man standing by a wagon in front of the dry goods store. A box with flour and coffee was lying by one of the wheels, the slats of the box broken and the bags of flour and coffee spilled out into the muddy road.

The white man was middle-aged and nearly too fat to bend over, as far as I could tell. He was looking down at a young black man who was kneeling in the dirt trying to gather up the pieces of the box. But the white man surprised me because he did bend over, agilely and without any wheezing, and picked up a chunk of iron ore lying near his boot. He threw it full force into the side of the black man's head without ever saying a word. Neither did the slave. The only sound I heard was the crack, like a pine limb splitting under the weight of ice—that's what the skull sounded like as it opened up in front of us.

People milled around the body for a time and looked a bit disgusted with the whole scene, but half an hour later the man had carted the body off in his wagon. You could barely see where the dark blood had mixed with coffee and flour in the road.

That night Martha said she wasn't up to any fireworks and went home. I didn't much feel like it myself but had no place else to go. It wasn't practical for me to go home too early, so I just sat next to Sam and watched the sky catch fire and thought about Martha's expression as she looked at the slave's empty stare into the muddy road. Martha looked grief-stricken—as if it had been Sam or me lying there.

That wasn't the last time that summer that we saw a dead man or the sky catch fire. Before July was done we watched the undertaker carry two more bodies to the cemetery. The first death might have been our fault. Sam and I were walking past the old jailhouse when we heard a hoarse whisper spit out, "Hey, boys. You, boys." When we looked up, there was an old man with a grizzled white beard and a thick scar across the bridge of his nose and another under his right eye. If it hadn't been for the bars that separated us, I might have run then and there.

"Be Christian boys, won't you, and get me some matches for my pipe."

We did it and his face softened beneath the scars and hair, and he said, "God bless you boys. It sure is white of you. God will bless you."

But if God was going to bless us that night, I wasn't able to notice it then. Instead, it seemed as if we were cursed. At about ten o'clock, as we were heading back from the river, we saw the sky on fire. When we came to the jailhouse we saw the flames licking the whitewash off the brick. The bars on the windows were red with the heat, and smoke billowed out of the very spot where the old man had spoken to us, begged us for the matches that most likely burned him to death.

It wasn't but a few days later that old Sam Smarr was shot down in the street as if he was a dog. Sam Smarr was a harmless old drunk. He wasn't like my father. Sam didn't have a mean streak in his skinny body. He couldn't have hurt a body even if he'd wanted to, and he wasn't the type to want to.

It was Friday at noon, cloudless, and the sun made everything so clear that it hurt your eyes to look around at all the peeling paint and lost hopes in the town. Sam Smarr was drifting down the middle of the road, drunk again. That was nothing unusual. Neither was his conversation with himself. Talking to himself like there was two of him staggering down the street. Loud enough for anyone around to hear, he was talking about what was wrong with the town. It was hard to take it seriously or to be angry with him because he was the gentlest soul on earth when he was sober. He wasn't a man who was made to drink. It's like it changed him into a different person.

This time he was talking about William Owsley, the shopkeeper, and how he made his money from other people's hardships. He was right—Owsley was an old skinflint—but he probably had no right to say such things for everyone to hear on Main Street. It's probably never a good idea to speak the truth that loud in a town like Hannibal anyway, especially on Main Street.

If he had been sober, he certainly would have been smart enough not to say, "Owsley, you're a damned pickpocket, a damned son of a bitch." On the other hand, it wasn't a killing offense, but that's what Owsley made it. He shot old man Smarr twice in the chest and left him lying there until someone came to pray over him as he took his last breath. I heard one of the men say that Smarr was as honest and peaceful as any white man in the state of Missouri. It was too bad, the man said, that drinking made him a little turbulent.

A group of men carried him to Dr. Grant's place, the apothecary's shop. I heard that some of those men and others went to Owsley's house on the edge of town and threatened to hang him. They yelled and threatened and talked in brave language until Owsley appeared on his porch with a cocked shotgun in his arms and an amused expression on his face and made them scatter like scared children. A few weeks later, Owsley was acquitted because the jury decided that Smarr could have been a threat as he was carrying a gun and besides Owsley had just cause anyway. Owsley's lawyer said that he had been sore provoked. Nobody checked, of course, to see if Smarr had ever fired a pistol in his life. Or if he had ever raised his hand to another man in anger in anyone's memory.

Sam, Martha, and I watched from the crest of Holliday's Hill as Smarr's

daughter and a few townspeople walked behind the undertaker's wagon to the
cemetery. From our height the procession looked like a sad, silent line of Monks on
their way to church. The string of people seemed far away from us. They weren't
far away from us, though, and we knew it.

Before the summer ended, we followed Sam down the same road to the cemetery in the line behind his father's coffin. Sam's father had been sick for only a
short time. In a sense, a final pipe dream did him in. Judge Clemens had gone off
to Palmyra, the county seat about ten miles to the west of our town, on another one
of his wild goose chases. The night he left, Sam and I stayed out most of the night.
The Judge had some kind of a court case against William Beebe, but he was really
looking for enough money to finance his campaign for clerk of the county court.
He went to Palmyra, but the case didn't get resolved that day. It didn't matter
much, though, because on his way home he got caught in a sleet storm that soaked
him clean through to the bone. By the time he got to his house, he was tired and
sick. As the days went along, he just got worse. First pleurisy, then pneumonia. He
was forty-nine when he died. Two years younger than my own father was then.

Dr. Meredith convinced Mrs. Clemens that it would advance the cause of science to allow him to do an autopsy. That night, Sam and I stood on a wooden box
peering into the lamplit back room of Dr. Meredith's office. The office was
cramped and the lamp didn't do much more than make the darkness a shade of
gray, it seemed to me. Outside, where we stood trembling in the evening air, a
half moon painted shadows all around us and appeared to reach the corpse itself.
The body was wrapped in a dirty white sheet. A tall black man, silent as petrified
wood, stood next to the doctor. The black man was strong. Even in the shadows I
could see how powerful his arms were. When he lifted the Judge's body, picking up
the edges of the sheet and tossing him onto the worktable with a thud as if he was a
sack of meal, I could see the muscles in his arms ripple like the wind against high
wheat. A copy of the poems of Longfellow dropped out of the Judge's back pocket.
The doctor kicked it aside and, with the help of the black man, took off the Judge's
clothes, leaving him exposed in a way that made me feel naked myself.

The doctor took up a large knife that looked like an oversized scalpel and cut
a Y into Judge Clemens's chest from each shoulder to the bottom of the breastbone.
Then with a smaller knife he began to peel the skin and muscle off the Judge's
chest. The doctor looked over at the black man, whose eyes were closed tight and
mouth open in a wide yawn, and said, "Jackson, hand me that saw on the other

table." I knew that I was going to be sick at any moment. The air smelled as sweet as raw lamb.

Down by the river, the air smelled empty as the night, and I breathed deeply until the sweet smell disappeared and the sickness along with it. I waited for Sam to come for a long time, it seemed, thinking of what I would say to him when he appeared, but when he did sit down next to me, we didn't say anything. As hard as I tried, I couldn't think of anything to say. Both of us just kept looking in the direction of the dark river until we fell asleep near the shoreline.

That night I slept like a dead man. I never dreamed or stirred once that I can recall. When I woke up, the sun had already risen an hour or so before, and Sam was gone. I saw him again the night after the funeral, with Martha, on Holliday's Hill. It wasn't yet night when we met up with each other. It was dusk, and the air was beginning to look blurred and then bruised and purple. Sam didn't look at us as he spoke, and I didn't look at him either. He was really speaking to Martha, I knew, because I had been there. I had seen most of what he had seen. I remembered clearly the stern look fixed on the Judge's face and pictured his chest opened like a shocked expression. I knew what the saw was to do.

"I'm never going to say this again or tell anyone after this one time," Sam said. "But I need to say it once. I don't know why, but I know that I do. So, I'll say it now. I watched Doc Meredith cut into my father's body last night. I should have turned my eyes away. But I couldn't. Or, I don't know, the thing is—I didn't. It was like watching someone cut into my own body. I felt ashamed for my father that I didn't look away, and sorry for myself that I couldn't bring myself to do it.

"Maybe I was looking for the Doc to show me something in my father that I had never seen before. When he died, we were all gathered around his bedside— my mother, Orion, Ben, me, and Pamela. My sister was crying so hard that the tears were splashing onto the bed. My father reached out his arm and pulled her head toward his lips and kissed her. 'Let me die,' he told her. That's the first time I ever saw him kiss anyone.

"When Doc laid him open—heart and lungs and intestines all crowded together—I looked as closely as I could to see if there was room for what seemed to be missing in him. There wasn't much room for anything but what was there, it seemed to me. There just wasn't even any room for a soul, as far as I could tell. I couldn't see any place for a soul at all. There was room for the brain. I didn't wait, though, for him to show me that, too. I turned away before he took that from me as well.

"So I can still believe that there's room for a brain in a human being. I

learned that. There's room for ambition and intelligence. There's still room to be-
lieve in that. And I plan to. I plan not to become my father or like either of my
brothers. I plan not to believe in some daydream of Tennessee land making me
rich. I plan to believe in one thing only—in myself. I plan to forget what I saw
and remember what I didn't."

He looked like he had more to say, but I could see that he wasn't going to and
that he wouldn't bring up his father's death ever again and expected us not to either. Martha looked at Sam in a way that made my stomach knot in jealousy. But
even then I think I knew that her look wasn't romantic but rather some form of
quieter love, a sense of security that comes from being with a person who will care
for you no matter what you tell them about yourself.

We sat there without speaking for a good long while before Martha finally
spoke up. The words came out in a rush like she had held them in for a long time
and now they were climbing all over themselves to get the thing said.

"I've longed to tell you and Tom something all summer," she said. "Ever since
I met you." This seems to be the time to tell it. We all have our secrets, I suppose,
and in our own hearts we can't change them. I've come to love the two of you and
want you to know who I am.

"My grandmother was a slave. I don't think I've ever said that out loud before.
Not even with my mother. We let it all go unsaid, knowing what's not to be spoken.
Some things are too dangerous to talk about. But to say it aloud is like coming off
the stage after so many performances that my limbs ache from the acting.

"My grandmother was part black, just enough black blood coursing through
her veins to make her a slave. By my calculations, I've got one-sixteenth of Negro
blood in me, and that's all it took to make me a Negro in Kentucky or all it would
take in Missouri to make my mother and me slaves. We left Kentucky so that we
could forget one story and remember another. I understand what you mean, Sam.
When my father died, we found a way to make our own truth and let the world fit
itself into it. We were tired of trying to fit our lives into some design that didn't
make any sense to us at all. So we just made up our own story. Like your talking
about doing. We just made a story that's as true as any other. More true maybe."

I kept silent, not having any secret to share. Everything about me was out in
the open, it seemed—my father's drunkenness, my brother's disappearance, my
rags, even how I felt about Martha. There was not much to hide and no place to
hide it, I suppose. Having things out in the open can be a burden, surely, but it
can also make things a lot easier at times, too.

I was surprised at how long the silence lasted. It stretched into the swelling *buzz of the cicadas, Sam staring straight ahead the entire time. Silence is a language in itself, and this silence spoke its message as clear as any preacher at a pulpit. It lasted too long, so long that it created its own sound, like creaking boards about to snap. It lasted long enough for each of us to realize that Sam and Martha were telling two different kinds of stories. What she saw that they had in common, Sam didn't want to see.*

At the point I thought he was not going to speak at all, he finally said, "I'm not sure what's true or not any more. I'm not sure I really want to know the truth all the time." Then he paused again and stopped long enough to make me wonder if he had said all that he would. He still had not looked at either of us. He turned his eyes from the river to Martha. "That's a lot of surprise to deal with in one evening. I need time to think on it. Let me have some time to think on it."

With that he walked down the hill toward his house.

Martha didn't raise her eyes from the ground. "Don't worry," I said, "he'll get over the surprise of it, all right. This won't mean anything. Not anything at all. I don't care what—it doesn't mean anything at all. It doesn't change a thing."

Oddly enough, I was telling the truth—at least for me I was. I didn't care if her grandmother had been a slave or if Martha was part black. It didn't seem to matter at all. I wasn't sure why it didn't—because it should have made a difference, all the difference in the world.

Over the next few weeks, by his absence and his silence, Sam made it clear that it did matter. It wasn't long after that night that Sam disappeared from view entirely, first becoming a printer's apprentice for Joseph Ament at the Missouri Courier and a year or so later leaving for St. Louis and the larger world as a printer. I spent those years learning the carpenter's trade and trying to redirect any affection Martha had for Sam to me. He had disappeared, but I had no plans to go anywhere.

Even after he left for St. Louis, Martha seemed to expect him to return any day and to have taken her secret and turned it into the purest love and friendship. But when his brother Orion published Sam's first letter from New York in the Hannibal Journal, Martha's eyes clouded over with resignation.

Sam wrote: "This trip was a very pleasant one. Rochester, famous on account of the Spirit Rappings was of course interesting; and when I saw the Court House in Syracuse, it called to mind the time when it was surrounded with chains and companies of soldiers, to prevent the rescue of McReynolds' nigger, by the infernal abolitionists. I reckon I had better black my face, for in these Eastern States niggers are considerably better than white people. I will give you a motto, and it will be useful to you if you will adopt it: 'Consider every man colored till he is proved white.' That's the only way to survive in the East, at any rate."

When I read that letter in the newspaper, I couldn't help but wonder if Sam had written it as a message to Martha and me. It was as if he was saying that too many things had changed in his life, and he was going to hold on to some of the old ways to keep his balance. As if he was saying, I don't want to be taken off guard any more. From now on, all the shocks will come from me. I'll create them with my pen.

He also wrote me around the same time and said that he had journeyed to the beach to put his feet in the Atlantic Ocean where he imagined not warfare because of slavery but his name marking history. As far as I could tell, Sam wouldn't let his dreams turn toward Martha or friendship. Either he didn't want to crave the comforts of home—or he simply didn't crave them. His dreams were of his future. He longed for movement. Only movement. He wanted only the surprises he could create himself along the way.

Martha made her own move shortly after that first letter in the paper. She went to San Francisco with her mother to open a school. She was going, she said, to the very edge of America, as far from slaveholding as she could get. When we kissed goodbye and said farewell, I knew that I would follow her as soon as my apprenticeship was done. In my heart, I believed that she knew it too.

16

*I*t took me a year and a half to finish my apprenticeship and become a journeyman carpenter. It took another year to save the necessary money to get ready to leave Hannibal for the West. During those years I heard from Martha every other week and I wrote as often. Sam I heard from or about intermittently—sometimes in letters and sometimes in newspaper accounts.

The printer's shop became Sam's college. In one of the books he wrote later he described his feelings about the printing business, "One doesn't spend years in this trade without setting up acres of good and bad literature, and learning—unconsciously at first, consciously later—to discriminate between the two . . . and meanwhile he is consciously acquiring what is called a style." It was years later that I read something Sam wrote about how he found his true calling—as a writer—when he was still working in the printing business. According to Sam, one day as he was walking home from his printing work, a page of a book blew across his path. He grabbed it out of the air and read it. It was a few paragraphs about the life of Joan of Arc. Sam said that it stunned him that a book could hold such truth. That's when he began to read serious literature, he said, and that's when he started to think about writing it as well. Sam was always good at changing the plot of his life to fit the story he had made up for himself, so who knows if this tale of Joan of Arc is true, but surely he was impressed by the bravery she showed in her life.

I thought of being a printer myself, but saw the drudgery it was watching other apprentices in the trade. For a time I watched Wales McCormick do the work and that mostly settled it for me. An apprentice printer had to build the master's fire in the morning, fetch water from the village pump, sweep the office, wash the rollers, wet and turn the newsprint, set type, distribute it, work the press, fold the printed newspapers, deliver them, and pursue delinquent subscribers and advertisers. Besides, I reasoned that I needed to not feel I was following in Sam's footpath. Work with a saw and hammer seemed less complicated to me or at least a more direct contact with the world—and it left me more time for reading the books that I wanted to at night.

No pages of a martyr's biography, carried on the breeze, floated in my path to change my life. My story was a lot less dramatic than Sam's. The boardinghouses where I stayed in those last few years in Hannibal became my schoolroom. I read to make myself the kind of man I wanted to be, the kind of man Martha would be proud to have. I read to understand the world and the kind of life she had chosen. Both Sam and I were trying hard to invent new selves, I suppose, and maybe our reasons for doing it were not as different as we might have imagined. Maybe there is only one reason for wanting to transform yourself.

During those years, as far as I could pick up from bits and pieces of information, from newspaper accounts and plain rumor, Sam went from New York to Philadelphia and then on to Washington, D.C. Eventually, he wended his way back to his brother Orion's businesses in Muscatine and Keokuk, Iowa. He was the same old Sam. Always half serious and half not. Some of his articles he wrote under the name W. Epaminodas Adrastus Blab, and they always made me laugh, even if I had to cringe at the cruelty of some of them. His letters in Orion's paper revealed a sense of humor that was forged in sadness or disappointment.

From New York City, he wrote once to me, "I've learned a great deal traveling about the East, seeing the World's Fair and other phenomenons. I've learned, for instance, that technology could improve everything human. Except human nature, that is. There's no machine that will likely be invented to do much to improve that. When you have a chance, Tom, let me know how things are in H____L."

Sam was always funny, to be certain, and took a dark view of most small towns, Hannibal included, although, strangely enough, he loved our hometown, too. He seemed to see it as a kind of dreamy lost paradise, a place that—no matter how hard he tried—he could not find his way back to as he got older. He was apt to make jokes about life in Hannibal, though, at times even when we were boys. And he never had too high an opinion of the average human being who lived there, either. Even himself. But a town like Hannibal could never hold a young man like Sam Clemens.

I had heard at one point that he was headed to South America to make his fortune in the coca business but had gotten sidetracked onto the river. Being a riverboat pilot had been the dream of half the boys in Hannibal—so it seemed to me that things worked out mighty well for him. For a couple of years he lived as high as a man can, like a prince on the Mississippi. And if the war hadn't come along when it did, he might have ended his days as a pilot, a legend on the river like Horace Bixby.

Sam wrote to me once or twice during his years on the river. "I'm learning a lot of things as a river pilot," he said. "Mainly, I'm learning the prodigious vocabulary of curses available to a man who listens carefully and applies sound memory to the task. I've learned enough boasts to educate a humble man. If only I needed some humility. Or believed in its value."

I never received a fully serious letter from him until the summer of 1858, when his younger brother Henry was killed in an explosion on the paddle-wheeler Pennsylvania. His letter was probably written less to me than it was to himself— "If I hadn't lobbied for a job for Henry. If I hadn't fought Brown over family honor. If I had done something more to help Captain Klinefelter find another pilot. If I had done more to stop the race in November before the boiler suffered damage. If I had not pressed the physician for more morphine for Henry. If, damnable word. If only I could have saved him, I would gladly be struck dead this instant."

Death was still shadowing Sam, and he felt haunted by some curse, guilty in some way that neither he—nor I—ever fully understood. When his nineteen-year-old brother Henry asked him to help him get a job on the river, it seemed like a good idea. When William Brown, the pilot of the Pennsylvania, who proved himself to be a mean-spirited, small-minded, foul-mouthed little tyrant, lied about Henry to Captain Klinefelter, Sam thought it his duty to exact justice with his fists. And when the dream he had of Henry dressed in Sam's clothing and laid out in a metal coffin with a bouquet of white roses with a single red one in the middle of his breast came to him one night, Sam dismissed it, as seemed right, as mere foolishness.

"But," as Sam wrote in his letter to me, "it was all planned long before I was born. This is just somebody else's dream, and I'm acting out my part in it. Somehow, though, knowing that doesn't stop my conscience from tearing at me like a wild beast. I wish that I had never had to stop anywhere a month. I do more mean and stupid things the moment I get a chance to fold my hands and sit down than I will ever get forgiveness for in two lifetimes."

I felt sorry for him then, at least I did until I got his next note, dated July 25, 1861, from St. Joseph, Missouri: "The war ended my piloting days on the Mississippi, and two weeks of the Confederate Army ended my inclination to be a soldier. I'm on my way to the Nevada Territory and west of that one day, I hope."

He had not asked one word in all those years about Martha, but he knew where she was. I knew that, or sensed it at any rate, and he knew that I did. So I took his note as a gentleman's warning, although I'm not exactly sure of what. Soon after that letter, I left for San Francisco myself. I wanted to get there before Sam did. It took me about two years to work my way to the coast, but I still got there before Sam did, although not before his name arrived, his new name, that is, Mark Twain.

Hundreds of thousands of others had led the way for both Sam and me, of course, following the pipe dream of gold to Nevada and California. Without realizing it until a little more than a decade later, after reading Roughing It, I had followed in Sam's footsteps a good portion of the way West. I took off from St. Jo as he had but not on an overland stagecoach. I hired myself out to a family heading out with a wagon train. We moved slower than any coach, bouncing our way through Kansas and Colorado. A few of the hired men left when we first hit Utah, but I waited until we arrived in Salt Lake. I worked for six months help-

ing to build a church and a hotel. That gave me enough money to board a coach to Silver Springs, Nevada. There was plenty of work for me as a carpenter in that town. I saved every penny I earned, even though I discovered in that place more ways than I ever dreamed of to spend time and money.

I was sorely tempted to do some prospecting. Most men in Silver Springs thought I was a bit slow-witted not to. James Mitchell, a carpenter like myself, had been the one to discover gold in the millrace of the sawmill that he was building for John Sutter in Coloma in '48. The story had it that he lived in a mansion on Nob Hill in San Francisco. But another rumor had it that he was a drunk in a mining camp in Colorado. I wasn't sure where the truth lay or how my story was destined to turn out. I just knew that it wasn't gold I was after exactly. I just needed enough of it to discover if there was a new life waiting for me to begin living it.

Prospecting seemed like too much of a gamble to me. I was afraid that I'd lose the money I had saved and then lose what was most precious to me—time—in making it up. I wanted to get to San Francisco as fast as I could with enough money in my pocket to make a new beginning there. If I wasn't a rich man, that was all right. Being rich was not what I was after anyway. If I thought Martha cared about such things, I might have myself. I guess I was a gambler, though, after all because I headed to San Francisco as if I was meant to be there—and I had no sure proof that anything like that was the truth. I had her letters and a kiss when she left Hannibal, but the rest was what was in my heart. Love is always a foolish gamble, something of a bluff. That's part of the excitement of it, I guess, that you never play it with cards that you're sure of.

I knew that there were faster ways to get to San Francisco, but probably not with the money I had saved and not starting out from Hannibal. Most people traveled to San Francisco by boat, many rounding Cape Horn in a six-month journey. The shortest way was through the isthmus of Panama. A few years before I started out, a whole host of ships came to San Francisco because it was the closest port to the silver and gold mines. Schooners, whaleboats, steamers all seemed transformed, people said, as ships entered the glistening bay of the city. Captains and crews abandoned their vessels and headed off to the Sierra Nevadas. At one time, more than six hundred ships swayed sadly back and forth, ghost vessels at anchor in the harbor, waiting for their crews to discard the hopes of a quick fortune. Some of the ships broke anchor and floated out of sight like forsaken lovers slipping away into the fog.

In Silver Springs, I started to see Sam's name in the newspapers, the Virginia City Territorial Enterprise mainly. I remember the first account I read by him, what at first seemed a sad story about the discovery of a petrified body of a man up by Gravely Ford. The man had died of a protracted exposure more than three hundred years ago, the story said. The whole account turned out to be a hoax, and when I read it again, I saw pretty clearly what I had missed on the first reading— the corpse petrified into a sitting position and one hand placed unmistakably in such a way that it was thumbing its nose at onlookers. I heard that Sam was paying back a personal debt with the local coroner. He paid back a lot of personal debts over the years, it seemed, and he was good at it.

It was around that time that I received a letter from Sam. It found its way to Nevada even though he had sent it to Hannibal, thinking I was still there. It didn't have a return address but I knew it came from somewhere in the Territories.

It was the old Sam: "Some people are malicious enough to think that if the devil were set at liberty and told to confine himself to the Nevada Territory, that he would come here and loaf sadly around, awhile, and then get homesick and go back to hell again. But I like it here, at least for the present. I suspect that it will not be long before I'm on the road again. I need to keep moving and keep my eyes wide open."

Not long after that letter, a travel story in the Enterprise was datelined Carson City and signed "Yours Dreamily, Mark Twain." That was an old riverman's term from the Mississippi meaning "safe water," but it was also a phrase I'd come to hear a lot in Nevada saloons when a customer wanted to mark up two drinks on credit. It was just like Sam to wink in such a way.

I made it to Sacramento a few months after the war ended. Sam had already gotten there, to that part of California, in a sense. His story "Jim Smiley and His Jumping Frog" had made him a celebrity in the East as well as the West. I read the story in The Californian. I knew the tale was bound to be the start of his fame, and that he was at the beginning of getting what he had always most desired in the world, fame and money, mainly, I think, because he thought they would protect him, it could be, against false dreams. But I wasn't sure how much he wanted such things for their own sakes or if they were leading him back to Martha.

I got to San Francisco the next week.

That's where the journal ended, as if the writer intended to tease whoever read it forward into the next leatherbound diary or into the world itself. There was a note written by my great-grandfather, Thomas's son, taped to the inside cover. Dated June 4, 1957, three weeks before my great-grandfather died, it was two sentences, printed with the kind of attention a man would give to a message he folded into a bottle and dropped into the sea.

If the house still stands, at 17 Fulton Street in San Francisco, the other journal should be where I left it in the attic. On top of the crossbeam where the wood meets the slant of the roofline.

—*James Blankenship*

17

The rest of Thomas Blankenship's story would be in San Francisco. It was as if my great grandfather left the journal for me, knowing one day I would get to see it and one day need an excuse to embark on a journey, to head toward the compass point most important to my heart.

The direction seemed a familiar one, somehow. So many before me had been drawn west. The West was where my blood and my story might have been mixed with Nada's. If I had a fraction of black blood, it was not even enough to erase the freckles from my cheeks or to darken the blondness of my eyebrows, but if Martha had become my great-great-grandmother, perhaps the past and the present would become part of one coherent story for me instead of seeming to be disparate tales that had little to do with each other. How they were connected exactly I wasn't sure. So I went on the road out of fear—afraid that I would find the next journal and afraid that I wouldn't, not sure whether I wanted to discover that Martha's blood was part of mine or that my great-great-grandfather had found a way to live contentedly without her, wondering if I wanted to discover a way to connect all that was gone and all that was to come or to live outside of both forever. Wondering if I wanted Nada's story and mine to be different or so intimately connected that no one could ever separate us.

I was going to go on the road, as my ancestor once had, but unlike him, I wasn't sure exactly why I was going or what I was looking for. In a way, we set off in the same direction for opposite reasons. He left in search of Martha. I left Nada behind. Of course, simply, I was looking for the journal, but I didn't know what I wanted it to offer me. San Francisco was a long way to travel for a history lesson, even one in which a central character bears your name. I realized that I may have been more like Sam Clemens than I was like my great-great-grandfather, running from something rather than running toward it. More like my father than my great-great-grandfather. I wasn't sure why I needed to go. I wanted to be more like Thomas, I suspected, or maybe less like him, and I guess I hoped in going I would find out how to do one or the other and be happy with my decision. I wondered what form of cowardice I might be proving to myself, though, in taking off. Was I afraid of what Thomas Blankenship was not daunted by with Martha? Did I run from the consequences of the fight at the Home? Or from a future that included Vietnam? Did I run from a future that meant finding myself in a past like Andrew Weiry's? Or did I simply run from Mr. Calabria and Martha and Fitz and anything and anyone that put a name to who I was? I wondered if I ran from them. And why.

That afternoon I ran, though. I said goodbye to Andrew, left a note for Nada, and set off to hitch a ride to New York City. It didn't take long to find one. I had just gotten to Route 97 over the Barryville Bridge when Patrick McAwley screeched to a stop a few yards in front of me. Everyone in Yulan knew Patrick. He was a legend on the road. He always drove over the speed limit, but he had a magic card that kept him safe from the cops. Legend had it that he was stopped four times in one night on Independence Day, going from Yulan to New York City a few years before. Each time he was stopped, he flashed the card and said, "I'm on the job," and was sent on his way. It was as if he couldn't be touched by the ordinary forces of the world. He was outside the laws of man, maybe even the laws of physics.

Patrick had gone from the FBI to work for a sheik who lived in a forty-room mansion on the Raritan River in New Jersey right next to a house owned by Frank Sinatra. The sheik paid huge amounts of money into the widows' funds and the children's funds for the New York and New Jersey State Police organizations, and everyone who wore a badge in the Northeast knew his name. The sheik gave Patrick the magic card that the head of the New Jersey State Police had given to him, and with the card, even after being stopped for traveling 130 miles per hour on the turnpike, Patrick was sent on his way, most of the time with a smile, occasionally with a gentle admonition.

Three weeks before he picked me up, Patrick had been in an accident on Route 55 between Yulan and White Lake. He had been cruising along at 115 miles per hour when his car left the macadam and turned, like a love letter caught in a wind, toward the treeline. It was going so fast that the car went airborne and cut the tops of a row of pines, decapitating them like a scythe in the high grass. The car may have seemed to float a long time in the air before it lost its momentum and crashed to the ground. When the police arrived, they scooped up most of the five hundred bullets and half dozen guns that had sprayed from the trunk as it snapped open. The ambulance driver found Patrick's $5,000 jeweled Rolex, a gift from the sheik on New Year's Eve, winking in the moonlight. The police took him to a local hospital. The X-rays showed no broken bones, and Patrick went home to bed. On the police report, the officer wrote that the driver lost control on a patch of ice. Neither the police nor God, it seemed, wanted to exercise any wrath against him.

So, even though I was looking to get away immediately and make it to the city as fast as possible before I changed my mind about going at all, I hesitated when Patrick opened the passenger door and smiled like Norman Bates showing a motel room to a customer.

"Get in, kid. Where you heading?"

When I told him Grand Central Station, he said, "No problem. I'm heading through Midtown on my way to the Village. I'll get you there before it turns dark."

It was close to dark already, as far as I could tell. Before I had even closed the passenger door of his Corvette Stingray, the tires howled and burned and pebbles careened off the hubcaps. A dust cloud trailing behind the car, he headed down Route 97, and within a few minutes we were on the Hawk's Nest curve, cutting the winding road into a straight line at 85 miles per hour. I held tight to the sides of my seat, imagining what it would feel like as we flew over the low stone wall and sailed into the canyon and the Delaware River hundreds of feet below. Patrick looked over at me, taking his eyes off the road long enough to make my skin tingle with despair.

"So where are you headed, kid? I mean after Grand Central?"

I couldn't return his gaze. I kept my eyes fixed on the road, hoping to set an example—or at least see the end before it came.

"San Francisco," I said. "I'll be visiting family in San Francisco."

He continued to look at me.

"I've always wanted to go to Frisco. Never have. Seems like the whole world is heading out there these days. I may drive there this summer. Where does your family live? I'll look you up."

I offered up the first street name that I could remember from recently looking at a detailed map of San Francisco, an address that I prayed—just on the off chance that he would decide to drive in a mad rush across the country in some forty-eight-hour delirium—was far from the section of the city where I might end up.

"Polk Street, 423 Polk Street, across town from the park. My family are the Clemenses."

I kept staring at the road in the faint hope that by sheer force of will I could get him to look toward it himself, that the inclination of my head and the fixed direction of my eyes on the blurred white line would compel him, like a magic spell, to concentrate on the world that exploded all around us, but it was a car horn screaming as it came around the curve, the driver wild-eyed in terror as he saw the Corvette in his lane, that pulled Patrick's eyes back over the steering wheel. He turned away from the oncoming car without ever acknowledging that it was there, without ever pausing in his conversation.

"All those beautiful hills," he was saying. "It must be crazy driving up those hills. It must be wild coming over the top of one of them and not knowing what's on the other side."

He didn't stop at any lights in Port Jervis, New York, or Matamoras, Pennsylvania, as he headed onto Route 6 and into the country south of the town of Milford. The Palisades Parkway in New Jersey was a tight, two-lane highway, and we passed every car along the way as if it were parked. We sped past the Mad Anthony Wayne exit and across the George Washington Bridge, the city in front of us ablaze with lights, and got onto the Major Deegan Expressway. I barely had time to wonder who Major Deegan was and if he had any connection to Mad Anthony Wayne as we sped past Yankee Stadium and the apartment buildings that rose and fell along the avenues of the Highbridge section of the Bronx. Before I could gather my thoughts, we had bounced to a stop at the Third Avenue Bridge around 138th Street.

The light was red and cars were lined up in front of us. Two men in woolen caps and grease-streaked brown jackets sprayed water on the car windows and wiped them with cloths that added more dirt than they took off. Drivers handed them some change or a dollar bill, more out of fear, it seemed, than any sense of tipping for a service well performed. When one of the men, gray-whiskered and toothless, leaned over Patrick's windshield and began to spray,

Patrick rolled his window down, reached into his jacket pocket, and pushed a gun into the man's face.

"Get the fuck out of here," Patrick said. "My windows are clean enough."

Patrick then turned to me.

"I hate these guys. They think they can intimidate every driver coming through here into paying a toll. You don't give them some change and they throw a rock at your fucking car. Well fuck that. I'm not giving them a fucking penny."

He held the gun up between us and waved it.

"No taxation without representation, eh? This is goddamn fucking America, goddammit!"

By the time we reached 42nd Street and Lexington Avenue, I felt as if I had gone farther than I had expected to go, as if I had exited some hallucination and was damp with exhaustion after it. It was not completely dark, but the terminal was bright and seemed to have nothing to do with the streets outside or any wild ride with Patrick McAwley. Patrick was gone like something I had only imagined and could just vaguely recall in the bright lights and polished banisters of the station.

Grand Central was a cathedral of marble and glass, a church with no clear religious affiliation. Its spirit seemed to be in the human voice, hundreds, maybe thousands, of voices echoing throughout the waiting room. The clock on top of the information booth read 6:07, and a voice, as deep and calculating as I imagined God's to be, said, "The train to New Haven is boarding on Track 18. Train to New Haven. Track 18."

Arched windows rose up the length of each wall above the east and west balconies. Long, cylindrical chandeliers hung in the north and south corridors. The lights of the trains, fixed red eyes in the distance, stood waiting off to my left. There was no place to sit but the stairs leading to the balconies. If there had been seats, some people might have sat there in awed silence as they did in St. Patrick's Cathedral. They would have sat there, I'm certain, praying to no other God than the collective voice and mysterious movement of humanity. All around me, sound and action swirled purposefully but just beyond my exact understanding of it. All of these travelers seemed to know exactly where they were going and why. It seemed so simple watching them. Life seemed so simple. Just do what they were doing. Head home from work or head out on vacation. There was a time to catch a train, a time to return. Check your watch, read the schedule. Arrive at your destination.

San Francisco seemed no more real to me at that moment than the island of Atlantis. San Francisco was just another one of those places that I had seen in books, read about and dreamed about. I might as well be going to Venice or Paris or some Greek island. When I looked at the train schedule, the times and dates swam in a blur of black ink. Past and present, dream and wakefulness, all seemed equally unreal and aligned to some scene I watched but wasn't part of at all.

I had enough money to get a sleeping car to Chicago, but I decided to save the seventeen extra dollars and to sit up for the night. As uncomfortable as that train seat was, I felt too excited by the thought of the journey to feel stiff or cramped at all during the night. I'd never been out of New York State, except to cross the river into Pennsylvania and Shohola Falls when I was at Washington Lake Boys' Home, and I wanted to see what I could of the country, even if it was squeezed into the frame of the train window and I had to squint into a darkness that would become at times as deep as the bottom of the sea.

As the cars of the train shook their way out of Grand Central, I kept my gaze on the world that was appearing and disappearing with each tick of the wheels. Outside the station, the train halted for a few minutes in the gray-black light. Stopped in her car at the corner, a woman sat at the steering wheel, weeping like a person alone in her bedroom. No one was near her car, and she seemed unaware of the train. She didn't know or appeared not to care that she was framed in my view as if she were an actress in a silent film. The train began to move, and she continued to sit there, her eyes straight ahead, weeping openly, unashamedly.

For some reason, I wanted to hold her in sight. I didn't want to lose the memory of her but was afraid that I would. I forced myself to visualize my arrival in the West when I would remember her, remember the moment that I saw her and dreamed of entering San Francisco. If I could remember her, I thought, I could hold the past and the future together. Maybe I could hold on to the present in the process. For a moment, though, sitting on that train, I couldn't make sense of the present at all. The present seemed less real than my memories or my dreams of the future, as if it existed only between those two imagined points. But at least the past and the future could be held in the imagination. The present disappeared before you had a chance to think about it. It was lost in the living of it, it seemed.

Within seconds the woman's image was gone, the train entered a tunnel, and in the utter darkness her face became mine reflected in the glass. All I could see was my own face, dry-eyed but no less mysterious to me than hers had been. My face, a shadow in the glass, reminded me not of what the future might hold but of the past, of my face in the window of the hospital waiting room, years before as my mother fought once more to return home.

I remembered sitting in that hospital waiting room, all chrome angles and white walls, and not being able to think about anything in particular. It was like I was watching myself think. I had spent the night before dreaming about my mother but somehow the dream got confused with me being the one in the hospital room. When the doctors operated on me, I was wide awake, staring into their eyes. They cut into me and took everything out, organ by organ, until I was hollow and weightless.

That's the way I felt that afternoon in the waiting room as I stared at a painting on the wall. It was a painting by Claude Monet, dreamy and out of focus. It pictured half a dozen sailboats on a deep blue inlet. A group of sunbathers stood on the pocked white sand—men in gray coats and Panama hats and women in long beige dresses, sun bonnets, with parasols dangling at their sides. A stately old mansion perched on a dune behind the people on the beach who looked out toward the boats and the horizon. One man stood with his back facing me, and he peered intently, it seemed, at the beach, which curved like a pale dragon's tale past sails and clouds.

I remembered the painting more vividly than I recalled anything in the hospital. More vividly, I was ashamed to admit to myself, than I remembered my mother's suffering at that time. I remembered looking deeply into the painting, maybe hoping to lose myself in that soft landscape, maybe wishing to see what that man with his back turned was able to see.

The hospital overlooked the East River, and in the late afternoon sun that broke through the window in the corridor outside the waiting room I could see the waves of light play on the water. The wind blew ripples along it from the Manhattan piers to the shores of Roosevelt Island. It was the dark pools, though, that I found the most hypnotizing. Each pool was like a leaf floating on a sun-flecked river, and I watched each one as it disappeared downstream.

From that window, I could see planes angling down into Queens and kids bouncing balls in playgrounds below me, women walking poodles, and streams of yellow cabs along York Avenue. So much life appeared in that one tiny window that it took my breath away—so much happiness and indifference and sadness. How could anyone ever keep up with it all? I couldn't take my eyes away from it. Any more than I could take my eyes from the woman crying in the car. And I didn't take my eyes from that window, not even to look into my mother's room—until the sun went down and the glass turned black and reflected my own face more clearly than it had the streets below.

It was my own face that made me turn away, that made me turn, blinking, into the stark light of the waiting room. It was my mother's face, then, that I once again tried to store in my mind the way I wanted to hold that woman's in the car. If I lost them, I was afraid, there would not be enough air to breathe. So I tried, like a man desperately seeking to catch his breath, to remember. I needed to remember.

18

The train to Chicago stopped first in Albany. The trip between New York City and Albany followed alongside the Hudson River. It was wide and beautiful and to me appeared to be a more breathtaking escape route than Twain's Mississippi. I opened my great-great-grandfather's journal, which I carried in my jacket pocket, and reread the last few pages, thinking about his entry into San Francisco and my following him a century later. "On top of the crossbeam where the wood meets the slant of the roofline." That's where his story ended and mine began. That's where I was headed.

The car I was in made chirping sounds as the train shook its way along the tracks. We chugged along, a heartbeat at a time, slowing with a moaning at small towns along the way and then building speed until we became a racing pulse. The trees on the east side floated by, shades of green and brown in the rectangle of streaked glass. Occasionally the doors between cars opened and the sounds of the wheels came sweeping into my compartment in a blast of cool metallic air. Into the night the train shuddered, a sound like wings beating in the darkness.

As we got close to Albany, we passed over bridges spanning murky green streams and alongside ditches strewn with concrete and brick. We rattled by discarded railroad ties, a slough filled with gravel pits, old shoes, scrap iron, and broken bottles, past mudholes, shredded tires, twisted vines, and thousands of telephone poles and birds on the wires. It all seemed wonderful to me. In the gray morning light, the city appeared confounded and depressed by the color of the air that hung over the worn Victorian buildings—but even that uninspired city looked bright with the possibility of the road.

From Albany we headed west, passing along the lower edge of Canada, across the tail of Lake Erie, and into Detroit. It was barely light when we pulled into the station in Detroit. It seemed as if, during the night, the train had leapt to Michigan, jumping into the Midwest by magic. I had enough time before we departed from Detroit to step off the train and walk along the platform. I wrote a postcard to Nada. I had the time to write a letter if I had known what to say. But how could I explain to her what I was doing or why I had left when I didn't understand it fully myself? "I'm on my way west," I wrote. "There is something I have to do. I need to go. Please find a way of letting Fitz and Mr. Calabria know that I'm all right. I'll be back. Wait for me. I'll be back."

It made me feel like a liar because I didn't really know if I would be back or not. How could I know for certain that I would return if I didn't know all the reasons that I was going? I didn't sign the postcard, and then to be safe I put it in an envelope addressed to her so that no one else would read the card.

The ride to Chicago went through parts of Ohio and Indiana. Wheat fields stretched to the horizon and cows drifted across pastures as if they were cloud formations. I had never seen such open ground before. Everything I had known up until then had been enclosed—by apartment buildings in New York City or by the Catskill Mountains surrounding Shohola Falls. It seemed a door was opening to a wide, uncluttered room. There was more than enough air to breathe, more than enough space to disappear into forever.

The layover in Chicago was four hours. When I stepped out of Union Station into the afternoon sunlight, I realized that I had not been out of doors for over thirty-six hours. From the station I walked to Michigan Avenue. My idea of the city was shaped by Al Capone and Elliot Ness, gangsters and bootlegged liquor, but that notion soon vanished in a city that appeared larger than the slice of history created for me mainly by television shows. An icy wind blew hard and followed me around every corner I turned. Each street had its own character—five-story limestone buildings or gleaming glass high-rises. The tallest building I passed seemed taller than the Empire State Building, but it was at that moment, craning my neck to get a better look at the top, that I recalled that I had never seen the Empire State Building except in photographs.

Chicago was like an outdoor museum—scrollwork, gargoyles, and sleek towers, marble staircases spiraling toward tapered forms crisscrossed by wind bracing, all polished glass and steel girders everywhere I looked. As I walked along the crowded streets I remembered some lines of a poem by Carl Sandburg we had been forced to memorize in grade school: "Hog Butcher for the World / Tool Maker, Stacker of Wheat." I didn't much like Sandburg's poetry, even in grade school, and now it seemed even more out of place. His was not the city I saw in front of me, but I did see in those buildings some sort of precarious balance between art and commerce as if the soul of human beings and their business sense had made a pact.

I walked to Grant Park and sat across from Buckingham Fountain, watching the water spout from the sculptures. Clouds had begun to blot out the sun and the temperature dropped a few degrees. A young woman sitting by the fountain took a light jacket from her bag, stood up, looked directly into my eyes, and smiled as she put the jacket on.

"Business?" she asked.

"No, I'm not on business. I'm just traveling to San Francisco. Just roaming. Heading to visit family."

She looked at me and smiled again, this time in a way similar to how my mother did when I was a little kid and had said something she thought was funny, or like Mr. Calabria, raising his eyes in mock disbelief.

"No, no. I mean do you want to have some business with me? Business. You know . . . sex."

She wasn't much older than I was. Light brown hair, cut shorter than mine, and a pleasant, round, freckled face, not beautiful but sweet. A kind of pale skin that seemed to have seen the sun only on rare occasions. She looked like a Catholic schoolgirl, out of uniform on a school day and slightly uncomfortable about it.

Paying for sex had never entered my mind, although I used to see the prostitutes at night on Garrison Avenue in the Bronx and wonder about them. They had always seemed much older than I was, foreign and indecipherable. They dressed in high heels and tight shorts and had such a knowing, ironic glint in their eyes that they looked more like battle-weary soldiers to me than young women interested in sex. But even though the streetwalkers I saw on Garrison Avenue made me think of bombed-out buildings and war-torn cities, sex had been on my mind plenty during those years, even if paying for it hadn't been. Sex had been part of my thoughts all the time—in churches and school, on the buses and subways in the Bronx, even in hospital corridors. Not even my mother's dying could stop such daydreams. I had thought about it at times that made me feel selfish and guilty, but I had never considered paying for it. It seemed a thing for old men and ugly ones to do.

But there I was, looking into her eyes and noticing the curves of her body and after the first wave of guilt—as I thought about Nada—washed over me, all of a sudden it didn't seem like such an impossible idea. The thought of having sex with a stranger was exciting and one more part of freedom and escape, a way to be anonymous, to become someone I didn't know, maybe to find out who I might be. At least I wanted to convince myself of that, and I wanted to keep the conversation going, even if it ended up being nothing more than a flirtation. It was an odd word to use—flirtation—in thinking about a conversation with a prostitute but that's the word that was in my mind, and it probably says more about my confusion and desires than it does about the facts of the world or what was happening between us. I wasn't sure what I was doing, but I wanted to keep talking to her anyway.

I hadn't been on the road long, but I was lonely already. Lonely enough to want to disappear and come back a different person. This wasn't me talking to this girl but someone else, a man on the road to nowhere with another name and history. It felt good allowing myself to disappear. I had no responsibility for the past and no connection to the future. There was only the present to live.

"So, what do you say?" she asked. "Would you like to spend some time with me?"

I stuttered out a few disconnected sentences.

"I don't think so. My train leaves in three hours. I mean, you're very attractive and all, but I've never done this. I mean, I've done it but not in this way. I've never been in Chicago before. Do you live around here?"

Her smile widened, a beautiful, crooked-toothed grin, a look on her face like a tomboy getting ready to go skinny-dipping. This felt like a date, not a negotiation, a generous-hearted young girl trying to deflect an awkward situation with a smile that turned, after a few seconds, into an earnest expression, to tell me, it seemed, that she took both of us and the situation seriously. How could she, though? What did I mean, after all, by saying that I had never done this before and that I'd never been to Chicago? Were the two supposed to be connected? What sense did they make? If this were a date, it would have been off to an embarrassing start.

"I have a place around the corner," she said. "It's not very fancy, but it's close. What's your name?"

"Thomas Calabria." It came out as naturally as if it were my real name. Sometimes I surprised myself how readily lies sprang to my lips.

She said that I didn't look Italian, and then she narrowed her eyes slightly as if she were trying to get my face in focus.

"Are you sure you wouldn't like to come to my place?"

"No, I'm not sure of much."

That's all I had to say, I guess. She took my hand and said, "Twenty dollars. Half price because you're cute." And she led me across the busy thoroughfare, holding my hand gently like a teenage girl guiding her boyfriend toward a shady spot on a sun-scorched afternoon. We could have been walking to the candy store or going to an afternoon movie.

She had a studio apartment across from the elevated train tracks—just a kitchen big enough for two people to stand in, a closet-size bathroom and a living room with a bed, a chair, and a chest of drawers. The window in the living room had yellowed shades drawn below the edge of the sill. The glass rattled as a train pulled into the station above us.

My body shook a bit—from the cold, the pulse of the train, guilt, anticipation of what would happen next. I clenched my teeth to stop the shaking. My heart was beating fast. I thought of Nada. I couldn't imagine her doing what I was about to do, and it made me feel dishonest and disloyal. But at the same time I was visualizing this girl taking her clothes off, my hands on her breasts, her hands on me.

I couldn't think of anything to say when we crossed the threshold but "Do you have to eat standing up?"

She smiled at me again as she had in the park, and for a moment I imagined I was falling in love with her, that I would stay in Chicago, and she would change her life and mine. Like me, she had no identity—or a false one that she discarded, I guessed, at the end of work each day or had lost somewhere along the way—so why couldn't we vanish into one another, leaving not even a trace of ourselves behind? We could create new names for ourselves.

"I eat out," she said. "Or I sit on the bed."

It was depressing to think of her sitting on the bed, looking at the chipped paint on the walls and eating cereal or a piece of toast like a sick kid staying home from school on a Tuesday afternoon. Only she wasn't a kid exactly and there was no school for her to stay home from.

"Why don't we get the money out of the way?" she said, like some spirited but soft-hearted girl who says before you go into the gymnasium for the junior prom, "Why don't you kiss me now so that we get that awkwardness out of our systems and we can enjoy the evening without worrying about how we'll lead up to that moment?"

Of course, all of those fanciful thoughts didn't change the colder facts that I didn't want to face—I was hurting Nada, lying to her in what I knew would be my future silence about this girl. Hurting her even if she never found out about it. This was an exchange of money, an act of commerce, not affection or trust. I handed her two ten-dollar bills, which she put in the top drawer of the dresser, stuffing it among the kind of underwear you would expect your sister to wear, not a prostitute, a kind of ordinary Woolworth cheap white cotton that you could imagine hanging on a clothesline in Indiana.

She turned off the lamp near the bed, leaving only the bulb from the kitchen to spread a faint yellowed light around us. She took off her clothes unhurriedly and stood before me in the half-light. She was skinnier than I expected. Her legs and arms were like a young girl's. The bones of her hips jutted out and her rib cage and collarbone stood in sharp relief against her pale skin. Her breasts were almost too big for her small frame, round and upturned, the nipples hard points of darkened flesh.

I started to speak, but she looked at me and shook her head. "Shhh, just take off your clothes," she said.

I did, more clumsily and hurriedly than she had. She placed her hands on my shoulders and pushed me gently onto the bed. Bending over, she brushed her breasts against the side of my face and kissed me intently on the lips. Then she pressed her tongue into my mouth. When I pushed my tongue into hers, she held it with her teeth and drew it in farther, holding it firmly without biting it. She kissed my neck and let her tongue slide down my chest. I couldn't tell if the heat was from her tongue or my own body. As I lay there, it seemed that I could hear the hot blood rushing through me and toward her mouth. I felt like everything inside me was searching for a way to disappear.

When she got on top of me, her legs straddling mine, she placed her small hands on my shoulders, bracing herself as she moved slowly up and down and after some time faster, making muffled cries like a trapped animal, her breasts touching my lips and finally, one and then the other, in my mouth, the nipple pressing against my tongue like the tip of a finger. She arched her back and looked toward the stained and shadowed ceiling, and I came, not seeing her eyes and thinking before the pleasure had even subsided of Nada, who seemed as distant and lost to me now as my mother.

I stayed around for a few minutes afterward. But I didn't have much to say and she didn't either. We had lost interest in one another, like two people who know a date has not gone as hoped and that there would not be a second one. It seemed as if sex had changed the room, made the lamplight so bright and metallic it hurt my eyes. The anticipation had made the room so charged, and the realization had made it so empty. I saw every crack in the walls and ceiling and every stain on the bedcover. My own face in the mirror over her dresser was too familiar. I wanted to see something new in that reflection, but I saw a face that held no surprises, just disappointment. I had not lost myself or found myself either, as I had hoped.

As I left, I muttered "thank you" and gave her a kiss on the cheek. It wasn't the right thing to do, but what is the right thing to do in such a situation? What is the right form of parting after you've had sex with a stranger you will never see again? It had started off awkwardly and ended the same way. At least I stopped myself before saying "I'll call you," and walked into the welcoming silence of the hallway.

By the time I was walking down Michigan Avenue again, I felt not only guilty but stupid, too. I was even less sure what I was heading off to find, why I had left Nada, but I knew it wasn't to meet this girl in Chicago. I hadn't even found out her name. I would never know her name. Did I want to disappear completely like her or travel far enough so that I could reappear as my true self and would I even know that when I saw it? As I walked along the crowded street toward the train station, I imagined that I was invisible, slipping in and out of the fast-moving groups without being seen. Untouched. Unnoticed. Hidden from my own life. I felt like a man who has tripped on the uneven pavement in front of a crowd and has escaped the scene of his embarrassment, turning the corner to find his anonymity again. When my train pulled out, heading west, I was happy to be gone, happy to be invisible and on the road again.

19

Heading out of Illinois into Missouri, I had reached the beginning of something in me. The train crossed the Mississippi River between La-

Grange and Quincy, some miles north of Hannibal. The river had a wide, gentle look that I knew had to be a deception. The current led down to the town where my great-great-grandfather, Thomas Blankenship, had lived and dreamed and made his point of departure. I had been there, with him, in my imagination only, but I felt, crossing the Mississippi, that I too was leaving that washed-out river town and heading toward some piece of myself that had been lost.

The train glided across the windswept plains of Kansas as if it were sliding along frozen ground. When the conductor called stops for Wichita and Dodge City, I knew I was in the West of myth and legend, in the stories of Wyatt Earp, Bat Masterson, and Doc Holliday. The train hurtled through the purple sunset and into nightfall, through the Wild West of tall tale and violent history, through my childhood dreams of heroism and adventure and simple justice.

As fast as we were moving, I had never felt safer in my life. The stranger the landscape the more at home I was, the more easily I breathed. I was perfectly still and at the same instant racing across the country. It was as if I were sitting still watching the land move in front of me. I watched it all, part of the landscape but separate from it, turning the clock back from one time zone to another as I headed into the future—or was it the past? The black blur of the highway stretched out into the distance, car lights flickering like fireflies in the night to the north of the rail lines. The softly rolling hills rippled far from the lights, and the small towns were only a dream beyond them but no more real or less so than the Dalton Gang or Billy the Kid.

I was not sure why being on the train moving west made me feel so content, so protected. But I had the feeling that nothing could touch me—or even see me—as the train cut its path through the land. It was as if my daydream of invisibility in the Chicago streets had become true. It may sound crazy, but it seemed like movement erased time altogether—or slowed it down to where I could measure it like a heartbeat. A line from one of Sam Clemens's letter in my great-great-grandfather's journal kept coming back to me—"keep moving, keep your eyes open." I couldn't help but feel that the faster I moved the more weight that flew from my chest until the air that came into my lungs had an unaccustomed lightness and sweetness to it.

I also had this odd sensation that if I traveled far enough and in the right direction I'd meet up with myself like Tom Sawyer did at his own funeral. On the train, everyone I loved was gone—my mother, father, Nada—but it didn't matter because I would be gone soon too. I was no longer Tommy Blanks. I was a stranger, not connected to anyone, moving too fast for sorrow, moving too consistently for time or tragedy to catch up.

And maybe there was no way to return. Maybe the trip was all outward and not back. Perhaps that had always been true. For the time being I just closed my eyes and decided I could not say where the beginning place was until I got to the end of the road. Then perhaps I'd know where I had started and where I was meant to be.

The train pulled into the station on Wynkoop Street in Denver early the next morning, and I stretched my legs by walking down Lawrence Street to the oldest part of the city. The state capitol building looked like photographs I had seen of the U.S. Capitol. The sky was light blue and cloudless, clear enough to make you believe that you could see Pike's Peak miles away. I watched a woman count her way aloud up to the fifteenth step, holding the hand of a small red-haired boy and say, "Steven, you are exactly 5,280 feet above sea level on this step. That means you are exactly one mile above our home in Maryland here."

Listening to her, I realized that I was farther from home than I had ever been. But I wasn't sure where home was any more. I didn't know for certain if I wanted to know or if I had ever truly known. As the woman was talking to the boy, a girl in a red halter top and tight white shorts walked toward me with the kind of smile on her face that I recognized from Chicago. Even though the layover in Denver was scheduled for three hours and some of the guilt had already evaporated from the day before, I cast my eyes down, took three steps at a time, and headed back to the train station.

The southern Rockies descended into the high desert in New Mexico. There was a broad view all around, land and sky. For miles the sky was crystalline, but far off I could see reefs of clouds, and beyond them lightning cracked the horizon into white fissures. The world seems to come into focus when the spaces are so wide. There is something peaceful and frightening about such open spaces. It was like being able to see into the future. The high desert landscape wasn't desolate but various if you stared long enough (and if you had met someone, as I later did, who could point out all of the things you would likely miss seeing)—a landscape with all kinds of colors if you looked close—yellow, gold, purple, and brown. The desert flatness was broken by rabbitbrush, tumbleweed, and clusters of stunted junipers punctuating the spaces like parentheses on a wordless page. For miles on end there was nothing that my eyes were accustomed to seeing, no cars or buildings or people. Instead, red rock buttes and a few windmills and water tanks took over the view. Adobe-walled huts, the color of burned sand, were as much a part of the natural landscape as the canyons and the arroyos.

In Albuquerque there was a derailment up ahead that the conductor said would take at least thirty-six hours to fix. I had spent many a rainy afternoon as a kid reading about Taos and Santa Fe, and the layover gave me enough time to get to see them and to get back in time to catch the same train. As a kid in the Bronx, I had read everything that I could about New Mexico. I'm not sure I can explain all the reasons for my fascination with the place as a young boy—perhaps it was simply that the openness of New Mexico seemed to me so different from the walled-in Bronx. Maybe it was that my mother had gone there once as a young girl, sent to a ranch for a few weeks by her parents in the hopes that the dry air would help her recover from a case of bronchitis that threatened to turn far more serious. My interest in New Mexico in the last few years was easier to explain. The last book my mother read was Willa Cather's *Death Comes for the Archbishop*. She had read it three times in the months before she died. I hadn't the courage to read it when she was sick or immediately after she died, but in a bookstore in Denver I had bought a paperback copy.

As luck would have it—good or bad, I wasn't sure at first—I hitched a ride as soon as I got out of the station with a man who called himself a preacher. He never told me what denomination he was, but he kept saying things like "connecting to the ultimate power" and "sensing the presence of the Great Spirit." That kind of talk made me nervous, but he seemed harmless enough and, besides, right away I sensed that he knew the territory and could name the mountains and the plants and understood the people, too.

At first I didn't learn any more about where he expected his vague missionary zeal to take him than I did about his religious affiliation. I did find out, though, that he was going to Santa Fe and Taos. Sometimes things work out that way, I suppose—I mean, you want to go some place and there's a ride waiting to take you. He was on a pilgrimage, he said, that would take him in a circle through Acoma Pueblo, Canyon de Chelly, and Shiprock and then through Taos and Santa Fe and back to Albuquerque.

"C'mon, son, you're in God's hands," he said, "but I'll get you back in time to catch the train. And even if God's time and the train schedule don't match up, there's always another train west. Take the ride that fate offers—that's my motto."

So I went with Marvin the preacher—he never told me his last name—in his brand-new 1967 Pontiac Tempest to see the cathedral that Willa Cather's archbishop built in Santa Fe and the adobe home of my boyhood hero, Kit Carson, in Taos. If I had to go on a pilgrimage and suffer the threat of salvation along the way, it seemed like a small price to pay for a free ride into the western past, into my mother's past.

Marvin was only a few years older than I was but his bushy black beard made him look as if he were much older.

"I found my calling," he said, "in the jungles of Vietnam. Humping it alongside rice paddies, that's where the Great Spirit came to me."

He kept the windows of his car rolled down all the way, the hot air exploding through the car, shaping his hair and beard into a wild, dark tangle. The wind forced him to shout, a red-faced John the Baptist in the red rock country of the American West. Maybe that's why he kept the windows wide open—so that he would sound to himself like a preacher seeking to convert the multitudes, even if he was just pointing out a jackrabbit dashing across the road and speaking only to one lonely traveler. We drove on the highway that ran parallel to the Sandia Mountains until we were about an hour west of Albuquerque. Then we turned south toward Acoma Pueblo. The whole way he held an unlit joint in his fingers, occasionally putting it to his lips.

With his green eyes red-streaked from the sun and his hair matted into knots from the wind, he looked as stoned as one otherwise conscious man could get by the time we reached Acoma Sky City, but in truth he was more sober and clear-headed than I was. As we approached the mesa that Acoma sat upon, he took the unlit joint and put it into his shirt pocket.

"I used to smoke a lot of pot in 'Nam," he shouted into the wind. "I mean a lot of weed, you know. The way some guys might smoke cigarettes, I'd smoke pot. Ten, maybe twelve joints a day. Sometimes I'd light one from the roach of another, sort of chain smoke them, see. I could barely feel my own skin over there I was so high most of the time. That's the way I liked it. I didn't want to feel anything over there, let alone my own skin. God Almighty, everybody over there was looking to get out of their skin if they could.

"About two months before my tour was up, I was sitting in an open field with Charlie Whitegoat, one of the guys in my company. Some of the guys called him Skinwalker because he was an Indian but also because he was able to disappear in the jungle when we were on patrol. He could make himself invisible. He was there and we could see him, but the enemy couldn't, you understand? I know it sounds impossible and insane, but it's true. He could make himself invisible to his enemies.

"People died all around him for months and months, but no bullets ever came close to him. He could walk out in the middle of a firefight, and the bullets that were headed toward him would bend away in another direction or drop at his feet. I liked Charlie, but maybe I liked being around him because deep down I hoped his magic would rub off on me. Some guys started to hate him, though, I think. Sometimes people hate someone who's blessed, you know what I mean? Sometimes they want to see a man who they think is too lucky suffer misfortune. I think I started to feel a little that way in my own heart. Without saying it aloud to myself, I think I began to wish for bad luck to find him. It's natural sometimes in a place like Vietnam to hope that bad luck strikes someone else, even someone you like—in a place like that, you figure that there's a certain amount of bad luck and the more people it strikes around you, the greater the odds, in the long run, that it won't be you.

"Then one afternoon it happened. The guys were spread out all over the field in twos and threes. We were on our way back to base. The war would be over for a week. I was dreaming about lying in a hammock on China Beach, not worrying about being killed. Charlie and I were resting against our packs, handing a joint back and forth, when I heard a shot. It was like one note of a bell. No, it was more like a puff of air, to tell you the truth. Like somebody exhaling real quickly. At first I thought it came from Charlie, but he never made a sound. The bullet hit him in the middle of his forehead. He didn't even have a chance to look surprised, just sort of struck dumb, the same dumb, stoned expression he had on his face a second before. I got down and everyone started firing their weapons toward the tall grass. It was like that one puff of air had unloosed all the sound and fury in the world that was bottled up. Guys started screaming and cursing and firing round after round toward something they couldn't see.

"I reached over to Charlie and touched his face, but I couldn't feel anything. It was like my fingers were numb. My body was so numb it wasn't even a part of me anymore. I looked into Charlie's eyes, but he was gone. I don't mean dead. I mean he had disappeared, vanished into thin air. His body was there, but he was invisible, finally and for certain.

"It didn't hit me right away, but gradually I realized that I had let Charlie slip through my fingers. I started to wonder if I had wished enough bad luck on him to kill him. If I had cared enough about him or had enough guts, I might have wished him the same luck that I wanted for myself.

"All he'd ever been to me was a ghost. He had been invisible to me. I didn't realize that until he was dead. Right then I decided that the kind of numbness I felt in 'Nam I didn't want to feel anymore. Even if it meant not protecting myself from bad luck. I decided at that moment, with Charlie's empty body lying next to me, that there were worse things than bad luck.

"I guess I came out here to see if I could find Charlie's spirit in this place."

So we headed past Acoma Pueblo, a village perched on a mesa four hundred feet above the seven thousand-foot-high desert floor, Marvin searching for a ghost and me not really knowing why I was there with him, but recognizing that his war could be mine too. I couldn't enter Mr. Calabria's war or Weiry's, but Marvin's story could become mine.

The hours passed. Storm clouds began to fall like streamers in the eastern sky. We parked on the west ridge of the Canyon de Chelly, and as we followed the rocky path down into the valley, a breeze pushed us from behind. When we reached the bottom, it was like a huge crack had opened in the earth. The walls of the canyon rose up over a thousand feet in places. Sounds echoed. The very nature of sound changed. It deepened and held its place in the cool air. Parts of the canyon were wide, but in some places the walls were no more than fifty yards apart.

Marvin seemed to know a lot about the canyon. He told me that the name de Chelly was a corruption of a Spanish word that meant "inside the rocks." Inside the rocks was exactly the way to describe where we were. As we walked down into the heart of the canyon, the temperature dropped a few degrees and sounds changed timbre again. Every sound felt as if it came from inside of me, a voice rattling inside my own skeleton. Black streaks, what Marvin called canyon varnish, painted the walls and cliffs along with pictographs made by the Navajos and their predecessors, the Anasazis. "They painted them with a mixture of gypsum and yucca leaf," Marvin said as he led me toward a stand of cottonwoods next to a stream. We sat in the shade of the trees, listening to the water run over the red rocks, and Marvin pointed toward one of the shadow lines that cut into the cliffs.

"For the Navajos," he said, "this is the Garden of Eden. Can you believe that? The Navajos once thought, and may still think, for all I know, that this place was the center of the universe, the place where their ancestors emerged from the lower world into the light. Once, before the Spaniards and then Kit Carson led their soldiers in here, they thought this canyon was impenetrable, a sacred ground that could never be touched by their enemies. See that peach tree over there? That's what's left of their orchards after Carson's men got through burning them."

He held his palms up like some sort of holy man about to begin a chant and closed his eyes.

"You can barely feel the wind," he said. "You know the Navajos have more than thirty ways to say wind? Their language is like Chinese. The meaning of a word is changed by the pitch of the voice. I'm going to learn their language, study with a medicine man. Maybe I'll stay right in this country. Maybe Whitegoat will find me.

"We're all looking for something, but whatever it is, it will probably get around to finding us if we just sit still long enough. The Navajos believe to keep safe and holy that they should stay in the territory between four sacred mountains—Mount Blanco, Mount Taylor, the San Francisco Peaks, and Mount Hesperus. For the Navajos, the land has spirit. For them, there's no religion as we usually think of it as white men. Everything is part of the Navajo's religion—his hogan, his fields, his livestock, the sky above him. It's all holy. The natural world is a church."

When the sun began to sink in the western sky, we walked deeper into the shadows of the canyon until we came upon a sheep ranch. A man stood by the weathered wood of the corral stroking the neck of a horse and leaning in such a way that made it seem that he was whispering some secret into its ear.

"Ya ta hey," Marvin said as we drew near the man.

The man smiled and said nothing. He was a head shorter than I was but barrel-chested and muscular. His cheekbones and eyes looked Asian, his brown skin darker than the bronzed earth at his feet.

"We're looking for someone," Marvin said. "Well, looking for the home of someone who might have once lived here. Charlie Whitegoat. He died a few years back in the war."

The sun slipped almost fully behind the cliffs as the man waited to see if Marvin was finished speaking, looking off into the distance at the charred remains of a hogan, probably a *chindli* hogan, Marvin later explained to me, a house in which someone has died.

"Those houses are usually abandoned or burned," he said. "Death and everything connected to it is repulsive to the Navajos, a dark wind one shouldn't breathe."

The man's eyes had a pale fire in them that flashed against his brown skin.

"Nobody comes here except on purpose," he said. "Charlie Whitegoat never lived in the canyon. But he had an uncle here, a third cousin, some said, of Manuelito. A few around here thought he was a skinwalker, that he changed shapes when he wanted to, but he was just a man who went to live among the Bilgaana in California somewhere. He went like a white man to find gold and maybe he did."

He waited to see if we had anything to say and then he pointed to the east.

"Charlie Whitegoat lived up around Shiprock somewhere. I heard he went to fight in a Bilgaana war and disappeared. Head north over the Chuskas to Shiprock. That's where you'll find his people."

Early the next morning Shiprock floated before me like a ghost boat on the flat desert air. We bedded down in its shadow. The diamond-shaped head of the dragon lay to the west of the Little Dipper, and a new star blinked into existence, it seemed, every time I closed and opened my eyes. I realized as I stared at the sky for a while that most of the stars I was gazing at were just dreams of the past, light floating toward me from planets that were gone for centuries, memories coming to me in the form of light, no different, perhaps, than my own imagining of the past. But the light from those stars seemed as much a part of the world as the stars themselves. In them, the past seemed real. What would the present be without such light? Like those stars, we were made of light coming from the past and the present, and none of us could fully separate the two.

There were nothing but a few lamps from the town of Shiprock to blur the sharpness of the starlight in the endless blackness. The sky was wide enough to change the meaning of time, and I lay there staring into it for minutes or hours—it was hard to know. But after a while sleep seeped into my blood-stream like a drug. Every part of my body became heavy and numb, and I fell into sleep like a man learning how to die.

I dreamed of Charlie Whitegoat and Marvin in Vietnam. I was with them on patrol. The jungle we trudged through was dark and unfamiliar, stands of narrow limbless trees like prison bars separating us from the mud-choked stream we tracked. The familiar and the unfamiliar merged, as often happens in dreams, and the jungles became the rocky stream of Shohola Falls. It was Shohola Falls, but it was filled with terror. The rocks moved under our feet, and the water was more a sucking green slime than a liquid. Whitegoat stumbled and fell headfirst. Before I could bend down, he was gone—chest, waist, calves, boots—into the thick ooze. In front of me, in the shadows, was a dim figure that looked familiar. As I walked toward the shadows, I saw it was my mother. Her head was down, chin resting on her collarbone. When I got within a few feet of her, she looked up and took one step forward. Expressionless, she took another step and, like Whitegoat, disappeared into the ooze before I could even reach my hand out to her.

I turned behind me, but Marvin was no longer there either. He had disappeared, and Nada had taken his place. She had a smile on her face. I stepped backward to reach her, but she kept drifting farther and farther away from me, drifting up to the high plateau of Acoma. As I stepped back into the darkness to grasp her hand, I slipped and fell, but there was no solid ground to fall onto, just a dark space, a seemingly neverending darkness.

I woke up, falling toward the muck or into some mysterious, endless space, with my heart and stomach rising up as I went down, catching myself before my face touched the ground. My eyes opened wide to the sheer eastern cliff of Shiprock and then adjusted to the hot lights strung out across the sky.

I lay there until the sun licked the edges of the horizon and the wind purred from the north. Marvin stretched under his blanket. He stood up and folded his bedding.

"Come on, it's time to get you back to your train."

We rode through Taos and Santa Fe. The trip wasn't long, but it gave me enough time to dream of Nada, dark-skinned as a Navajo or the bride of Kit Carson, and to think of my mother as I finished reading *Death Comes for the Archbishop*. As Marvin drove, unlit joint hanging from his half-opened lips, I examined Cather's novel as if it were a map to my own heart, reading over and over again the last chapter, which describes the archbishop's peaceful and noble death and his burial in the shadow of the building he willed into existence. The young priest who attends the sick archbishop voices his fear that Latour will catch his death of cold, but Latour laughs and says, "I shall not die of a cold, my son. I shall die of having lived."

My mother, too, had died of having lived. How could one manage that, I wondered, being happy with the world that was offered? Being content with the story that fate or chance or God concocted? How did one find home, recognize it for certain, and not feel compelled to look further? Contentment was a mystery to me. My mother's. Nada's. Even Marvin was a mystery. He seemed content to drive me in my circle. He seemed content to search for something he could not name, as if happiness came from unanswered questions, not answered ones.

We had to race back to Albuquerque to get to the train station before it left that evening for San Francisco. Marvin never once mentioned Whitegoat on our way back. He parked his car and walked with me to the gate of the train station, like an older brother sending a younger one off to college.

"Where now?" I asked him.

"I'll be back in Shiprock," he said. I realized at that moment that Marvin had not done any preaching to me after those first few minutes we had been together in the car. I couldn't figure out if in the circle we had traveled he had followed me or I had followed him. I sensed, though, that Marvin and I were more alike than I had ever suspected. We both were looking for ghosts from our pasts, and I wondered if I would have any more luck than he had in finding mine.

"I'll be in Shiprock," he said. "I think I'll spend my time there."

The train was waiting at the station, and as I found my seat and looked out the window I saw Marvin standing beside his car, looking in my direction, smiling. I wondered then if it were possible to live a life in which one could be solitary and part of everything at the same time, in the same instant willing to die and finding a way to live?

20

The train to San Francisco ran through the center of Arizona, into a heat that was a vapor, beading up on the windows, a heat that waited to attach itself with fierce energy to your skin and lungs if you were foolish enough to step into it. It was a heat that made it hard to breathe. People all around me dozed. Families with small children and elderly couples. Soldiers heading home, I supposed, from boot camp one last time before they left for war. They reminded me that the war was part of me, too. It was inside of me, even if it was thirteen thousand miles away. These soldiers, only a few years older than I was, some maybe the same age, looked lost already, as if they had been there and back in their dreams so many times that they had worn themselves out, made themselves older than they ever expected to be. Their eyes were blank and defeated. They made me glad not to know exactly where I was heading or precisely why. I knew for certain, though, that I was headed away from school, the draft, and everything connected to the government and its knowledge of me. For the time being, I didn't exist. I was disappearing into the West. I wasn't sure if I was Tommy Blanks or Thomas Blankenship. White or black. Running away or toward. Whoever I was, the government would find it difficult to hunt me down and make me a part of its war. Like Whitegoat, I was a ghost, and as long as I kept moving, the government would never know I was there.

The train hurtled through the desert and slowed down as we approached the old part of Las Vegas, allowing me to squint into the bright bulbs of the city. The Strip was a twisting ribbon of electric lights, enough power to blot out the night sky and make people forget to sleep. There was no sun or moon, no clocks or time. It was an artificial planet of whirring machines and neon. The train stopped long enough for me to walk into one of the casinos downtown, smell the stale air, and put a five-dollar chip down on number 17 on the roulette table. I walked back to the train with $165 squeezed into the pages of my great-great-grandfather's journal.

Outside Las Vegas, the dark came back like some cautious wild animal. When I closed my eyes against the blackness, all I saw was Nada, her wide gray eyes. The expression on her face told me that I had hurt her by not being brave enough to stand still. And I could hear myself saying to her, over and over, "If I could, I'd be who you think I am." Staying demanded so much more energy than leaving, and I was exhausted. Nada never seemed to get tired. She never seemed to lose heart. My heart felt like a lead weight.

As the train crossed the border into California, her eyes stared into mine, looking sadly at me as if she felt pity for a friend who ran not from her or school, not from the shading of her skin or the bullying of Adam Delano and Brother Boniface, but from something near and inescapable.

The train pulled into Barstow at sunrise. Barstow was the sort of small town in which kids spent most of their lives dreaming of ways to leave, dreaming of ways never to return. They were there, some of them, still up from the night before, leaning against cars and looking wistfully at the train as it teased its way slowly across the back roads of the town, away from the hardware stores and gas stations, past the discarded tires and rusted barrels, and out into the pale emptiness that surrounded the place.

Once out of Barstow, the train headed north toward Bakersfield and San Francisco. I fell into a troubled sleep for a short time and dreamed of Nada. I sat with her in the living room of my apartment in the Bronx—books were stacked all around me in the room, on shelves and in high piles alongside the chairs and sofa. I was half hidden by the books. Next to me on the sofa lay a copy of *Huckleberry Finn* and my great-great-grandfather's journal. Nada was telling me calmly that she couldn't see me any more. She wouldn't wait any longer for me. It was clear to me that she didn't need me any more, that she had found a way to imagine her life without me. I could see myself crying in my sleep, an anguished sort of sadness that feels true and unusual. I awoke with a start and felt sharply the sorrow that had taken me in my dream. I touched my cheek to see if there were any tears because I had remembered shedding them so freely. They had felt real as any wakeful tears. My cheeks were dry, but my stomach had the same ache that I recalled from the dream.

"Are you okay, man?" A hand touched my shoulder. At the stop in Barstow a kid, probably a year or two younger than I was, had taken the seat next to mine.

His name was Welcome William Ward, and I had never met anyone quite like him. First of all, his actual first name was Welcome. It wasn't a nickname or some private family joke. When Welcome was born, his father had been a fifty-six-year-old textile mill worker in LaGrange, Georgia, a town of antebellum mansions and tarpaper shacks on the banks of the Chattahoochee River just across from Alabama. His mother had been forty-seven, and they had given up on the chance of having children, assuming that their nightly prayers had not reached God's ears. So, when their baby was born, they wanted to tell God, the baby, and the world how much they appreciated this miracle. When the baby was baptized, Mr. Ward, still with factory lint clinging to his scalp in patches almost the same color as the tufts of dark gray hair that draped over his ears, shouted, "Welcome, Lord, Welcome!" His mother and father had waited and prayed all of those years, but they weren't prepared for the flesh and blood of rearing a child.

Over the years, as he was growing up, Welcome drifted away from the back yard and got lost on the dirt roads off Red Line Alley, where the blacks who

lived there sat on the front porches of houses balanced precariously on cin-
derblocks. William regularly got into fights and skipped school. He forgot to
go to church and rode his bike through the neighbors' rose gardens. His parents seemed to know that he didn't mean any harm. He just didn't act like the
rest of the boys on Callaway Street. As Welcome got older, his mother and father seemed to him like a country farmer and his simple wife in a children's
storybook who learn that not getting what you wished for might be a stroke
of luck.

All of this Welcome told me before I had fully awakened from my dream.
Then he said, "You sure you all right? You looked like a troubling dream had
taken ahold of you. I've had those before. They don't mean too much, I don't
think. Although it's smart to be careful after you've had one, at least for a time."

While he said this, in a southern accent that dripped honeyed vowels,
every *o* and *a* hanging onto time with a sad leisureliness, he loosened his green
tie and unbuttoned the collar of his starched white shirt. He took off his sport
coat and folded it neatly in his lap.

"I like to dress when I ride the train. Look presentable, you know?"

He looked to be a year or two younger than I was. He couldn't have
passed for much more than sixteen years old, even in a suit. He was as skinny
as one of the birch saplings on the path to Shohola Falls. His bright red hair
was the same shade as the setting sun, and it exploded, I found out later, every
which way over his ears and forehead when he wasn't wearing enough Vitalis
to coat the axle of a truck. He had freckles that traveled from his cheeks to his
ears, floating upon the sort of white skin that always seemed to be blushing.
He looked a little like Tom Sawyer grown up to be a mad scientist, light blue
eyes the color of china and as wide as tea saucers.

"Where ya headed?" he asked but continued talking before I could answer.
"I'm going to San Francisco for a while. I've heard a lot about the place. It's
the kind of place where kids go to be around their own kind. Not much com-
panionship in Barstow. I'm going to slip away for the time being. I guess you
could say I'm on the run, and San Francisco seems to be as good a spot as any
to get lost in. What about you?"

I wasn't sure at first if I shouldn't just lie and say I was headed to Los Angeles, but for some reason I told the truth.

"I'm going to San Francisco, too. I have some stuff to find out about my
relatives, and that's the last place I know that they were. Or maybe I'm just on
the run like you. It's hard to tell exactly."

"Well, maybe we should be on the run together," he said. "We may can develop a partnership. Even outlaws need some company."

So Welcome William Ward and I became traveling companions. I found out that he wasn't younger than I was. He was a little more than a year older. He had turned nineteen the week before and had graduated from LaGrange High School that past August, a little behind schedule because of a fight in a chemistry class that sent a tray of test tubes and a Bunsen burner crashing to the floor. We had talked for a few hours on the train that day. Mostly, I'd listened to him. I had drifted off to sleep when he nudged me awake. My eyes opened to the cold window glass against my forehead and the desert holding itself like a lunar landscape in the gathering darkness.

"Can you keep a secret?" he whispered. "First, what do you think of the war in Vietnam? I need to know that before I tell you anything."

"I think it's a damn mess. And I feel sorry for the guys over there."

"Okay, then. I'm on the run from the draft board. I guess I should be in Canada, but it knots up my insides to think about living in another country. San Francisco may not be Georgia, but it's still part of America, right? I'll still be an American there, maybe not a patriotic one, but I'll still be an American. I'd be ashamed not to be an American. I've shamed my parents enough not going to war. I think it would kill them if I was a foreigner, to boot."

I said I guessed San Francisco was still part of America and I supposed he would still be an American citizen as long as he stayed there, and we headed off together.

The train pulled into the Oakland depot, and we got on a bus that took us across the Bay Bridge and to the Ferry Building on Market Street in San Francisco. We walked west toward Golden Gate Park, out of the business district, and onto the winding, fogbound streets. North Beach was alive with crowds of people, signs flashing for Carol Doda, the queen of striptease, and men in clownish hats waving people into the clubs like carnival barkers lost in the bright sunlight.

We passed City Lights, the bookstore of my dreams, the bookstore of Kerouac and free-falling escape, and then we turned onto Polk Street as the fog lifted and a row of two-story houses appeared before us like flashes of golden light jutting through the clouds. Each house was a rainbow of colors. One, in particular, was an artist's dream and a painter's nightmare, with scrollwork and arches and columns painted yellow and blue and green and orange.

Welcome looked over at me, "What is it, a house or a painting? I've never seen anything in Georgia like it. This city has more colors than I've ever seen outside of a picture book."

We didn't end up finding an apartment in San Francisco but in Berkeley, a college town across the bay. I had more in common with Welcome than I at first thought. Like him, I had never seen any place like San Francisco—or Berkeley, for that matter. They were surprising in their own ways. San Francisco was nothing like New York City. There were no tall apartment buildings that shut out the sun. Instead the city opened itself to the sky and water. San Francisco seemed to be on the edge of the world, and it was hard to imagine anything beyond it.

The city was the end of something, surely, a place bursting through the currents of fog as gracefully as a dolphin playing in the waves. San Francisco stood at the other side of the continent from Shohola Falls, as far away as it could be without sending me across an ocean. In every way, it seemed to be the opposite of my hidden world at Shohola Falls. The magic of San Francisco was its very openness. Its mystery lay in its bustling frankness and unselfconscious beauty. It was all sky and diffused light, mixing Victorian charm and utopian craziness as if they were meant to be part of one another. My first impression was that the streets were filled with young people, long hair reaching below their shoulders, dreamy-eyed kids about my age wearing tie-dyed shirts and sandals. And music seemed to come from every window and storefront. I felt like a pilgrim who had stumbled onto a celebration. The city was alive with its own sense of being the destination at the end of many roads.

And that's the way I'll always see San Francisco—the way it seemed to me then and still does—a flash of brightness and color, streets rising breathlessly toward the clouds, the wind made of salt spray and sunlight, a city of past and present, dream and truth, a memory almost before it was an experience. It was one of those places—like Shohola Falls—that I knew before I even saw it.

Welcome and I trudged up and down the hills of the city that first day, looking for a place to stay, but either the apartments were too expensive or the agents were reluctant to rent to two teenagers, even when one of them had on a sports coat and a green tie. We had better luck in Berkeley. The rents were cheaper and, because of the university, there were more young people, and most of them were by far more disheveled looking than we were.

We found an apartment on Ashby Avenue, right off of Shattuck, one of the main streets that ran north and south, cutting a line from the alleyways of Oakland to the tree-lined edges of the Berkeley campus. The apartment building was a one-story pink stucco place that looked more like a storage shed than anything I had ever seen people renting as living space in New York City. There were eight studio apartments, all exactly alike, with a kitchen large enough for two thin people, a bathroom slightly larger than a closet, and a living room that had a pullout bed. I had the bed on Mondays, Wednesdays, and Fridays. Welcome had it the other days. We weren't afraid of touching each other exactly, but he had a sleeping bag that was probably more comfortable than the bed. The apartments branched off the main corridor of the building, and in a short time we got to know everyone who lived with us. Our apartment was in the front, one window facing the constant flow of traffic on Ashby Avenue and the other facing west, looking directly into the alley between our apartment and a three-story Victorian house next door that had a rainbow-colored sign on the front door: "House of Enlightenment and Good Karma."

Toward the end of our first week in Berkeley, Welcome and I walked down Telegraph Avenue, past a gauntlet of street people asking for handouts and dealers whispering, "Want to get high? I got some premium dope." When we got the Sproul Plaza at the entrance to the south side of campus, a crowd was gathered around a man with a thick nest of curly black hair tied in a ponytail and a fantastic beard flowing wide and long over what looked to me like a Bedouin's robe. It was hard to see anything of his face entangled in all the hair. His words flew liked birds flushed from a jungle.

"My name is X Swami X and I'm called here to start the Revolution," he said. "I'm here today because my mother didn't breastfeed me long enough," he paused, scanning the crowd sitting on the steps of the plaza. "She stopped abruptly when I was twelve. Without any warning she just stopped. I could never get used to the milk they sold in stores. It made me a malcontent."

He started to dance up and down the steps, sort of like a Fred Astaire from another planet, his robes floating in the breeze he created, and he pulled a sheaf of papers from the depths of his right pocket. They looked as weathered and frayed as it was possible for pages to be and still remain intact.

"Here, children, we have the history of the world." He shook the sheets of paper like a tambourine.

"I'm writing the oral history of the world, and that's the story of Revolution. Most of our history books are stories about civilizations. Civilization is a pus-filled plague. Our civilization is worse than the Black Death that destroyed half of Europe. Civilization in America kills three-quarters of the people before they have time to reach puberty.

"Those of us who haven't been killed off, who haven't had our souls sucked out of us by television and schoolrooms, need to be ready to die at any time. Expect to die at any time. That's the only way to live."

I tried to imagine what brought this X Swami X to this place at this time. My own reason for being there was complicated enough, I suppose, but it seemed simple to me compared to his possible reasons for ending up pacing across Sproul Plaza in front of me and fifty or sixty other people sitting on the steps. He was a clown, but he was something else, too.

"Who wants to eat their synthetic food?" he shouted. "Who wants their Ring Dings and their Cheerios and their Twinkies? Who wants their refrigerators and Chevrolets? What will you give up to live free? Will you get rid of your Timex and your color television?"

For a minute I got a little worried that he was going to call on me—third seat, third step—as if it were a class and this were a quiz. Okay, Mr. Blanks, are you ready to die? What will you give up—love, hope, the past, the future—to be free? Nada? The memory of your mother's death? The safe world of anonymity and escape? As much as he sounded like a familiar schoolmaster, he was another species entirely. He was the clown in a Shakespeare play. Henry David Thoreau at an Alcoholics Anonymous meeting. An actor playing the part of a mad scientist who accidentally walked onto the staging of a high school version of *Our Town*.

"Let's blow up the factories and the schools to start with. Let's make them all into parks. People's Park can be everywhere. Every factory is an insult to our right to sunshine and pure air. Every school is an affront to our freedom of expression. This place behind me is a swamp of lies."

He pointed his arm over the heads of the crowd. "They don't tell you one word of truth in those buildings. It is the same old lies about who owns what and how you can get a piece of it. But who owns the water? The air? The forests and the mountains, the sun and the stars? The government, and this school is part of that government, would have you believe that they own all you can breathe. I have a friend who says that she never wants to own more than she can carry away on her back. How much can you carry away with you right now? If you don't leave it behind, it will kill you.

"It's no different than escaping from Alcatraz. Every kid in every grade school and high school in this country is a political prisoner. They should all be set free. Everyone with a draft card is a political prisoner. Burn down every school and toss the draft cards into the blaze. Then dance and make love. If we get out of the people's way and leave them alone, if the government disappears, if the pigs stay in their pens, and the storm troopers go on a permanent vacation to Las Vegas or Disneyland, maybe everyone will just let their hair grow and make love, watch their dope and their gardens and their hair grow, and make love.

"Remember this, you smiling potheads, advocating the violent overthrow of the government of the United States is a crime. But actually overthrowing it is nothing but a revolution."

As he spoke, smoke rose up alongside him and curled along the steps and into our eyes, making them smart. For a moment, I thought it was a wonderful special effect. Talk about revolution and make the smoke appear like a gossamer curtain on a stage, let the smoke burn our throats and nostrils just enough to compel us to pay attention. But if it was a stage effect, it was part of a production larger than someone like X Swami X could master, I knew even as I imagined doves being pulled out of his sleeves and flying off into the smoky sky.

Down Bancroft Way, the wide avenue that hugged the south side of the university campus, a line of helmeted Berkeley police—all blond-haired and broad-shouldered, all over six feet two, all under twenty-five years old—came in a phalanx that stretched across the road. At first, watching the police march down Bancroft Way from the heights to the west was like viewing a movie. It seemed no more real than seeing a hundred police with billyclubs and shields in a dream. Everyone in the crowd stood frozen—apparently as hypnotized as I was. We all stood there as if we were waiting patiently to see what would happen next on the screen in front of us. The smoky arcs of tear gas canisters crisscrossed in front of the police like fizzled fireworks on the Fourth of July. It was as if we were all there to watch a parade.

Then, as if an explosion had occurred, everyone spun into movement, and the world was a blur of people running and shoving one another past Sather Gate, the entrance to Sproul Plaza, and out onto the traffic of Bancroft Way. The cars came to a screeching halt. This was California, I realized, where drivers stopped as soon as a pedestrian stepped into the roadway. Even in those troubled times, there was this California etiquette. In New York City, the dead bodies would have piled up in front of the student union building. It had always seemed to me that drivers in New York City took it as a personal affront when someone stepped off the sidewalk onto their sacred ground. But here, amid the tear gas, there was a sort of courtliness.

Screams and shouts merged with the smell of chemicals in the air. As the crowd started to run in all directions into the heart of the campus and out onto Telegraph Avenue, the police broke ranks and charged after them. I felt swept along by smoke and bodies, fueled by fear, and hardly able to get a fix on what street I ran along until I saw Welcome in front of me darting in and out of the moving crowd. I tried to call out to him but didn't have enough breath to get the words out. So I kept my eyes on him as if he were a light in a dense fog and I had no other marker to tell me where to go. I thought I had found a way to escape the fierce complication of the world. I had left the riot at the Boys' Home behind. I had left Nada and my mother behind. But the world had caught up with me, swept me up like a tornado.

After a few minutes I could see that we were going south on Telegraph and angling toward Bowditch. We were approaching People's Park, and I sensed, even as I kept on in the same direction, that it wasn't a good idea to end up there. Everyone in Berkeley knew, even after a few hours in the town, that the city officials were searching for any excuse they could find to remove the squatters who had taken over the park and made it a little city of tents and sleeping bags, cardboard huts and campfires. When we cut across Bowditch onto Dwight Street, the crowd of people in the park had already gotten so large that the grassy area couldn't hold them all. I caught up to Welcome and touched his elbow.

"What the hellfire shit and goddamn is going on?" he said.

It wasn't really a question, even though the intonation was there, so I didn't waste my breath answering. Around us stood hundreds of students and street people, panting but still, as if this were a game of ringolevio in the Bronx and we all had reached the sanctuary of base.

The police appeared on the rise to the north, but nobody moved. Even the police stopped. It got quiet enough to hear the ticks of time. And then there was a moment in which all silence turned to sound and all stillness into structureless movement. The crowd became a rushing stream, and we were pulled by its current onto Haste Street. I had enough time to smile at the irony, and even enough to decide not to nudge Welcome to look at the street sign, before the press of human bodies flared out in all directions, toward alleyways and back yards and into the roadway itself.

Welcome and I ran, too, and were again separated by the crowd. I spent much of the late afternoon searching for him. I hid in alleyways and ran alone down streets that were usually crowded. I ran until dusk turned into darkness. Windows all along Telegraph Avenue were shattered. Homemade barricades, made of old chairs and trashcans, blocked roadways. Blood dripped from walls and bonfires burned around the city. In the flickering darkness, people ran in small groups, and occasionally a police car screeched to a stop, and someone was thrown against a parked car or down onto the pavement.

When I got back to our apartment on Ashby Avenue, there were no lights on and Welcome was not there. I went out early the next morning looking for him. Bulldozers were churning up the gardens in People's Park, and by the time I circled back in late afternoon an eight-foot fence encircled it. A large crowd had gathered across the street from the park, and Alameda County sheriff's deputies in blue jumpsuits, looking as skittish as U.S. Army paratroopers who had just landed in the middle of a Vietcong-held village, were holding shotguns tightly against their chests. Someone in the crowd threw a piece of brick, and then a bottle, flung by someone on a nearby rooftop, exploded at the foot of one of the deputies. Then the sound of shotguns merged with screams and broken glass.

When it was all over—and I didn't find this out until I read it in the paper the next day—one man had been killed, his stomach torn apart by pellets and another blinded. Many others had been shot, beaten, and arrested. I still didn't know where Welcome was. All I knew for certain was that the fury of the world had once again found me.

21

W hen he did return to the apartment, two days later, his blue eyes were white with excitement and his red hair knotted with grass and dirt. I was sitting near the front window, and he came in with the Berkeley Barb in his hand, saying, "Listen to this!" He read sentences out of order, jumping from one paragraph to another: "We need to make Telegraph Avenue a strategic free territory for revolution. . . . Students must destroy the senile dictatorship of adult teachers and bureaucrats. . . . The people of Berkeley must arm themselves and learn the basic skills and tactics of self-defense and street fighting. . . . Unite with other movements throughout the world to destroy this motherfucking racistcapitalistimperialist system. . . . We need to establish a drug distribution center and marijuana cooperative."

He looked up breathless and smiled.

"Just calm down a second. Take a breath, and before you read me every slogan for the brave new unracistcapitalistimperialist world," I said, "could you tell me where you've been? And try to remember that you're a small-town southern boy who still likes grits and pronounces the word racist with seven syllables."

"Of course, of course, you're right. I guess I'm a little excited. Seven syllables? Five at the most."

He raked his hand through his matted hair and sent grass and dirt spraying onto the floor.

"These last few days have been. Well, I don't know how to explain them," he said. "It seems like I spent most of the time in this girl's apartment, although I'm not sure if it was the girl's apartment or if she was just visiting a friend. It was hard to figure that stuff out the last couple of days. But she was an awfully pretty girl, I can tell you that. People came in and out of the place like it was the post office back in LaGrange. I may have been a tad confused, though, because someone gave me some LSD and all I can remember for certain is listening to The Who play 'I'm Free' and Janis Joplin sing 'Piece of My Heart.' You know something, Tommy, that girl can sing. I mean she can sing till you think the top of your head is flying off."

"So that's what you've been doing while I thought you were arrested or dead, tripping out on Janis Joplin?"

I was only teasing him, of course, but he got such a sad, guilty expression on his face that I started to apologize myself.

"I'm just glad you're back, safe and sound."

"And I got us both jobs," he said, the wide-toothed grin invading his face again.

We started working the next day, Welcome at Moe's Records and me at Cody's Books, a few blocks from one another on Telegraph Avenue. I needed to have some money while I tried to decide how to spend my time. Time, it

172 | SHOHOLA FALLS

seemed, I had plenty of to spend. Each day I said I'd get to San Francisco the next day to find the second part of the journal, but I didn't want the adventure of Berkeley to end. What the riot had left me with was the old stillness, the feeling that the world might be kept at bay if I just stayed quiet enough, kept to the shadows. I didn't want to pull myself from it for anything that would change my course at that moment or my life there. In Welcome, I felt as if I had found a brother, despite his age, a younger brother, with all the innocence and loyalty and passion of blood. In those months, the journal became a book that I loved so much that I didn't want it to end. I wanted the anticipation of a conclusion more than I wanted to discover what was actually in the final pages. So I spent my time writing to Nada, living each day listening to Welcome read passages from the *Barb* and Janis Joplin singing the heartbreaking blues.

I always had to smile when I walked into Moe's records and Welcome was there at the front counter, his name tag pinned over his heart—WEL-COME—as if it were a greeting for customers. It was strange how for a time Berkeley seemed to make Welcome more himself not less so. He didn't lose his innocence. It seemed to get stronger. He would come home from work and discuss the Revolution as if Moe's records were ground zero.

Most of the time at night there would be six or seven people crammed into our tiny apartment. Welcome and I were the only ones with name tags. He had his and I usually wore mine. It said "T. Blankenship/Cody's Books." For some reason I didn't want to use my old name when I got to Berkeley. So I used a false one or a new one or, I guess maybe, the true one. But just as I said at the outset, figuring out the truth isn't always as easy as it might at first seem.

Sometimes we sat around and smoked pot, drank the sweetened ice tea that Welcome made by the gallon, and played a card game called "Hearts." The object of the game was to get as few points as possible or to get them all, to "shoot the moon." Each heart was worth a point, and the Queen of Spades was worth thirteen. All of the cards were dealt out, and then each person passed three cards to the player on his left. Then someone led a card (as long as it wasn't a heart) and each person had to follow suit if he could.

Like all card games, it was a game of chance, but there was plenty of room for intelligence and strategy, too. Any little choice could affect the outcome of the game and how a person fared—which three cards someone chose to pass, whether the person dumped the Queen of Spades early or held it for later in the hand, whether the player tried to shoot the moon or played it conservatively.

Welcome always tried to shoot the moon, and he never did—not once in all the months we played. Most of the time he ended up with the majority of the points. I shot the moon a few times, but rarely. Usually, I played the game cautiously, never winning but never being the big loser either. John Nakatani, our neighbor from down the hall, always won. He never brought the woman who lived with him to our place. He never smoked any pot. He just drank Coke after Coke after Coke like he was at some business meeting and needed to keep his wits about him. Maybe that had something to do with his winning. He didn't just win most of the time. He always won. He never lost even one game. We may have been so stoned and he so wired that, for him, playing against us was like playing tennis against a man in a wheelchair. He was never a gracious winner, just an uncanny one, and as soon as he won the game, he would always get up abruptly, smile, and say, "I think Sarah needs the pleasure of my company. Thanks for being such good losers."

Ingle and Elmo, our neighbors across the hall, smoked so much pot that their baby girl seemed high most of the time. The air in their apartment was a cloud, and even the baby's cries had a lethargic, bemused sound to them. Ingle (the man) and Elmo (the woman) fingered the cards as if they were a Tarot deck and each game revealed the true direction of their lives. A few times their friend Errol Flynn came with them. I'm not sure if his real name was Errol Flynn or if it was just a name that he had taken or one that had attached itself to him like a barnacle. Whatever his name was, they called him Errol, and he was as out of place as the actual actor would have been in our game. Errol was balding and popeyed. Where everyone else seemed to be backing into a fog, Errol looked as if he were under a magnifying glass in a bright sunlight and as if he were ready to jump out of his skin. Every one of his movements was like a lizard's tongue, all flicking out and fast retreating.

Everyone was from somewhere else—from Indiana (Ingle and Elmo) or Los Angeles (John Nakatani) or Colorado (Errol Flynn)—and every one of them seemed uncertain whether or not they were heading toward home or away from it. Every one seemed to be a wayfarer, trying to figure out exactly what he was looking for. For this reason, some days Berkeley seemed exactly like home to me. The right kind of home. A place in which I could be whoever I wanted to be, a place in which everyone floated in a careless sort of haze.

A few months into our time in Berkeley, Welcome and I sat in our apartment with Nakatani, Errol Flynn, and Ingle, playing hearts and listening to the local radio newsman talk about what he was certain was Richard Nixon's case of syphilitic madness, when a tapping that sounded like the sort of noise you would expect to hear in an Edgar Allan Poe story made us all look up from our cards. The sound came from the window that faced the alley between our apartment building and The House of Enlightenment and Good Karma next door.

When I pulled up the shades, I saw a slim young woman with long, silken black hair that fell to her waist. I opened the dirty window and saw that she was naked and her skin was the color of the early evening sky. She stepped into the light of the street lamp, and I noticed that she had some Japanese blood in her and that she was beautiful. She looked up at me, all sloe-eyed and as much a mystery to herself as she was to me and said, "Could I borrow a match?"

There was a lot of movement behind me, chairs banging into tables and people shoving one another to get a better look. I fumbled for a second and then handed her a pack of matches that was in my T-shirt pocket. Before I could take my eyes from her breasts, she had taken the matches, said "thanks a lot," and turned away into the shadows toward The House of Enlightenment.

"Jesus, you're a smooth talker," Nakatani said.

"God, she was good looking," Welcome added as he stretched his neck out the window.

"I guess I acted like a schmuck," I said, "but the next time a beautiful naked girl knocks on my window and asks me for a match, I suppose I'll be prepared and be able to act like Cary Grant—or, who knows, maybe even the suave John Nakatani."

"Eat me, why don't you, Blankenship?"

"I wonder what that House of Enlightenment and Good Karma is?" asked Welcome. "Do you think it's a commune or something?"

"It's a counseling center or something," Ingle said. "Who knows, maybe for people with drug problems." And as if his own words reminded him of something he had been trying to remember, he relit the joint that he had put out and left in a bottlecap fifteen minutes before the girl tapped on the window.

"She sure was good looking," Welcome said again.

"I'd sure like to fuck her," Nakatani said.

"I guess Sarah would have something to say about that," Welcome said.

"Maybe she would," Nakatani responded, stretching his legs out in front of him, "but it wouldn't matter. Being with one person for too long is nothing but a failure of the imagination. It's just a dumb-ox kind of devotion. Nothing like that really lasts, at least not in the right way. How could it? And who'd want it to? After too many years it would turn itself into some dreary habit that was hard to shake, that's all. If you just accept the fact that change is the only constant, then you'll be content."

"She sure was pretty," Welcome said.

"Whose deal was it anyway? Let's finish out this game," Nakatani said, picking up the deck and shuffling them expertly.

Welcome started to change shortly after that night. Maybe, like me, he was thinking about what Nakatani had said, about nothing really lasting for long—love or friendship or truth. Maybe he had fallen in love with the idea of that naked girl and couldn't get her out of his mind. Maybe there were just too many people searching for too many things in Berkeley, and it all made him confused and lonely and homesick. Maybe there was too much talk for him in the town about the need for change and never enough, finally, about what should remain constant. Maybe the war had finally caught up with him, caught him by surprise like the riot and left him with only his shame or his fear or loneliness. Maybe he missed the red clay of LaGrange but couldn't figure out how to go home. Whatever his reasons, he started to smoke pot as often as Ingle and Elmo and often with them—until they headed out in their van to Alaska—and then he sat on the back steps of the apartment building rolling joints by himself. He spent time walking around Telegraph Avenue with Errol Flynn trying to score speed and LSD—until Errol Flynn, or whatever his name truly was, disappeared one day. Welcome never read aloud from the *Berkeley Barb* any more, and even his innocence seemed to take the shape of lethargy most of the time.

Every weekend since we had gotten to Berkeley, Welcome and I had gone to Live Oak Park, which was a mile or so north of the campus, to play basketball. He loved the game almost as much as I did. And I think we loved it for the same reason. The game existed absolutely in the present. There was no past or future. The game allowed for some luck, certainly, but most of what happened on the court was the consequence of what you did and how well you did it. The game wasn't perfect, but it seemed so much fairer than life, so much more just.

Even after Welcome started to smoke more pot, we still went to Live Oak Park every Saturday and Sunday afternoon. We spent the hours from noon to four running and passing and shooting. It was the running I think we both loved the most, a movement that led us nowhere but into our own bodies. There was nothing during the time of those games to think about. There was only movement for its own sake. Welcome's red hair flew behind him like flames and his freckles widened like pools of dark light in the sunshine, and at those moments he seemed to be exactly who he had always been and would always be. This is where we were supposed to be—our hearts beating wildly, our breathing coming in quick, passionate bursts, our minds and bodies undivided. But then, one day, even Live Oak Park and basketball became something different for us.

It was a Sunday afternoon in late spring. I had written to Nada that morning, telling her everything I could about where I was and why I hadn't yet found the other journal in San Francisco, trying to make her understand—when I didn't know myself—why I hesitated in searching for the other journal. I couldn't tell her that I had roamed the streets of San Francisco on my days off from work at Cody's, that I had fallen in love with the mists and fogs of that city, that I had found a place in Berkeley where I could be everyman among every man, among any man, so many people like me in so many ways. I couldn't tell her that I had strolled past my great-great-grandfather's house on Fulton Street a dozen times and had walked up to the door half a dozen times but had never rung the bell, had always taken the bus back across the Bay Bridge. I told her that I loved her—and I did—but I couldn't explain to her or myself why I wasn't with her then.

No explanations were required on the basketball court. That afternoon Welcome and I played better than we had ever before. I couldn't miss from the outside, and he was a magician with the basketball, stealing it from whomever he was guarding, slicing through two players to the basket, dribbling behind his back and through his legs and finding the open man with a pass that fell like atoms of light through the outstretched arms of the defenders.

We won game after game until it seemed only darkness could defeat us, only death could stop our run. We played together like twin brothers, two halves of the same person, knowing where we would be at every instant on the court, reading each other's minds as if there were really only one mind at work, one soul to account for in the afternoon's ledger. I could sense the old Welcome coming back to life, like a man stepping out of the fog into the clear sunlight. And, as simple as it was, I think that's all it would have taken—just one series of games like that where everything made sense, where all meaning came from action, where all action came from desire, where everything transformed itself in the flutter of an eyelid but where the order and rightness of things never changed.

We were both tired, and if we had stopped playing before the last game, everything might have turned out differently. But we didn't stop. It's hard to end things when you're winning and every move of your body seems to you like a gift from God, like some unpromised good luck. The guy who was guarding Welcome was taller than he was and a lot stronger but not near as fast or as skilled with the ball. He was a black guy with glistening muscles that shone like waxed metal in the fading light. He wore a thick gold necklace that hung down to the middle of his bare chest.

From the outset of the game he didn't like Welcome. I had seen him standing along the sidelines, leaning against the chain link fence as we played, and watched his eyes narrow in jealousy as he watched Welcome float toward the basket for a layup. When he started to guard Welcome, he put his body right up against his, and when Welcome made a move around him, the black guy used his arms and hips to stop him. Welcome didn't call a foul. He just bounced off him and passed the ball to the other side of the court. But Welcome was too fast for him, even when the black guy put his hands on Welcome's hips to slow him down or reached his arm out to stop him from bursting past toward the basket. Near the end of the game, with the score tied, the black guy simply knocked Welcome to the ground, shoving him with two hands when Welcome broke free for a layup.

"Get up you little white motherfucker. I'm sick of you elbowing me when you dribbling the ball. I'm going to kick your ass if you do that again."

Welcome just lay on the ground looking a little stunned, catching his breath. He stood up slowly and turned away from the court. He looked over in my direction, "That's all for me. I'm not playing any more. I can't play with some crazy nigger."

When he said that, the black guy threw the basketball at Welcome's head. It banged with a lot of noise but harmlessly against the fence.

"I got a gun in my car and I'll shoot your motherfucking white ass."

A few guys on the court held him back, and I walked alongside Welcome. "Let's get out of here."

As we walked down Shattuck Avenue toward our apartment, we heard the black guy's voice at our backs. "That's right, you white pussy. You better stay away from here. I'll kill your ass if you come back. See if I don't."

I don't think it was that Welcome was afraid to go back to Live Oak Park, but I think the park and the game, like Berkeley itself during the last few months, had been ruined for him. The game was no longer about movement or even pure skill, any more than the city was about pure love or social welfare. The game was connected to the past and the future in a way that it hadn't been before. For him, the game now had a complicated sort of human politics to it that made it part of Berkeley and John Nakatani's world. Welcome had come to California to escape the war in Vietnam, but the war had not taken the meaning out of his life. It had done the opposite. It had given him something to travel away from, and for a while Berkeley had given him an alternative way of seeing the world. Now all he seemed to think about was home, even if that meant the draft and the war. He seemed too tired to do anything but go home.

He called his mother and father to tell them that he was thinking of coming back to Georgia.

"Hey, Papa, this is Welcome. How's Mama? How's everyone in La-Grange? I'm thinking of coming home Sunday week. I may can be there even earlier. I'm thinking of leaving tomorrow."

His father had a voice that boomed from the telephone like a used car salesman's making an announcement over the lot loudspeaker.

"Your Mama's not here right now, son. She's over at Miss Park's house. Her son Jamie got killed last week in Vietnam."

There was a silence. Then Welcome said, "I'm sorry, Daddy."

"I know. We are too, son. There's a lot of anger and hurt in town right now. It might be best for you to stay put. It's not a good idea for you to come home next week. Maybe things are better left the way they are right now."

"I was just playing with the idea. I hadn't made up my mind for sure or anything. I might head up north for a time. I was even thinking about Alaska."

The voice boomed from the telephone. "It's not that we don't want you, but it might not be the best thing for you to come home for a while yet. Alaska sounds like a good idea. The last frontier, eh? Adventure. That's what a young man needs. Why not call again in a few weeks?"

I could see that Welcome had the same expression on his face that he had when he walked away from the basketball game at Live Oak Park, as if he'd been betrayed but he wasn't sure by whom or why.

22

What happened next led me once again to my great great-grandfather's journal and Mark Twain. I needed to find my way home, and the journal had been a map there all along. Sometimes you need to hear from someone else what you already know in order to see it as a truth worth believing.

Welcome died the next day. I watched him die. So did half the population of the Bay Area. It was on the television news at six o'clock at night and in all the newspapers the next morning—even the Berkeley Barb—of course, they connected him to the antiwar movement and suggested he was a martyr to the cause of peace and freedom.

But his death had nothing to do with the antiwar movement, at least not in the way the paper suggested. I think Welcome had always wanted to find a way to run and to stay still at the same time. He had been running for years, maybe his whole life. Like me, he had been searching for something unchanging in an unsteady world, maybe some way to escape death. He hadn't found it in movement or revolution or games or drugs. So he decided to take flight one last time, one last flight that would never change. He may have decided that the only way to escape death was to give himself over to it entirely. In some way that I didn't understand and still don't, Welcome's death freed me to go find the journal and let it lead me wherever it would. I no longer needed to stay at a safe distance from what the world had to say to me—or do to me. Somehow, his death gave me that.

On Sunday morning, Welcome put on his starched white shirt and his suit. He knotted his green tie tight to his neck and slicked his red curls down behind his ears. His eyes were the same color as the sky that day, and they shone happily in a way that they hadn't in months.

"Tommy, I'll say a prayer for you at church today." He winked as he went out the door.

He didn't go to any church, though. And although no one knows all the facts, the police and news reporters came up with enough information for me to believe that I have as much of the truth as I need or anyone can ever have. Welcome took the bus on College Avenue across the Bay Bridge to San Francisco and then took another to Golden Gate Park. It was a cool day, and he walked through the park with his jacket on, past the hillside where they perform the Shakespeare plays, where the two of us in our first weeks in town had come upon actors performing *A Midsummer Night's Dream* as if it truly were one. He went past the DeYoung Museum and kept on going until he stopped for a while at the buffalo paddock and then he quickened his pace and got to the beach that runs along the Pacific Ocean. He trudged past the Cliff House and Seal Rocks, Point Lobos and Mile Rock Lighthouse. For a time he sat on the sand at Baker Beach and gazed up at Golden Gate Bridge, which was floating in the clouds even though it was a clear day in the city.

Traffic on the bridge wasn't heavy, and only a few people walked across on either side. But there was a camera crew from Channel 3 News filming a story about the men who repair the bridge year-round. The newsman and his camera crew stood on the bridge across the car lanes from Welcome who looked directly into the eye of the camera before he turned away forever. Welcome waited for a couple to pass by as he stood at the center of the bridge, gazing back toward San Francisco. He said "good day" to them and even tipped an imaginary hat in their direction as he probably remembered the old timers at the post office in La Grange had always done. When he stood up on the railing, the wind making him grip the cables to get his balance, a few cars slowed down but none stopped. The news camera followed his movements as if it were recording some ordinary movement in time.

The waters more than two hundred feet below him boiled and the cables above his head moaned in the wind. The sun began to break through the remains of the fog, and the bridge looked as red as blood. Welcome stretched out his arms in a vee like a man about to pray. He raised his eyes toward the sky and he let himself fall. It seemed he fell forever, but the news camera didn't record it or the news station decided not to show its audience. The passersby said that he floated like a piece of paper on the currents of wind until he disappeared into the churning sea. He didn't even make a splash in the turbulent waters. One second he was there in the air, and the next instant he was gone.

Someone on the bridge had time to take two photographs, which the newspapers printed in the morning editions. In them, Welcome looks to be flying, not falling, rising on the air like a bird, a young man coming to life instead of dying. But the truth is that he fell to his death. Even though his body was never recovered, he fell through the air for those last few seconds, as mindless, perhaps, as a creature on the wing, but to his death.

I mourned for him then and miss him still, but the day he fell I just stared at the photograph of him—arms outstretched, green tie flying like a banner behind him, and his red hair blending in with the steel silhouette of the bridge. His image looking back at the camera or the photographs of him falling were shown throughout the night on the television news. The next day I stared at Welcome's image in the newspaper. The image was always the same, though. He was always falling, and there was nothing I could do to change that.

I called Welcome's parents that night and told his father what had happened. He didn't say much. He didn't even seem very surprised—as if Alaska or death were not all that different. As if he expected the call, like the parent of a soldier in Vietnam might wait for such a message, have imagined it so many times that the actual call seems just a retelling of an old story.

The next day I went in search of the journal again. I knew that Welcome had drifted from the world long before he fell from it, and the only way for me to keep from falling too was to go to 17 Fulton Street. I needed to find out if there was a voice from the past waiting for me there and I wasn't afraid any longer to hear what it had to say.

HOME

23

I left for San Francisco on the morning of May 22. It was windy and the air had a dampness that made it feel colder still. I hitched a ride across the Bay Bridge with a dark-haired, middle-aged man who never said anything after "Where ya headed?" Every once in a while he looked at himself in the rear view mirror and brushed aside a few strands of carefully combed hair that had strayed onto his forehead, but he never said anything, and that was fine with me because I had no intention of making conversation.

He left me off on the lower end of Fell Street, about where the Panhandle section of the city begins. I walked down Haight, past head shops and street musicians. Psychedelic posters marked every other doorway, and young girls in wide bellbottoms and long sundresses sold the *Oracle* on the corner of Ashbury.

At the corner where Haight intersected with Stanyan Street, a young man about my age sat slumped on the bottom steps of a purple and gold Victorian house. He wore a dirty white T-shirt with an image drawn on it of a small cartoon figure with a beard down to his sandaled feet. The figure had on sunglasses and a wide-brimmed hat with a feather in it. The young man was curled up on a bed of newspapers, and at the very point where the long nose of the bearded cartoon figure touched the papers beneath the man was the image of Welcome, falling through the sky. I stood there and stared so long that the man opened his eyes and looked directly into mine, but then he just closed them again as if he too had fallen and couldn't gather the energy to speak, had nothing worth saying, nothing he wanted to hear and no message to offer anyone.

I crossed Stanyan Street into Golden Gate Park and followed the same route that Welcome had before me until I got to Spreckels Lake. Then I turned north up to Fulton Street. The house I was looking for was nearly as far west as you could go. It was past La Playa and close enough to hear the roar of traffic from the Great Highway, to pick up the whisper of the distant surf, and to suggest the silent memory of Welcome's fall into San Francisco Bay.

The house my great-great-grandfather, Thomas Blankenship, lived in on 17 Fulton Street was the one he died in on March 21, 1910, the same one in which he had spent more than half of his life. The house had weathered the great earthquake and the more than half a century of salt spray and fog that came after it. The people who owned it, a young couple from Indianapolis who inherited it from their grandparents, showed me around after I told them that my ancestor had once owned the house. They let me sift through the old chest in the attic. Among the trinkets and old photographs was one letter. It was postmarked March 22, 1910, and addressed to Thomas Blankenship. They had read it and kept it as a worthless token of the past but a conversation piece nevertheless. When they offered it to me, I decided not to tell them that the Sam who wrote it was Mark Twain, not at least until I had a careful look at it. It was probably worth some money although not enough to change their lives. But I read it as if it could change mine.

Dear old Tom,

I should have written this fifty years ago, not waited until I was about ready to die of tobacco heart, but I was always a coward, and I knew that it would be easier to speak from the grave. Besides, I hadn't lived long enough then to be worn out properly so that I had only the unvarnished truth to tell. It takes so much energy to tell a good lie. I have the strength these days only for the truth.

I feel a whole world of shame for so many things. I never did stand as a friend to Martha. The skin of every human being contains a slave. Too often, I've been a slave to my own fears and the desire to find a place in society. I loved Martha— and you too. You must have always known that. Martha knew, I'm sure. I loved you two as much as I loved Livy and the girls. Now Livy is gone and dear Susy and Jean, too. I've often wondered during the past two decades—Why was the human race created or at least why wasn't something creditable manufactured in place of it? God had His opportunity. He could have made a reputation for Himself. But no, He must commit this grotesque folly. Sometimes I think that human nature is the worst consummate shame and lie that ever was invented. Isn't man a creature to be ashamed of in pretty much all his aspects? Is he really fit for anything but to be stood up on the street corner as a convenience for dogs? All I care to know is that a man is a human being—that is enough; he can't be much worse.

These past years I have given up drinking, most of my smoking, and have settled in Redding, Connecticut, in order to get rid of Mark Twain, but up until the last few days, I haven't been able to stop the performance entirely. Maybe good liquor and twenty or thirty cigars a day was necessary fuel to keep such an act going. Without it, I'm lost. But I guess I've played the part so long that it's about impossible to take the makeup off altogether. Until now.

I'd like to write with uncompromising honesty, but I have too many flaws to confess—I'm a failure and a coward, to match it. But I came in naked with the comet seventy-five years ago, and I suppose I'll go out the same way, at least trying to get near speaking the naked truth. Compared to most men, I haven't received poor wages for my life's work. I made a fortune, lost one, and made a second one in my old age. I've been feted and despised, and I'm not sure which one was more of an honor. I've seen every part of the world a man needs to see and some that a man should have no obligation or desire to encounter in a lifetime. I've probably loved and hated as much as any man in history before me.

I've been betrayed by those I've trusted and watched just about every person I loved be torn from me. But I suppose this is the fate of every man. Only the lucky—those who die before the bloom of youth is off their cheeks—escape that fate. Death should not be sad, though. Living is sad enough without making a blessing like death carry that same responsibility. And I'm about through with it. I have no envy for the living—only the dead need fear my jealousy.

In the course of climbing this seven-terraced summit, though, I've inhabited the paradise of the intellect and the imagination. What better place to live? I feel guilty about my daily and nightly emancipation from the world's slaveries and sorrows. I feel guilty, as well, and disgraced over my betrayal of Martha and you when we were youngsters in Hannibal. I was a coward. I knew it then. I admit it now. I've tried to balance the ledger by helping some young Negroes get a proper education in this country, and I've tried to do something in my books to change the way men think. Maybe that's still possible—to change how a man thinks—I'm still enough of a fool to believe that after all these years.

I wanted to write you when I heard that Martha passed, but it struck me like a thunderbolt and no words would come. I had hated life before on many occasions—from the time I was 18—but rarely had I been indifferent to it. After Susy died and then Livy, I felt like a dead man going through the motions of life. I was a mud image, and it puzzled me to know what it was in me that wrote and had comedy-fancies and found pleasure in phrasing them. I no longer have any interest in fiction, unless it provides answers to why human beings exist except to provide Someone's sadistic entertainments.

But now, while I have one remaining chance to speak, I wanted to say that I've always envied your courage and open heart. You never ran from experience, as I had once thought, but toward it. To move in such a direction may be foolhardy but anything worth admiring is surely foolhardy. Fools are the only humans we should admire, ultimately. I suppose. But, of course, in this country we have time only to honor the wealthy.

Soon I'll be heading toward the only experience left to me—and the only one I truly desire—the final one. Fame has brought me what most men dream of, but I've often thought that your dream would be the way to sleepwalk through this world. I have nothing left but the dreams I make up as I sit in my bed and dictate to my secretary.

I'm working on what will be my last book. It probably has too much truth in it for a living man to publish. It says all I have left to say. All I have ever had to say, perhaps. It will be my voice speaking from the grave. It's told by an Austrian man who looks back on something he learned in his boyhood when he met a mysterious stranger. The boy lives in a sleepy Austrian town, away from the world, and still drowsing in the Age of Belief. What the boy learns about life, what the stranger teaches him, is this: "You perceive, now, that these things are all impossible except in a dream. You perceive that they are pure and puerile insanities, the silly creations of an imagination that is not conscious of its freaks—in a word, that they are a dream, and you are the maker of it. The dream-marks are all present; you should have recognized them earlier. It is true, that which I have revealed to you; there is no God, no universe, no human race, no earthly life, no heaven, no hell. It is all a dream—a grotesque and foolish dream. Nothing exists but you. And you are but a thought—a vagrant thought, a useless thought, a homeless thought, wandering forlorn among the empty eternities!"

I wish I had a pleasanter truth to end this letter, but I have breath left only for this simple wisdom. I can't rightly imagine why I have spent so much of my life running from what I now most seek. I used to hate the vulgar temerity of death, but everything but death seems no more than a stupid hoax now. It's another one of those strange jokes played on us, I guess. I'll have no more to do with jokes any more, though. I shall never write any more.

—Sammy

I was sitting in the half darkness of the attic with the letter in my hand when the owner came up and said, "My wife and I will be out back in the garden if you need us, but please take all the time you want up here. See if you can find anything that belonged to your ancestor. We'd be happy for you to have anything you can find. One of these days all this stuff is just going to get cleaned out and thrown away. Why not have someone who cares about it have it?"

I sat there for a moment before I decided that after I had read my great-great-grandfather's second journal, I would give the letter to the young couple. It might get them a new car or a trip to Europe, and, besides, it reminded me too much of Welcome's falling into nothing and I didn't need more reminding in the years ahead.

The other journal was exactly where my great-great-grandfather had left it, I suppose, on a crossbeam in the shadow of the roofline, where you would never find it unless you were looking for it or doing a drastic cleaning of the attic, and it was obvious from the cobwebs and the clutter that no one had done that over the years.

It was the twin of the journal I had found in my great-grandfather's house in the Catskills, the same scarred and dappled leather and gilt-edged pages, the same small, faded script. Probably, my great-grandfather, James Blankenship, had come home to San Francisco shortly after his father's death in 1910. James would have been about thirty-three years old at the time, a man with his own life back east. My guess is that he read the journals then, brought one or both back with him to the Catskill Mountains. He either left the second journal on the crossbeam then in 1910 or, more likely, he went back after the war and his own son's death and his argument with his son's wife. My suspicion is that he found a way years later, a man bordering on old age himself, to get into the house on Fulton Street and place the second journal on the crossbeams in the hopes of drawing me or my father back home in some future he imagined as he waited alone in the mountains.

That May afternoon I sat against the warm bricks of the chimney and in the slanting beam of light that came from a dormer window and seemed to contain more dust motes than illumination, I read my great-great-grandfather's journal, arched forward toward the half light as if I were straining to hear the distant whispers of ghosts.

24

I made my way down Fulton Street toward the ocean on a warm afternoon in late December. I was hoping that I wasn't just like the man in that frog story that Sam had written who didn't see what was right in front of him. I hoped that my heart was allowing me to see clearly. As I walked along I wondered if love might not blind a man at times as much as hate. I had to believe that the right kind of love wouldn't do that. What else was there to believe?

On my left were the beginnings of Golden Gate Park. Saplings and bushes were being planted in what was thought of as unpromising soil, and I had read in the newspapers that many residents were calling it the Great Sand Park. They thought it was a waste of tax money and would never amount to anything. The park seemed promising enough to me, though. Everything did on that sunny day, I suppose. A cool breeze blew in from the Pacific and the hills rose all about me more majestic than any of the bluffs around Hannibal. To me, it seemed as if a new world was being built on the edge of paradise itself.

San Francisco in those days was a city trying hard to figure out what it meant to be—boomtown or fancy metropolis. On some of its sand hills you could still see wooden shacks, but if you raised your eyes a few degrees, marble mansions glittered in the rays of sun that broke through the fog. Downtown, the streets were paved with gap-toothed cobblestone, but wooden planks or plain dirt lined many of the streets around the city.

Nothing around me appeared to be older than a few minutes. Everything was in the process of being built—schools, churches, libraries, theaters. There had been plenty of saloons and bawdy houses for quite some time. It hadn't been long before I arrived that gold fever had caused the population of the city to jump from thirty pioneers to twenty-five thousand prospectors, prostitutes, businessmen, and preachers in little more than three months' time. People must have woken up some mornings rubbing their eyes to see if it was all real.

That's why everything had such an unfinished look. So much had happened so quickly, what chance had there been to finish anything? It was a city of gold in which adventurers blown by the four winds had landed. The city was taking shape before my very eyes, not a memory but an experience, rising up before me faster *than I could describe it. When I arrived, it seemed that the city had no past. Its future was uncertain. It existed only in the present. In that respect, for me it felt like the perfect place to be. Like the city, I was ready to believe in possibilities and new chances. I was ready to base my life on what might be the truth.*

When I saw Martha, she was standing outside her gabled home and school-house, partly framed by the ocean in front of her and the emerging park to her left. Her thick hair was pulled back, showing the light brown skin of her neck against her white dress. When she turned, it looked as if she did so with a purpose, as if she knew I was walking toward her. She turned as though she had heard her name called in the distance. But I had not spoken.

"You are the same," we both said in a shared breath and laughed happily at the coincidence.

"I've waited for you forever," she told me. "Or so it feels."

To me it seemed as if time had sped forward to that very moment, that now everything would slow down to a more natural speed, that the past was all squeezed together and the present and the future would stretch out in a way that would make sense. I wanted to tell her so much, but all I could think to say was, "Everything will be all right now."

"And you don't mind," she asked. "I mean it doesn't matter . . ."

How could it matter? I just smiled and drew her toward me.

We both knew that Sam would show up one day soon. He had written to her a couple of times in the past few months. The last one was two weeks ago:

"I don't know what to write—my life is so uneventful. Some times I wish I was back there piloting up and down the river again. Verily, all is vanity and little worth—save piloting. To think that after writing many an article a man might be excused for thinking tolerably good, those New York people should single out a villainous backwoods sketch to compliment me on!—'Jim Smiley & His Jumping Frog"—a squib which would never have been written but to please Artemus Ward, & then reached New York too late to appear in his book. But no matter—

*his book was a wretchedly poor one, generally speaking, & could be no credit to ei-
ther of us to appear between its covers.*

*"I think the critics missed fire on that subject, but I suppose it is better to be
praised for the wrong thing than not to be praised at all. I thought the flush times
were past, but I'm beginning to suspect that they are just about to start for me.
Bret Harte & I have both quit the Californian. He will write for a Boston newspaper hereafter, and I for the New York Weekly Review and possibly the Saturday
Review sometimes. I am too lazy to write oftener than once a month, though. I
need spare time to sit and contemplate my sins. And even more time, perhaps, to
be forgiven for them."*

Sam may have traveled with more than his share of guilt but he was never
lazy, no matter what he said. He was always writing something new, always moving. In the next few months he seemed to be everywhere at once—in Jackass Hill
in Tuoluma County and then in Angels Camp in Calaveras County, in Sacramento and Marysville and Red Dog and You Bet and Virginia City. It was like
he was circling around San Francisco trying to figure on a good moment to land.
Maybe waiting for guilt and fear to blend together and shape themselves into
some new emotion that he had never experienced before.

It was not long after I got to San Francisco that I saw a copy of an article by
a man named Fitz Smythe in the Gold Hill Evening News. The writer must have
hated Sam. He called him a Bohemian from the sagebrush and said that Sam
"had lost $40 in the house of a lady, under peculiar circumstances and had lost his
watch in the aforementioned establishment." Smythe said that Sam "thought the
police had stolen it on the night previous, having been oblivious to the fact that his
friend had taken it from him early in the evening, in order to save him from loss."
He said that Sam "probably had a venereal disease" and that it was understand-
able that he was disgusted with the West. Smythe ended his article by saying,
"Well, my boy, that disgust is mutual, and I don't wonder that he wants to leave.
He has been a little out of health of late and is now endeavoring to get the chance
to go to Honolulu, where he expects to get rid of one disease by catching another. If
he goes he will be sadly missed by the police, but then they can stand it."

Sam had become famous, but that fame had brought along its fair share of
enemies. When Sam saw that article in the Gold Hill Evening News, I was certain that he would pay that writer back for his time double. As I thought about it
some, I wasn't sure who I felt more sorry for—Sam or Fitz Smythe.

I settled into doing some repairs on the schoolhouse and began an addition to the classrooms. I was an expert carpenter, but I was beginning a new apprenticeship. I would soon become Martha's student so that I could teach alongside her.

We waited for Sam to arrive.

We saw his name in the papers even more often now and Martha received another letter from him in the winter of 1866. "I never had but three powerful ambitions in life," he wrote to her. "One was to be a pilot and another was to be a preacher of the gospel. I accomplished the first one and failed in the second because I could not supply myself with the necessary stock in trade—i.e., religion. I have given up that sort of belief forever. But I have had a call to literature, of a low order—i.e., the humorous. It is nothing to be proud of, but it is my strongest suit and if I were to listen to the maxim of stern duty which says that to do right you must multiply the one or the two or the three talents which the Almighty trusts to your keeping, I would long ago have ceased to meddle with things for which I was by nature unfitted and turned my attention to seriously scribbling to excite the laughter of God's creatures. Poor, pitiful business!

"My third ambition was to love purely and innocently, and that too I've lost the chance for because I'm not honest enough or brave enough for it. But I want it, deserving or not, I still want it."

The next week he stood at Martha's door, hat in hand. Controlling his surprise at seeing me at the dinner table. He stood on the porch with Martha for half an hour talking at first excitedly and then in a sad, urgent whisper. He had turned to leave like a man walking away from a funeral sermon when I came out onto the porch. He looked at me closely, as if he was seeing me for the first time, and said, "Tom, I guess I'm doomed to despise you for a disloyal scoundrel, even if it's me I really hate."

Maybe he expected me to be loyal to his idea of the love that was supposed to be between Martha and him. He forgot that I loved her too or maybe didn't care. Or maybe he had already become Mark Twain and figured that sort of love was his right and not meant for an uneducated carpenter.

Sam and I never talked face to face again, but three months later, when he returned from his trip to the Sandwich Islands, Martha and I heard him lecture at

Maguire's Academy of Music on Pine Street in San Francisco. It was a packed house and a great success. Right up on the stage there on that night Sam became Mark Twain for certain and forever, his eyes flashing, his drawl slower than poured molasses, and his lyrical descriptions of the islands mixed with jokes that kept laughter exploding throughout the room. Sam appeared to have survived any hurt that had recently been inflicted on him or he simply used it to make himself into a star burning too bright and hot for anyone to touch. His eyes had a look in them that said he would have the sort of success that would protect him from any bad dreams.

The next month he sent a letter to us, addressed to the school and without salutation. It began, in Sam's careful script, this way: "I leave tomorrow for good. I sail on the America. San Francisco is no longer home for me. It is a prison. All the wild sense of freedom is gone from it. The city seems so cramped and so dreary with toil and care. Last month I put a pistol to my head but wasn't man enough to use it efficiently. But I don't mean for anyone to feel sorry for me—as I don't for myself. Pity is for the living; envy is for the dead. Many times over the past weeks I have been sorry that I did not succeed, but I will never be ashamed, I'm sure, of having tried. Suicide may be the only sane thing the young and old ever do in this life. But suicide is for the brave, not for me. I'll write instead. I'd like to turn this inkstand into Aladdin's lamp before I'm done. I want my books to be water; those of geniuses are wine, but everybody drinks water."

I wrote to Sam a number of times before The Innocents Abroad was published. During those early years of my marriage to Martha he never answered, though, except maybe in his books. He did send us short notes after The Innocents Abroad made him even more famous than he had already become, one in the early 1870s, a year or two after Roughing It was published. "My publisher is a quadrilateral, astronomical, incandescent son-of-a-bitch, but I doubt I could find a better one," he wrote. "Read my book and you'll see what I mean."

He wrote to Martha and me only one other time during those early years in our lives together, in 1877: "I'm sailing to Europe for how long I don't know. I think it's about time that I enjoyed some of the advantages of being dead." Perhaps he continued to write to me and especially to Martha in his books, telling us in the characters he created like Huck and Jim and Roxy what he wasn't able to in letters or in person. Maybe the books were his letters of love and friendship. Martha and I waited for them as if they were, at any rate, as if they were personal messages from a distant friend. In Huck and Tom I saw our past friendship. In Huck's willingness to go to hell to help his friend Jim, a black man and a slave, I saw Sam's tribute to my brother Benson and what I had always loved in him and convinced myself that maybe Sam had grown to respect, as well. I also sensed Sam's regret that he hadn't been able to make the same decisions himself as a young man that Huck had. In Roxy I saw his brutal memory of the all the fakery of race and caste and how it destroys everything it touches. By 1894, when he published Pudd'nhead Wilson, we were both getting to be old men, but he hadn't forgotten Martha or the fraction of blood that would have made her a slave when we were young. I knew from his story that he hadn't forgotten. And by that time we had both learned that there are different kinds of hell that can await a man. It takes a dangerous brand of courage to be willing to go to hell for a friend but a certain kind of cowardice brings with it a worse sort of hell, I think, and I believe Sam thought so too.

Sam was never one to forget and, in part, for that I never stopped loving him. And because he couldn't forget, he was never fully able to love me—or himself—again. Perhaps I reminded him of who he once was, Sam Clemens before he became Mark Twain. But he was always two people. One of them—Mark Twain maybe—was able to forgive enough to find a way to love, despite the past. Sam Clemens never could, it seemed.

Although he never spoke about it directly, Sam understood his double nature—at least he was aware of the existence of his two selves and a little afraid of the each of them, I guess. For our son James's tenth birthday, Sam sent a gift—a book. Not one of his books, mind you, and not one we were likely to read to James until he got a lot older. Sam sent The Strange Case of Dr. Jekyll and Mr. Hyde by Robert Louis Stevenson. Sam's note said, "Everyone is a moon, and has a dark side which he never shows to anybody. Just tell young James that when he gets older he should never show his complete self to the general public. Tell him to wear the clothes that fit the moment. He will learn that clothes make the man. Naked people have little or no influence in society."

Martha never stopped caring for Sam, I'm certain. We were able to keep him in our hearts through his stories. We waited for him to return to San Francisco, but he never did. It was as if he disappeared and returned in the shape of stories, bound neatly between hard covers, surprising us but with no surprises he hadn't crafted and controlled.

A year after the first cable car began operating in the city, a month or so after we celebrated our fifth wedding anniversary, I sat with Martha in a car traveling along Clay Street. She slipped her hand into her bag and opened a book and began reading aloud—"I fell in love with the most cordial and sociable city in the Union.

After the sagebrush and alkali deserts of Washoe, San Francisco was paradise to me." Martha looked up at me and smiled, her dark eyes steady and bright, the stores and houses behind her changing colors and shapes with the clicks of the cable car.

"He sent it to us," she said. "It arrived in the mail today along with this card."

The card had three lines of writing and a signature: "I feel as if I have just risen from a long sleep. One cannot change the dream one has awakened from but one can hope for better dreams in the future. I plan to keep moving and to keep my eyes wide open. —Samuel L. Clemens Mark Twain."

That was in 1872. There weren't many other letters from Sam. The more he moved about, the more firmly rooted Martha and I seemed to become in San Francisco and our lives together. After James was born in 1876, a miracle child that neither Martha nor I would have thought possible, we got younger, it seemed because of him. We had given up on having children after ten years of marriage. We were both old enough to be James's grandparents, but he made us a young married couple again. This was the sort of surprise that Sam could not have written about in one of his later stories because it seemed too strange to be true. But life doesn't have to be like fiction. As sorrowful as life very often is, at times it can be too wonderful to make for a very believable piece of fiction. You just never know what's in store for you. It wasn't ten years later that Sam's daughter Susy died of meningitis. Who could make sense of our good luck and his tragedy?

25

*M*artha and I had the advantages of both parents and grandparents for the next twenty years. Having a child made us feel young enough to have the necessary innocence to raise one and gave us a patience or endurance that we might not have had when we were younger. When a child comes as a complete surprise as James did, you don't consider much more than enjoying the company and good fortune, for however long it lasts.

We never had any other sons or daughters, but James always felt like he was *part of a big family, what with all the children at the school we ran. James learned his books but he also learned how to make and fix things from me, so, in a sense, he had the best of two worlds in him. James had my light hair and Martha's dark skin, my skill with a hammer and saw and Martha's with adding and figuring.*

I never did understand why I ended up being so lucky. I often thought about it as I stood in our backyard working on a bench or chair for the schoolroom. The world I had ended up in seemed as close to paradise as a man was likely to come to on this earth. Between the schoolhouse and my work as a carpenter, we got along fine over the years. We lived next to a park as lush as Eden. In front of us was the forever expanse of the Pacific Ocean. To the east stretched the city of San Francisco, something ever changing in its beauty. James had his brothers and sisters in the classroom to play with each day and Martha and I had each other and everything around us.

My only regret is that time moved so fast. James went off to school in the East when he was seventeen. After he left, it seemed right to close the school and relax for a spell. Forty years of marriage went by, it seemed, in a heartbeat. In the telling things move even faster, as if someone knew the story right from the start and jumped ahead in the storymaking.

Martha died before I even got the chance to see her as an old woman. She still seemed to me like a girl in her twenties. She passed away in her sleep one night as if she had given her breath to the soft breeze that blew in from the ocean the next morning.

It all seemed too fast, but who has the right to complain about such a thing? I was lucky, of course, that I wanted it to last—and had the memory of it. Writing it all down has been like living it again.

Toward the end of his life, Sam wrote Martha from Hamilton, Bermuda, the last letter she ever received from him: "I am so glad to know that you are happy! To know that you have had so many happy years! That is all I ever wished for you. Some are born for one thing, some for another; but you were especially born to love and be loved, and be happy—and so things are with you as they ought to be.

"I fled to Bermuda when the most recent disaster fell into my life—the double disaster, for Clara was gone into permanent exile 15 days before Jean was set free from the swindle of this life. Stormfield was a desolation. Its charm all gone and I could not stay there.

"My ship has gone down, but my raft has landed me in the Islands of the Blest, *and I am as happy as any other shipwrecked sailor ever was. I shan't go home till . . . oh, I don't know when. There's no hurry. Hurry? Why, there's no hurry about anything, suddenly the hurry has all gone out of my life.*

"If I were young enough to care about hurrying, I would care, perhaps, as well about changing things from the past. But what's the use of changing the past, even if we could? We are all sleepwalkers waking, finally, to an empty room. Changing the past would never change that final emptiness."

Sam was right in one respect. Life does seem to be a dream, but it doesn't have to be a grotesque and foolish one, I don't believe. Why not dream a more beautiful and courageous one even in the face of sure loss? I'm certain my old friend yearned for that or he wouldn't have kept on writing the way that he did—or the kind of stories that he did. All writing is some sort of hopefulness, a paying witness to what we cherish and despise so that some things can last longer and others can be forgotten.

Martha died a few days after his last letter came in the mail. We had lived more than half of our lives together, and it was the kind of life that I had imagined it might be when I gazed at her on Glasscock's Island as a young boy. No life is without miseries and moments of despair, but even in the darkest minutes I recognized that I had been given great and undeserved good luck to have followed her to San Francisco and found my life and home with her.

Sam was right when he said that what we love is eventually torn from us, but I believe he was wrong in thinking that it is then lost to us forever. If I had known Martha only five years instead of fifty, I still would have counted myself blessed—because such love is never earned. It's always a gift. And so is life itself, filled with surprises that will take one's breath away for all the sorrow and beauty. I'm not sure I believe in an afterlife any more than Sam did, but I do believe in the life I have lived. And I'm not sure that anyone can expect more than that opportunity, to live a life, that is, and to be able to see it whole. Sam expected more than fame and fortune and happiness. He expected those things to come without peril, I sometimes think—or if not that, then he expected them to last until he had had enough of them. Nobody ever gets enough of such contentments, if they are genuine. Adam would have never left the Garden if he had not been thrust out.

We have no choice but to build our Edens out of impermanence. What else can we do but make our lives and love out of what is temporary? That's the story of all human love. And, because there's no choice, that has to be enough. What's left is the story that we are left with to live by. Action becomes memory as surely as inhalation turns into exhalation.

Under the last word was the date *March 31, 1910.*

26

It was mid-afternoon and warmer outside when I thanked the owners of my great-great-grandfather's house for letting me browse around in the attic. I had to fight with them to get them to take the last letter that Mark Twain had sent Thomas Blankenship. "No, no, you keep it," they had said. But I refused and know that one day it will be worth something to them.

When I stepped outside into the late afternoon air, the sun had burnt through any clouds and fog. I carried my jacket with the journal snapped in the pocket. I walked back along Balboa and over to Turk Street, the jacket swinging against my side with the weight of the journal. I sat for a while on a bench outside the University of San Francisco and watched the men and women my age carrying books of their own and walking down the pathways with a purposefulness that I envied.

I walked down to Geary Street and hitched a ride with a guy who looked enough like Mr. Calabria to make me do a double take. I don't know—maybe I just wanted to see signs of home. He dropped me off at the highway exit and by the time I walked back to my place it was growing dark.

That night, back in my apartment on Ashby Avenue, I dreamed of the Bronx. I had dreamed the same dream or some variation of it many times before in the past year.

I was in the Hunt's Point section, but nothing was familiar. The streets were a maze, and I walked determinedly from one to another. I was heading toward something but exactly what was never clear. When I woke up, after each of those dreams, I could never understand how a place could be so familiar and absolutely strange at the same time.

That night, though, I woke up in the middle of the dream, and in the darkness its story for a moment seemed perfectly clear. The Bronx, like the dream, was only a memory for me. It was my past, not my future, and I couldn't change it, but I could make it mean what I wished. Some might understand me to be willing myself into blindness but maybe it was just another form of sight.

When I closed my eyes, I could see Thomas Blankenship, an old man writing the last lines of his journal, and my great-grandfather reading them and placing one of the leatherbound books on the rafter of the old house in San Francisco, as if he were leaving some enigmatic signpost for future travelers. I could also see Welcome falling through the fog-shrouded afternoon, appearing and reappearing, a strobe light in the mist that was like a woman's breath under the Golden Gate Bridge, until he disappeared forever. As if I had dreamed him into existence once and now had not the imagination to make him appear again. But I had not dreamed him to life. I suspect that he had chosen to jump because to disappear was less complicated than remaining part of all the confused life around him. It must have seemed less dangerous to him to fall away from experience than to find a way to live in the midst of it.

I sat there wide awake in the darkness of my apartment and realized that I would be leaving any day now. I thought for a moment about the naked girl who had appeared at the window and remembered the conversation with John Nakatani afterward. I knew that Nakatani had been dead wrong. It was likely that Welcome believed Nakatani when he said that nothing of value really lasts, that we make up all that stuff to make our lives easier to bear. But as I sat there in the darkness, things seemed clearer than they had been for me in a long time. Loving someone until there was no more breath left to repeat the words was not, as Nakatani had said, a failure of the imagination. It was the opposite—that kind of love tested the limits of a person's imagination and courage. Because you had to be ready to risk everything. You had to find a way to reinvent the world every day when it was so much easier to keep everything at a safe distance. Nakatani had been wrong. Welcome had as well for believing him. And Twain too had gotten it wrong. All of them—even if they were right, they were wrong. Desire was a simple thing, but love took all your strength and the full powers of your concentration. It took every ounce of fearlessness you could discover. What we were left with was the story of that love. And that was enough.

The next morning I put the two journals in the mail to Nada. I attached a note: "This is why I took off to California, to find out where I came from and where I belong. I know now." I put the journals in a padded envelope and printed her name and post office box in Yulan, New York, on the outside. For the return address I wrote "Thomas Blankenship/17 Fulton Street/San Francisco, California," but I knew that the envelope would never be sent back.

I had saved enough money at Cody's Books to get a plane ticket back to New York. I flew out the following Saturday, away from the fog-covered city and the glistening bay and into the deserts and mountains of the west. It seemed as if I were going backward and forward at the same time, into the past and future, into all that was familiar and unknown.

From the plane window I looked into the deepening shades of blue, clouds hanging like ghostly pictographs over New Mexico, and imagined Marvin below nodding slowly in the direction of the plane in the sky above him, a smile on his face—he knew where the plane was headed. Each cloud appeared to have its own story to tell, beautiful and sorrowful and enigmatic against the endless sky. The clouds crawled along slowly enough to make me feel that I might be dreaming, a dream in which I moved toward everything I wanted to know and would never know. For the first time in a long while I thought about my father.

Some things are simple enough to understand, if not to put into words. Some directions don't need a map. For the first time in many years, I felt as if I knew who I was. I had gone West to find my great-great-grandfather's story, but I had discovered my own. I had found out that Nada and I were connected by blood, just another story but one we could always share. Now I knew the way home by heart.

27

The afternoon of August 14 I was in Shohola Falls before the sun set. I expected Nada to be there. I don't know why exactly. I had written to her telling her that I would be back on that day, that I would be standing on the rock we had stood upon so many days to watch the rushing stream, but still there was no logical reason she should be there. I just believed in my luck. Not because I deserved it—I didn't—but because it was meant to be.

At Shohola Falls it was clear and warm that day, and an early moon sprinkled light between the leaves. The water was iridescent, shifting from silver and blue to green and white. Nada was there, as I had dreamed, changing, too, before my very eyes. I wasn't able to turn my gaze from hers. I watched her shift in the changing light, the sun and moon floating in the same mysterious sky peeking through the branches behind her. Looking at her there, I knew she would be a story I'd always know but never know for certain. And that, I realized, was as it should be and, despite anything I might do, the way it would always be. What story is worth knowing once and for all?

That afternoon we jumped from the top cliff. All we had to do was push ourselves out into the air and let the water and earth rise up to us. We held hands and fell together into the screaming chasm and sensed the cold thrill of the water before we even touched it.

We stayed there until night fell upon us as we slipped into the shadows that filled Shohola Falls. The dark fire of Nada's skin glowed in the moonlight, and I saw then that the beauty of her skin color was just another risk, like love itself, and one I couldn't live without or would never try to live without again. That was one of the gifts Thomas Blankenship's journal had given me, the story of someone who was able to forget the world in order to find a way to live in it. What was the use of living in the world in terror of Delanos or in fear of losing something precious? In such entanglements, we're lost already. Eden is always lost from the very beginning anyway—there's nothing to do but make the best of our way toward it again.

As I think now of Shohola Falls, no more than a few miles east of where I sit next to Nada on the porch of my great-grandfather's old homestead rocking our daughter Millie in her arms, I close my eyes against the sunlight and surrender to my dreams of that place, to the stories of the Bronx and Mr. Calabria and Fitz and Mark Twain and Welcome. Shohola Falls seems to me now not a haven from the world, as I once thought, but an entrance into it.

Afterword

This is a work of fiction, and even though the narrative contains several historical characters—the principal ones being Samuel Clemens (Mark Twain) and Thomas Blankenship (a companion of the young Sam Clemens in Hannibal, Missouri, who Twain claimed was the prototype for Huckleberry Finn)—it is a work of the imagination first and foremost and should be read accordingly. But fact and fiction do nurture one another in *Shohola Falls*, as they do in our daily lives, I suppose. For the "Blankenship Journal" sections, I have striven to be true to the biographical and historical facts of Twain's life and times. We know a great deal about the life of Samuel Langhorne Clemens, but there are some interesting gaps in his story. How did the young man who spoke in the typical racist locutions of his time become the writer who exploded our myths on race in books like *Adventures of Huckleberry Finn* and *Pudd'nhead Wilson*? I've allowed my imagination to fill in such gaps. Similarly, for the story of Thomas Blankenship, I have kept to the historical record—when there is one. But because little is known, I was left free to imagine what might have happened to the real-life Huckleberry Finn.

There are many pieces of the "Journal of Thomas Blankenship" that are based upon actual events or characters—the death of Sam Smarr, for instance (fictionalized by Twain himself in the shooting of Boggs in *Adventures of Huckleberry Finn*), or the story of McDowell's Cave, chronicled by many, Twain among them in his *Autobiography*. I have courted both history and biography in writing this novel but I have also paid attention to scholarly speculation about the facts. Therefore, my recounting of the young Sam Clemens's viewing of his father's autopsy is based upon the very real possibility that such a traumatic viewing actually did occur. Of course, I added Thomas Blankenship to the mix. Who knows, he very well might have been there. Mark Twain once said that biography is but the clothes and buttons of the man. Perhaps fiction gives us the chance to see the individual naked in the light of our imagination.

I could try to note each instance of the convergence of history and the imagination and each point where they diverge, but I won't for two reasons. First, there are mysteries in a book even for the one who wrote it, and I hope that along the way readers will point some of them out to me. Second, and more important, I'll leave the profound exploring of such territory to the reader. Creating too many road signs would only turn an adventure into a tour. To paraphrase Gabriel Marcel, I'd like this novel, like any significant experience in life, to be a mystery to be entered into, not a problem to be solved.